CRYSTAL MOON

COPPER RIDGE SERIES BOOK TWO

DONNA TAYLOR

Stalk me:

http://www.donnataylorauthor.com

Donna Taylor on Facebook

New Book Release Email List

For my mom, Nellie Gray.
Thanks, Mom, for passing on your love of books to me. You told
me once, a good book had to have good sex. Well, Mom, I hope
this is a good book.

PROLOGUE

Sawyer

"WHAT THE HELL'S the matter with you? You're squirming around like a kid about to piss his pants. You got something better to do than explain what's been going on with you lately? When did you decide it was okay to piddle ass around on a job instead of finishing it?" I gave the mechanic, Grady Wilks, my *don't screw with me* stare. I didn't waste time on deadbeats, but Grady had always been a friend worth spending time on.

"Hell, Sawyer, you know how it gets sometimes. More bills comin' in than money. I'm running a little short this month. It's got me scrambling. Picked up too many jobs trying to cover my ass and they've put me behind schedule."

Grady was putting a lot of attention into scrubbing his hands with a red shop rag. The restless hands, avoiding eye contact—all signs something serious had him twisted up.

"If it's just money, why didn't you come to me?

Wouldn't be the first time I offered to float you a loan."
And it wouldn't be the first time his stubborn ass refused
my help. I took a guess at what he was trying to not tell me.
"I thought you had all those hospital and doctor bills
caught up?"

Grady's dad had passed well over a year ago from lung
cancer. It hadn't been a long, drawn-out thing only because
he'd not gone to see a doctor until it was too late to do
anything for him. Short or long, the hospital and doctor
bills had been a staggering load for Grady to take on.

Plenty of people had told him it wasn't his responsibility to pay his dad's bills. That was all good and well,
except he would have lost his home and the garage if he
didn't pay up. Both were in his dad's and his name jointly.
He'd taken on his father's debts and been killing himself
ever since paying them off.

I sent as much work his way as possible, and that was
all the help he accepted. A few months back, he looked
happy as hell when he told me he'd managed to pay off the
last debt on his dad. Not many days after that, he was more
closed off and pinched than before.

"Yeah, I've got the medical shit handled. Just got
screwed up juggling things. Did a few quick jobs for the
fast money and it messed with the scheduling." Grady still
wouldn't look me in the eye.

Something had been going on with Grady ever since
he'd told me the medical bills had been taken care of.
Whatever he was hiding made him unwilling to ask for
help. The rope was dangling right there in front of him; all
he had to do was reach out and grab the line. I'd be the first
to say a man had a right to his secrets. But I also believed
that when a friend lied to my face, it was time to figure out
what was going on.

"If you'd gotten your head out of your ass and finished

the new traps in Colin's truck on time, your money problems would've already been solved. When I send work your way, I sure as hell don't want them coming back to me whining like a little bitch because the job is running behind."

"One more day and I'll have the job wrapped up," he said. "Already have the box installed, and the hydraulics that control the back panel are kickass. When that seat slides forward it barely makes a whisper, and the compartment behind it is the biggest one I've ever put in the cab of a truck before. Once the trim's replaced, ain't nobody gonna find it. Already finished the false bed in the back. It's seamless and watertight." Grady's enthusiasm over the new hides carried the first honest reaction I'd gotten out of him since dropping by and asking questions.

When it came to mechanics, they didn't come any better than Grady. He also had a real talent when it came to custom paint and body work, but his true genius lay in building hidden compartments called traps. There wasn't a big demand for them. They were too expensive and there weren't a lot of legitimate reasons to have one installed. Usually when he picked up a job for one, he'd be so damn stoked that it'd be all he worked on. Not this time, though. He was running two weeks behind on Colin's truck.

"I don't want to hear how close you are, just finish the damn thing," I ordered. "And you can cut the bullshit and tell me the real reason you've been dickin' around so long with it. You never could lie worth a damn." I should let it go, but we went way back. All the dumbass had to do was come clean, then I'd lend him the money or kick someone's ass. Problem solved. Money or an ass-kicking solved every problem out there.

The animation in Grady's face reverted to the pinched mouth and brow he'd been walking around with for weeks.

"I ain't lying. There's some personal shit been gettin' in the way. Said I'd take care of it, and I will."

"That personal shit have anything to do with Andrew Webber?" I watched him for a reaction.

Andrew's old man owned the Chevy dealership on the east side of town and the Ford lot on the west side. He also owned several other dealerships in larger cities located both here in Arkansas and across Missouri. Andrew ran the two car lots in Copper Ridge, meaning he had his own mechanics and body guys to take care of any work needing to be done on company trucks. Word had gotten back to me he'd been showing up at Grady's to drop off a different truck every few weeks. Since Andrew was a rat bastard, and him and Grady had never been chummy, I couldn't think of one good reason for the man to be popping up over here to help Grady out by giving him work. That left only bad reasons.

"What the hell, Sawyer? You spying on me?" Grady's glare told me all I needed to know. Now I needed the why.

"Did you forget this is Copper Ridge? Everyone's so fuckin' eager to stick their nose up everyone else's ass, I'd have to have the whole damn town on my payroll if you want to call it spying. That prick Andrew's been seen dropping off company trucks out here, and everyone's wondering what that shit's about. So, tell me, why in the hell would he do that when he has all those mechanics in those high-dollar shops of his daddy's?" This bit of info wasn't as well-known as I'd let on to Grady. Sure, Andrew had been seen coming out this way during the day, but those trucks of his had all been delivered at night. Just like they were being picked up at night when Grady finished whatever he was doing to them. Not that it was hard to guess what that was. The *why* was the real mystery.

"What I do in my shop is nobody's business but mine,"

he said. "You want me to start asking you shit about the bars you own? Or how about I stick my nose in those gambling houses you make a killing off of?"

"You want me to stay out of your business, you got it. You know where to find me when you're ready to drop all the bullshit." Turning my back on Grady, I headed out the open bay door. You can't help people until they ask for it. They're not ready before then. Until that moment, they're willing to look you in the eye and say, "I need help," anything you do for them can come back to bite you in the ass.

After I climbed on my Harley, I speared Grady with a last look. "Call Colin. Tell him what the hell's going on with his truck. I ain't your fuckin' secretary."

CHAPTER ONE

Kelli

I PULLED to a stop in the gravel parking lot and stared at the building that had starred in some of the most important moments of my life. Funny thing about that: I didn't even know of its existence until six months ago.

Needing a minute, I took in the mishmash of wood and cement block that made up the structure known as Skeeter's. The afternoon sunlight spilling across the front of the weathered building didn't exactly do it any favors. There were no signs attached to the top of the backwoods bar boasting the establishment's name. Apparently, if you were a local you knew what it was called, and if you weren't, nobody cared if you knew the name or not.

What signs the bar did boast were mostly old, rusty ones scattered in no particular order across the front of the building. They advertised everything from auto parts to liquor; snuff to pop. An especially classy one next to the entrance proclaimed *Get Your Woody Serviced Here*. A picture of an old wood-panel station wagon was centered in the middle of the words. No doubt that was a laugh that never got old with the drinking crowd.

Skeeter's definitely wasn't any kind of place I'd ever pictured working at. Six months ago, my privileged hiney wouldn't have stepped through the doors of this kind of dive. Funny how at twenty-seven I'd begun to figure out life didn't necessarily turn out the way you planned.

Shrugging off the what-could-have-been, I swung the car door open and climbed out. The gravel in the parking lot had me tottering worse than a drunk on my three-inch heels as I crossed to the entrance. Judging solely by the building's exterior, shoes weren't the only wrong fashion choice I'd made. Then again, I didn't own a single pair of Daisy Dukes, or have a stash of halter tops to pull from.

I'd struggled over what to wear before coming out here, finally settling on something I would have felt comfortable wearing to the boutique I used to manage back home. If the classic black pencil skirt showed off curves and the emerald-green silk shell reflected my eye color, well, those were just bonuses that might help me land a job. Sure, this was a bar, no need for a power suit, but still, I'd wanted to wear something nice. Basic 101 when applying for a job: dress to impress. Okay, the Louboutins might have been going too far, but it was doubtful the red soles would mean anything to anyone in this kind of place. Bitchy? I preferred to call it being realistic.

It was a relief when I reached the covered porch without a twisted ankle. Happily, there weren't any specta-tors loitering around the front of the building to witness my less-than-graceful approach. Seeing only one other vehicle in the front lot, and it was a monster motorcycle, I guessed there wouldn't be too many patrons inside.

Pausing on the wooden planks, I straightened my skirt

and made sure my blouse was still neatly tucked. Satisfied all was in order, I took a deep breath, gripped the door handle, and strolled through, owning the place.

The thunderous slam of the door closing had me jumping as if a bomb had just exploded in my panties. I landed with a wild wobble on the heels I was seriously beginning to hate. Apparently, the door didn't have one of those pneumatic thingies that kept it from waking the dead when it closed. Then again, I might have been a tad too enthusiastic flinging it open.

I'd wanted to make a statement with my entrance. Unfortunately, the impression was less *Confident Woman* and more along the lines of *The Clown Has Arrived*. Hopefully the room was dark enough that it hid the pink tide of embarrassment crawling up my neck.

Having already put on a floor show, I stalled just inside the doorway. Not a bad thing. No sense adding to the spectacle of my entrance by tripping over something and doing a face plant. Taking a moment to allow my eyes to adjust to the darker interior had the added benefit of giving me time to check out what I'd slammed my way into.

Back at the motel earlier, I'd asked the elderly manager, Mrs. Whatley, if she'd ever heard of Skeeter's. She'd been more than happy to launch into a litany of the shameful shenanigans people got up to in *that place*. By the time she was through, I'd conjured up a graphic picture of something that was a cross between an old-time saloon and a biker's hangout, with a side of cathouse thrown in for good measure. It was a regular Walmart of manly vices. When I'd asked for directions, Mrs. Whatley's self-righteous sniff was a clear indication that my moral values had taken a hit with the woman.

Scanning the room, I wasn't sure whether to be relieved or feel cheated. After preparing for a Den of Iniquity, the place turned out to be more of what I pictured a typical lower-class bar would be. Not as polished as a club you'd find in the city, but neither were there any diseased hookers or drunken bikers littering the floor.

There was nothing sinister about the polished bar that lined the right side of the room. The space between it and a quartet of pool tables was furnished with mismatched four- and six-top tables surrounded by equally mismatched chairs. Located in the very back was a raised platform where a band could set up, and next to it was a jukebox. They had the music options covered. An open area in front of the low stage provided plenty of room for anyone wanting to show off their footwork. In the back corner was the entrance to a shadowed hallway. Maybe that hallway was the road to damnation? The one Mrs. Whatley claimed everyone was on that entered Skeeter's.

"Can I help you, miss?"

The gruff question drew my attention back to the bar and came from a giant of a man owning the space behind it. Inked-up arms were attached to massive shoulders, and his thick neck was topped by a face that appeared to have been shaped by more than one fist throughout the years. It would be charitable to call his features "unique." It was a safe bet he wasn't one of those slick bartenders who impressed patrons by tossing bottles and glasses in the air while mixing drinks.

He wasn't alone at the counter. I shifted my attention to a petite brunette standing across the wooden barrier from him. The faint sneer on her lips made me think she wasn't exactly impressed with me. Customer or employee? If she worked here, she wasn't the stereotypical barmaid I'd expected to find. *Too young* was the first thought that popped into my head. But there was something about her eyes that made me think she'd seen some hard truths in her life.

My plan to take a quick peek at the third member of this little gathering stalled out when my eyes landed on the large frame of the man leaning against the bar. He was everything mommas warned their daughters to stay away from, and the very thing those same daughters wanted more than their next breath. I could almost smell the aroma of wild sex and broken hearts rolling off him. If Skeeter's was the road to damnation, this man was driving the bus.

There was nothing flashy about his appearance that screamed *look at me*. Everything he had on said comfort and not style. It was the body encased in the scuffed boots, relaxed jeans, and weathered shirt that snagged my attention. It was eyegasmic pleasure to let my gaze travel the long, sculpted length of him. Corded biceps were exposed by the bunched sleeves of a faded gray Henley. That square jaw of his hadn't seen the sharp edge of a razor in a day or two, and all that stubble surrounded well-formed lips.

Lips were kind of a thing with me. Didn't you just hate when a guy had lips that were barely there? I mean, come on. With thin lips you went in for the kiss and ended up with nothing but the skin between nose and chin. Gross. But these lips were a perfect blend of substance without being puffy. A hint of harshness around the edges teased a woman into wanting to try and soften them. Pulling my eyes from the temptation of his lips, they skimmed over a strong jaw line to focus on his thick hair. I'd never been a long-hair-loving kind of gal. While his was too long to be businessman trendy—my personal favorite—the dark waves that brushed the back of his neck were enough to make me a convert to the needing a trim look.

When I finally got around to looking into his cobalt

eyes, an overwhelming urge to slowly back away from his level gaze hit me. With his hip cocked against the wooden counter and an arm resting on the polished surface, he should have come across as relaxed. Should have. Instead, there was a sense of coiled readiness about him. I had this crazy Stranger Danger warning screaming in my head. Not a creepy-guy vibe, more *this is not a man you want to cross*.

Dragging my eyes back to the bartender took a conscious effort. He was the one who should have come across as the biggest threat in the room, but he was substantially less threatening than the other male.

I sincerely hoped Mr. Bartender was the person I needed to convince to give me a job. While I hadn't figured out whether the brunette worked here or not, I discounted her as being important. As for the one truly formidable presence dominating the room? I had a feeling it'd be a cold day in the corner of hell he ruled before anyone talked him into anything he didn't want to do.

"Miss, iffin' you're lost, just say so and I'll point you in the right direction. But you're gonna have to speak up. I don't read minds." The bartender crossed his muscular arms and rested them on top of his rounded belly. Cocking his bald head and raising an eyebrow, he tacked on, "Ain't nobody gonna bite."

The tiny brunette gave an inelegant snort. "Least-wise, not this early in the day."

Squaring tense shoulders, I moved closer to the trio and plastered an upbeat, confident smile on my face.

"Please, forgive my rudeness. My name is Kelli Radcliff, Mr....?" Taking the necessary step to get close enough to stick out a hand in greeting to the bartender, I held my breath. The wait to see if he would blow me off or actually take the offering stretched and stretched.

The pause seemed to last forever, but he unwound his

arms and completely engulfed my fingers in his huge paw. He carefully gave my hand a gentle shake before releasing it. "No mister. Just Charlie."

While I'd dismissed the girl as not being useful, it was never a good idea to ignore someone who might end up being a coworker. Flashing a smile in her direction, I again extended my hand for another shake. After half a beat, the girl offered up a hand. "Zanie Mae. Most just call me Zane unless they're pissed at me or want me pissed at them."

The sparkly little laugh I trotted out, as if Zane was the cutest thing ever, had me cringing inside at its falseness. These people weren't the type to practice social niceties, much less appreciate them. The eye roll the brunette flashed at Charlie was a good indicator I wasn't scoring any points.

Turning to the one person left to be introduced, I suppressed a shiver of awareness. *Down, girl.* I reminded myself I was here to find a missing piece of my past, not to become sidetracked by some macho piece of manliness. Still, I had this crazy desire to hear him speak. I was curious whether his voice would do justice to the image he projected. What a crime against nature if a nasally lisp came out of those sinful lips.

Cranking up the wattage on my smile, I extended a hand to Mr. Badass. He ignored my hand. Instead, he let his hooded eyes travel the length of my body in a parody of my earlier scrutiny of him. He just reversed the order, starting at my blonde hair and letting his eyes scorch a path to my feet. When he got to my heels, he lingered on them before returning to his detached role of observer. I got the feeling I'd been a lot more affected by his eyes traveling over my body than he'd been.

His callous rejection stung. I was used to men being a

little more excited to meet me. That was the only excuse I had to offer for what I did next.

Pulling my hand back, I examined it with a tiny frown, making it clear I was checking to see what was wrong with it. After a thorough examination, I spat in the palm then proceeded to give it a vigorous scrubbing against my hip. After examining it one more time, I nodded as if satisfied and again offered it with a brilliant smile. Momma would have been horrified by such an unladylike action, which only made the performance that much sweeter.

A moment of silence, so complete it had me worried I'd gone too far, was broken when Charlie and Zane busted out laughing. Zane belted out her amusement, making no attempt to sound cutesy or girlie. Charlie had the deep-chested, booming laughter a man his size was bound to have. While there was satisfaction in having achieved my goal of breaking the ice with at least two of the three, I never took my eyes off the beautiful stranger. The one who'd initiated my less-than-delicate approach to getting him to introduce himself.

I didn't have to wait long this time for a response. His body didn't so much straighten from where he leaned against the bar as uncoiled its long frame in a sensuous bunching and flexing of muscle. A hint of interest flashed in his eyes, where before they'd been cold, and those beautiful lips had the barest lift to one corner. I was determined to remain rock steady. My hand never wavered, although I was starting to worry my toothy smile was beginning to appear maniacal. But momma dogs would have kittens before I dropped either the smile or the hand.

"Sawyer."

One word and it was worth all the effort put into dragging it out of him. The deep huskiness of his voice sent a shiver of appreciation down my spine, and goosebumps skittered across my arms.

He took a firm hold of my hand, but instead of shaking it, he did the oddest thing. Turning it over, he examined the palm as carefully as I had done. Thankfully, he didn't spit in it. He ran the roughened pad of his index finger over the unblemished smoothness.

Realizing I was holding my breath, I gracelessly snatched my hand back from him. The burn left behind couldn't have been any hotter than if he'd traced across my palm using hot coal instead of his finger. A low, rumbling chuckle made me think he'd accomplished his goal, also.

CHAPTER TWO

Kelli

DETERMINED to maintain a pretense of control, I acted as though nothing unusual had taken place. I backed up, resisting the urge to again scrub my hand against my skirt. The need to erase the stain of awareness left by his touch was difficult to ignore. I could have kissed Charlie's ugly mug when he started talking and broke the staring contest between Sawyer and me.

"Miss, iffin' you're here for something to eat or drink, we ain't open yet. And iffin' you're here tryin' to sell something, we ain't buying." He crossed his arms back across his expansive chest.

"Oh, I don't know, Charlie. Someone here might be lookin' to buy whatever she's sellin'," Zane popped in with a smirk. She tipped her head in Sawyer's direction. "Or at least rent it for a while."

Sawyer drawled, "Shut the hell up, Zanie," in an offhand manner that carried no heat, then returned to leaning against the bar. If there'd been a spark of interest in him a moment ago, it was gone now.

"Zane, ain't you got something you need to be doin' 'sides embarrassing the hell out of folks?" Charlie's complaint sounded more resigned than angry.

I ignored her less-than-subtle remarks. Crude as they were, they weren't going to derail me from doing what I'd come here for. Raising my chin the tiniest fraction, I addressed Charlie. "Actually, I'm hoping you might be in need of help."

"Help doing what?" Charlie managed to sound both puzzled and suspicious.

"I would like to put in an application."

He continued to look puzzled.

"A job. I want a job working here." I spoke slowly. You'd have thought I was speaking some kind of foreign language from all the blank stares.

Zane was the first to react, and it wasn't exactly positive. She doubled over laughing. Charlie dropped the confused look and started his own rounds of chuckles while he eyeballed me like, *yeah, right.* Sawyer reacted the least but managed to convey the most by simply narrowing his eyes. He was the only one taking me seriously.

Before anyone could deliver a no, I launched into the speech I'd rehearsed over and over on the drive here. "I have wonderful assets to share, Mr. Charlie. I have several years of experience working with the public as a general manager of a very popular and upscale boutique in Little Rock. Close contact on a daily basis with the most demanding of customers has taught me the necessary skills to satisfy the most difficult clients. But please don't think I'm just some white-collar snob, because when it comes to getting dirty, I'm not squeamish. I'll perform quite enthusiastically no matter what position I'm placed in."

My verbal résumé set off another peal of laughter from Zane. And Charlie? He no longer looked amused, but appeared stunned. I couldn't resist glancing at Sawyer. Oh yeah, the bored detachment was definitely gone.

"Charlie, you gotta hire her after that speech." Zane didn't even try to control her giggles. "You ain't never gonna find another one like her around these parts."

"No."

One word from Sawyer and we all turned in his direction. He had eyes for no one but me. It wasn't difficult to read the finality of that "no" in the steeliness of his gaze. I turned to Charlie, hoping he might be more favorable to the idea, but he just shrugged.

"Aww, come on, Sawyer. Give her a chance. You know Sue Ann's boyfriend is making her quit now he's got her knocked up." Help arrived from the one person I'd written off as being of no importance. Zane was pleading my case.

"Besides, she's worth having around for a good laugh now and then."

Or not.

If any of them thought it was going to be easy to dismiss me, then disappointment was about to rear its ugly head. "This is not a joke, and neither am I. I need a job. Miss Zane stated you're in need of a new employee. I demand to be taken seriously."

"Don't go gettin' your panties in a twist. I'm just funnin' with you, but I'm serious as a heart attack, too." Zane might have been talking to me, but she stared down both men while doing it. "Sawyer needs to stop being so damn paranoid about strangers and let Charlie hire you."

I wasn't sure whether to trust Zane or not. I wanted to. Desperately. But I was having a hard time believing she wasn't setting me up for another round of *funnin'*.

"Zane." Sawyer shot her a warning glare. "The fucking

men will eat her alive and the women around here will rip her to shreds. Nobody's got time to babysit a fucking debutante."

"I'm saying she won't be a problem and she'll solve one of ours. By the time she's had her fill of working here, we can have somebody else lined up." Zane directed an assessing eye at me. "You ain't planning on tryin' to make a little side money, are you?"

Asking her to clarify her question felt wrong. I had a sneaking suspicion it had something to do with me joining the ranks of the diseased whores I'd expected to find thanks to Mrs. Whatley. Shaking my head hard enough to give myself a headache, I sputtered out, "No!"

Maybe it was wrong to let this strange girl do the fighting to gain me a job, but she had Sawyer listening. Something I chalked up to a minor miracle. It made me wonder if they were more intimate than simply boss and employee.

"See? She ain't gonna want in on no side action. That'll keep the regulars happy and out of her face. You know how bitchy they get when they have to compete with someone new. Besides, even if we did find someone from around here to replace Sue Ann, ain't none of them gonna have her classy ass… ets." Zane grinned and did this big hand swoop, showcasing my body in a classic Vanna White move.

As far as résumés went, I wouldn't be asking Zane to write me one anytime soon, but what she said seemed to carry more weight than the speech I'd prepared. Charlie was nodding. He appeared to be warming to the idea, which left Sawyer to convince. He was impossible to read.

Sawyer

. . .

WHAT THE HELL was Zane up to? She'd normally be first in line to give some socialite a kick in the ass to help them out the door. But right now, she was doing her damnedest to talk me into hiring one. There were good reasons not to bring in some stranger who had no local connection. Zane knew what every one of them were. This Kelli person didn't realize it, but Zane had taken a liking to her.

From the moment the woman exploded through the doors, my inner radar had been firing off all sorts of warnings. Course, those alarms were more to remind me it would be stupid as hell to get tangled up with a female who would be nothing but a pain in the ass. It wasn't until she started talking shit about wanting a job that I considered she might be a serious threat.

Everything about the woman screamed that she didn't belong in a country honky-tonk. From the way she talked to the way she dressed. She might as well have a neon sign hung around her neck flashing the words *High Class*. There was no denying she was southern with every soft word that rolled from her tongue, but she sure as hell wasn't country.

I'd been surprised at the way she'd stood up to me when I ignored her obvious maneuvers to find out my name. It'd been hard to keep from laughing when she'd spit in her hand then scrubbed it on that sexy, tight-ass skirt of hers. For me, that bit of sassiness added to the appeal of a beautiful face and a body made for sin. If she worked at the bar, she'd be a temptation hard to ignore. Never been big on resisting temptation.

I'd learned my lesson that women from her level weren't worth the trouble. They started out thinking they wanted some nasty from a bad boy, but it was only a matter of time before they went to work trying to smooth away all those hard edges that had attracted them in the first place. I stuck to women who were hard in their own ways.

To have a princess show up asking for a job didn't make a lot of sense. I wasn't a fan of mysteries involving a stranger hanging around one of my businesses.

Thanks to Zane's big mouth, this woman knew we needed to hire someone. Gotta hand it to her: she had balls to use that knowledge to her advantage despite being halfway afraid of me. I'd seen the heat in those green eyes when she was checking me out but had also seen the distrust. I gave her points for having enough sense to be leery. She had good reason to be. But she didn't let fear rule her and demanded she be given a job. Damn. I liked that about her.

Like her or not, the lady had an agenda. I would guaran-damn-tee it had nothing to do with a lifelong, burning ambition to work in a rough-ass bar.

When a woman as classy as her showed up in a rough-neck bar, it was a safe bet she was either hiding from someone or searching for something. The big question? If she was on the hunt, was she doing the hunting for herself or someone else? Might be interesting to keep her around until I figured out what the hell she was up to. And when did I start lying to myself and making excuses to keep a woman around? Especially one that was going to end up being a damn nightmare.

She wanted to insert herself into my world? Fine. But nothing said I had to make it easy.

"You ever wait a fuckin' table in your life?"

KELLI

. . .

"As a matter of fact, I have." I couldn't help feeling smug after his question. He'd been silent for so long as he studied me that it was obvious he'd been trying to come up with a legitimate reason not to hire me. I couldn't wait to knock that particular prop out from under him.

"I'll admit it's been a while, but in high school I was a cheerleader and worked the Sports Banquet every year. Then in college, my sorority hosted countless social mixers and charity events. I served at each and every one of them." When I completed my list of experiences, I might as well have added "so there." It was certainly implied in my tone.

"We don't host fucking tea parties around here." Sawyer's derisive drawl made it plain he wasn't impressed.

A groan erupted from Zane. "Hon, not helping. Maybe you should zip it and let me do the talking."

What had I said that was so bad? I'd simply pointed out I wasn't a complete stranger to delivering food and drink. Granted, it'd been a few years ago, but being a waitress wasn't exactly brain surgery.

Zane jumped in like she was afraid of what might come out of my mouth next. "Bottom line, guys, we need someone and she's here. I'll teach her everything she needs to know and keep an eye on her. You gotta admit, she's got nice tits, and don't forget her *ass...ets*." She cracked up again.

Good to see she was getting so much mileage out of that word. "That right there's enough to keep the male customers so distracted they won't even notice when she screws up. How bad can it be?"

That was it? My biggest recommendations were body parts and a "how bad can it be?"

"She's got a point, Sawyer. Sue Ann's already told me

she ain't coming back no more. The woman's here and iffin' Zane's willing to work with her, how bad can it be?" Charlie chimed in, sounding more stoic than enthusiastic. "Between the two of us, we'll keep her nose out of places it don't belong. She probably won't last long, but it'll give us a little breathing room and time to find someone else."

"Bad help beats no help." Zane summed up her pitch with a triumphant flourish.

I gritted my teeth and smiled as if Zane and Charlie's less-than-rousing words of support were the highest of praise.

Sawyer took turns leveling a stare at each of them. His harsh gaze lingered on me the longest. Not going to lie: sweat was running down the middle of my back. When he started walking in my direction, my smile faltered. When he passed by without a word, my shoulders dropped in defeat.

Convinced it was all over, I was shocked when, without turning around, he announced before walking out, "Hire her if you want. But if she becomes a problem, I'll be the one taking care of it."

I had no illusions. What I heard in his voice was not an idle threat but a promise.

CHAPTER THREE

Kelli

SILENCE DOMINATED the room after Sawyer walked out, leaving me to wonder if I had the job or not. I turned to Charlie, and his expression wasn't encouraging.

Zane was the first to break the silence. "He can be such an ass." She sounded a lot more cheerful than I felt at the moment.

Popping hands on hips, she grinned and said, "Hope you have something with you other than what you've got on. Those shoes are gonna be killers after the first thirty minutes. Lucky for you it's Monday and everyone gets kicked out at eleven on weekdays. Weekends are a different story. We don't close till one, but there'll be a lot more help. If they're not too busy working the back rooms. And just like the good Lord, you get to rest on Sundays. For the next few days you'll be working same schedule as me so I can keep an eye on you. That means you work six days this week and four next one. Any questions?"

Her barrage of information flew over my head. I was still trying to figure out what had just happened. "Does this mean I'm hired, and you want me to start right now?" Again, I looked to Charlie.

"Of course you're hired," Zane said. "Ain't that right, Charlie? Sawyer gave the okay, even if he had a piss-poor way of doing it."

He rubbed a slab of a hand back and forth across his bald dome before huffing out a sigh. "Yeah, I reckon so. We need someone and she's here. Just remember, she causes any headaches, it ain't just gonna be her ass on the line."

After giving his grudging agreement, he made for the swinging doors set in the wall at the end of the bar. Sounds of pans clattering and a greeting called out could be heard when he pushed through them. I imagined he was already complaining about the new girl to whoever was working back there.

"See? You're in. Now, about those shoes—any options?" Again Zane sounded way more cheerful than she should after Charlie's dire warning.

"No, not with me, I didn't expect everything to happen so fast. Is there time for me to drive back to the motel and change?" I crossed my fingers that the answer would be yes.

The drive there and back would allow time for what just happened to sink in. It felt as if I'd been caught in an undertow and was being dragged out of safe harbor into dangerous waters. Yes, this was what I wanted, but I'd been so focused on finding a way to work at Skeeter's that I hadn't planned beyond getting hired.

"Best not. It's already three thirty and we open at four. Don't want to give Charlie a chance to start second-guessing hiring you. He might change his mind. Don't worry; I always keep extra clothes here. Never know when somebody's gonna spill something, or worse, some light-weight can't hold his liquor and you end up wearing what-ever he'd stuffed in his stomach that day." Zane shrugged off my fish-eyed grimace of disgust. "Hey, it happens. Not often, but a girl's gotta be prepared."

Oh, lordy. What had I gotten myself into?

"I'd say we're about the same size." Zane narrowed her eyes. I could feel her mentally measuring me.

"My jeans might be a little loose in the ass. I've got more ham in the hocks than you." She slapped herself on the butt. "They'll be short in the leg, too, but ain't nobody gonna notice once you put the boots on. That is, *if* you can manage get them on. What size do you wear?"

"Do they run the same as shoe sizes?" The thought of wearing some stranger's clothes wasn't exactly thrilling. I was especially doubtful about the cowboy boots after studying the rather flamboyant blue ones Zane had on.

"You have got to be shittin' me, girl! You ain't never worn a pair of boots before?"

"Of course I've worn boots. Just not the type you have on." That came out way more defensive than I'd planned. But for the first time in my life, I understood how it felt to be the only kid on the block that didn't have the cool stuff everyone else sported. Which was ridiculous. My heels alone cost more than a closet filled to bursting with the type of no-name clothes Zane had on. There I went being bitchy again. Years of judging everyone through the eyes of my momma was going to be a hard habit to break.

"Never mind. I'll just run and get my backups. I've got an old pair of flip-flops out in my car that for sure you can wear if the boots don't fit. Don't worry; we'll figure out what works and what doesn't." Zane didn't wait for a yay or nay, just took off in the same direction Charlie had gone. Indecision glued my feet to the floor and left me wondering if I was supposed to follow or wait for Zane to return with the clothes.

As Zane walked away, she started rattling off something about introducing me to the cook, but stopped when she noticed she was talking to empty air. Looking back, she called out, "Well, come on. We ain't got a lot of time to get you fixed up and run through some of the basics around here. Good thing we've got a few days to get you geared up before the weekend."

That answered my question and motivated me into a fast walk to catch up. For someone as young as Zane appeared to be, she certainly had no problem ordering people around. I followed her into the kitchen, where a wiry older man was slicing tomatoes. He quit what he was doing when we stopped beside him.

"Lonnie, meet our new waitress. This here is Kelli." Waving a hand at the cook, Zane said, "Lonnie's been here longer than anybody. He can fill you in on a few things while I run out to my car and grab those clothes." She took off for the back door, not giving either one of us a chance to protest.

There was a moment of awkward silence as Lonnie took his time checking me out. There wasn't anything that screamed *dirty old man* in his scrutiny, though. More of a *well, I'll be damned* glint of amusement flickered in his eyes.

"So, you're what's got Charlie mumbling to himself as he shot through here." Lonnie chuckled. "Don't pay him no mind. He's a hell of a lot more bark than he is bite."

I decided it was going to be easy to like Skeeter's cook. The jury was still out on Charlie. He'd seemed nice enough, despite his scary size, until I'd asked for a job. Once Sawyer had made it clear he didn't want me working here, Charlie's whole demeanor had changed. He'd made it plain it didn't sit well with him, going against

Sawyer's wishes, despite having sided with Zane in the end.

Flashing a grin at Lonnie, I said, "Bark or bite, he's got me now."

Lonnie returned my grin, "You're gonna get on just fine here. Charlie might'a been fooled by them fancy duds you're suited up in, but you've got grit, girlie. You just remember that."

Lonnie's vote of confidence had me swallowing a lump in my throat. Funny how a few words of praise from a stranger meant more than anything I'd heard in a long time from people who were supposed to love me. Pushing memories to the back of my mind, I thought now was as good a time as any to start asking a few of the questions that had brought me to Skeeter's in the first place.

"How long have you been working here, Mr. Lonnie?"

"Now, none of that mister nonsense, girlie. It's Lonnie to a pretty little thang like you." He winked. "I've been here goin' on thirty-two years. Started out workin' for the original owner, Skeeter Louis. Course, he'd opened this here place years 'fore I ever showed up. When Louis decided to retire a few years back, Sawyer bought him out, and I stayed on."

A buzz of excitement shot through me. The old cook had been working here during the time period I was interested in.

"You must have seen a lot of changes over the years."

"Not as many as you'd think. The people that work here come and go. Most of the customers that have been coming here for years are being replaced by their kids now. Lot more strangers around since they paved the county road." He frowned as if he didn't much care for the idea of the strangers coming around.

"Been a few upgrades in entertainment since Sawyer

bought it, but we still have the same food now we had when I first started. Folks around here reckon it's the best burger you can sink your teeth into. Sawyer had enough sense to know you don't go fixin' something that ain't broke." His thin chest puffed.

"You mean Skeeter's had the same menu for the last thirty-two years?"

"No menu necessary, girlie, and that was true long before I ever started working in the kitchen. People have two choices, hamburger or cheeseburger. They want something to go with it, they can have chips or fries. Kitchen closes at ten. Can't get much simpler than that." Lonnie nodded at me.

"See here, girlie. This is mainly a bar, pure and simple. But we make a damn fine burger, always have, so we get a lot of folk in for supper. Families who show up with kids in tow generally clear out well before nine. Much later than that and it can get excitin' around here."

From the stories Mrs. Whatley had been eager to share, *pure and simple* were the last words I would've used to describe Skeeter's. That it got *excitin'* around the place was easier to believe. Still, it was a relief to find out there wasn't an extensive dinner menu to memorize. Before I could steer Lonnie back around to the topic that really interested me, Zane was heading back in our direction.

She showed up holding a pair of boots, with flip-flops sticking out the top of one of the boot shafts. In her other hand were a pair of jeans and a neon tee. I did my best to control a grimace at the screaming pink color of the shirt.

"Lonnie, I gotta steal your new friend and get her ready for tonight." Zane didn't even slow down as she walked past us.

Before hurrying after her, I flashed a smile at Lonnie.

"I'd love to hear some of your stories about Skeeter's. Maybe if I get a break later tonight we can talk?"

"Girlie, once them doors open for the night, I ain't gonna have a minute to call my own. Mondays and Tuesdays, I man the kitchen by my lonesome. You're gonna have to catch me earlier in the day and later in the week iffin' you're wantin' any stories. Now git. I've got work to do. You're gonna have your hands full keeping up with that one." He jerked a thumb in Zane's direction. Then he gave me another wink before turning back to the prep table.

CHAPTER FOUR

Sawyer

THE SCENE WAS one I'd stood in the middle of before. It might be on the other side of the county, but it shared the same destruction we'd found at Luther Hinks' operation last month, only on a much smaller scale. It was the fourth busted-up site I'd been to over the last year, and followed the same pattern as the others. Every bit of copper that had gone into the making of the moonshine still was missing. Only difference between this one and the Hinks site had been the number of kettles being cooked off. Harlen only had one large pot cooking compared to Hinks' half-dozen.

There was nothing left of the main kettle but the cooked mash that'd been splattered across the dirt. Beer from the busted thumper barrel soaked the ground, leaving a sour smell in the air that stung the nose. What couldn't be absorbed by the soil lay on top of the dirt like something someone had spewed after a hard night of drinking.

"How'd they manage to get the drop on you, Harlen?" I

shifted eyes from what was left of the still to the less-than-steady moonshiner, the owner of the mangled mess. Harlen was as tough an old codger as I'd ever laid eyes on. That was the problem. The man was old.

Took a special kind of asshole to beat up on someone in their seventies. I'd known one such cocksucker who'd had no problems pounding on old men. I knew for a fact that bastard was dead and couldn't have been part of this.

"Ain't never had no trouble in all the years been settin' up out here. Most thieving bastards ain't willing to work this hard for the amount of copper only one still will get 'em. Ain't rightly sure what time of night it was when I heard a noise outside the tent. Sum'bitches knocked me upside the head while I was crawling out to see what kind of varmint was prowling around. Next thing I knew, I'm waking up hog-tied with a sack over my head and listenin' to them tear the still to hell and back." Harlen leaned over and spat a long stream of brown tobacco juice on the ruined mash.

Joey, the grandson who'd found Harlen, made a grab for his grandpa, afraid the old man would follow the spit to the ground. Harlen shook him off with a peevish, "Git your hands offa me! I ain't worm meat yet, boy."

Joey threw his hands up and took a step back. Far enough away to appease the elder shiner, close enough to be in grabbing range.

"Ain't many of us old shiners left here abouts. This right here hammers the nail in the coffin for me." Wagging his head back and forth, Harlen resembled an old hound with his saggy jowls and sorrowful eyes.

"I'm gettin' too old for this. Ain't a single one of my kids or grandkids care nothin' 'bout carrying on the shine business." Harlen sent a resentful glare his grandson's way. "I'm gettin' out before I find myself on the wrong side of the grass, same as my ol' friend Donley went and did."

Wade had made the trip out with me to check on the damage. He kicked a clump of dirt over the nasty mix on the ground before complaining, "Well, hell, Harlen. If you're getting out of the shine business, why'd you bother to call us out here? There ain't any money in tracking your stolen copper."

Harlen puffed his thin chest out and pointed a finger, twisted with arthritis, at Wade. "I don't rightly recall *you* being the one I got a hold of. Sawyer's the one I made the deal with for the shine. He damn shor' had a right to know there weren't no way I could keep up my end of the bargain. Seems to me you dragged your sorry ass out here without me asking."

One look from me had Wade rethinking the smart-ass words he was about to fire back. I'd become his boss right out of high school. There were times he could speak his mind and get away with it, and then there were times it was healthier to put a sock in it. This was a prime example of when to keep his trap shut.

Turning back to the old man, I told him, "I appreciate the call, Harlen. Figure you've heard you're not the only supplier I buy from who's been hit hard this last year. Wanted to check what happened here for myself."

Wade was angry about losing another source for shine and being a dick because of it. My next words were as much for him as Harlen. "This is my problem, same as yours. It'd be a fuckin' insult if you offered to pay me to find the bastards behind this."

Harlen snagged the waistband of his pants and tugged them higher up his skinny frame. He spat another stream of ropy tobacco juice, barely missing the toe of Wade's boot, causing him to jerk his foot back. "Reckon you're better suited to figure out what the hell's goin' on than anybody else around these parts. Ain't none of us shiners gonna call the sheriff to track down the sum'bitches doing this."

"Don't worry. It'll be handled." After making the promise, I made my way to the faint trail that would take Wade and me back to where we'd left the truck.

It was a long hike through woods snarled with tangled vines and a short climb up a limestone bluff before reaching anything that resembled a dirt track you might be able to drive a truck down. Exactly as Harlen said, it wasn't the sort of place metal scrappers came looking to steal copper. It damn sure wasn't the kind of place you just happened to stumble on.

Harlen made quality shine in small batches that went for big money. He wasn't a major player in the world of moonshiners, which added to the mystery of why anyone would want to put him out of business. For the last five years, I'd been his only client.

Others that sold to me had been hit, but I hadn't been their only buyer. This latest had the feel of a personal attack against my operation. If someone was aiming to hurt me by taking out my suppliers, they were shooting up the wrong tree.

Losing another source for moonshine wasn't as crippling as they might be aiming for. In the last few years, I'd started to make adjustments to the line of services provided to men and women who didn't mind dipping their toes in the grayer areas of having a good time. Illegal gambling houses were way more profitable than illegal whiskey. It was almost a joke to call them illegal with the number of loopholes in the laws governing the playing of cards in private homes. Having the sheriff show up every Sunday after church to join in a high-stakes cash game of Texas hold 'em was a damn good insurance policy to boot.

I'd also been channeling money into legal businesses. Not as much fun, but the country was changing. I could either change with it or go down trying to preserve a way of life that simply wasn't possible anymore.

Hell, even the old moonshiner, Donley, had been smart enough to realize the days making a living by working stills hidden in the woods were over. According to Char, Donley's granddaughter, he'd been on the last liquor run he ever planned to deliver when he'd been killed.

Only stupid dickheads like the one who'd murdered Donley were too ignorant to figure out that way of life was ancient history. Not to say there wouldn't always be a handful of men willing to work their asses off trying to keep the tradition of illegal shine alive. Because there would. For those few, just like my dad and his dad before him, I'd always provide them with an outlet to sell their liquor.

It was the sort of gray area that a stranger working in any of my bars or gambling houses could easily stumble across and report to the authorities. As long as it was the local sheriff, it wouldn't be a problem. Bill Cantrell was more than happy to take the money I paid to make sure he turned a blind eye when needed. We both profited, but money wasn't the only glue keeping our arrangement from shattering. A secret that involved murder and Cantrell's family kept the sheriff on my payroll as surely as his gambling debts did.

The death of large moonshine operations had been coming for a while. For it to happen this way didn't make a lot of sense. I'd warned Char over a year ago that there was going to be a major shift in the shine business. It wasn't going to be shiner against shiner, or even shiner against the law. There was a new breed of bootlegger out there. One who had nothing to do with moonshine. One who provided a cheaper, deadlier high for those that the high was all they cared about.

Meth was sounding the death knell to a way of life that had been handed down with pride through generations of families. Nowadays, any halfwit with a list of ingredients and YouTube could cook a batch of crystal. A high that could be produced a hell of a lot quicker than moonshine could ever be brewed, with none of the hard labor involved. Hardest part to making meth was coming up with a couple of the ingredients. But just like anything illegal that made people rich, there was always a way to get the materials needed.

There was no reason for a war between the people who cooked meth and the men who cooked mash. Meth was winning. Old traditions and the men who kept them were dying out. The running and distribution of moonshine had made my family rich. I had no interest in expanding into drugs to make us richer.

"What the hell got you so jacked back there? Didn't think it was a big deal tellin' ol' man Harlen the truth."

I counted it a minor miracle that Wade had waited to start bitching until after we'd put some distance between us and the still site.

"You have a fuckin' problem when it comes to thinking. All those thoughts spill out your damn mouth."

"Shit, Sawyer, losing another still sucks ass. That old man closing up shop is damn sure gonna cut into profits." Wade slapped a branch out of his way. He was rewarded by the backswing knocking him across the back of the head as he passed.

I was enough of an asshole to enjoy listening to him cuss as he rubbed the sore spot. Having grown up running wild in the woods, I was managing to move through them silently with none of the flailing and stumbling Wade had going on. He may have grown up in Arkansas, but he was a Copper Ridge townie.

"You missed any paydays lately? Been shorted any money that was supposed to come your way?" I asked when he finally stopped swearing at the branch.

"Hell no. I'm just saying that with your connections you could—"

"Then shut up. I don't wanna listen to a whiny pussy." Time to cut Wade off before he got started with his big ideas.

Ever since I'd put Vernon in charge of a couple poker houses, Wade had had a bug up his ass. He wanted a territory of his own. With Vernon not around as much, I'd been letting Wade tag along more. The idea had been to give him more responsibility, but it wasn't happening anytime in the near future. Shit, who was I kidding? He was loyal to a fault, but the more I was around the dumbass, the more I realized he couldn't run a free blowjob stand in a maximum-security prison.

For the next few minutes, the only sounds breaking the silence were the crunching of dried leaves and the snapping of dead branches under Wade's boots. Silence was a problem for Wade. He hated it.

"Heard Charlie hired a new waitress. Boys say she's got a body on her that'll knock a man to his knees. Course, I'd rather sweet-talk her into dropping to hers." Wade thought he was a real ladies' man. He was always bragging about the women he screwed. And even though Wade didn't mention her by name, Kelli was the only new waitress he could be talking about. It pissed me off that the guys were "discussing" her, and it pissed me off even more that I cared.

"She's out of your class and theirs. I told those assholes to keep an eye on her, not stand around flapping their lips, trying to figure out ways to fuck her."

Wade threw his hands up in the air, "Whoa, if you want to call dibs, just say so."

"I'm not calling fuckin' dibs. What are you, ten?" I could feel Wade's overdeveloped sense of curiosity snap to attention. My overreaction to the normal bullshit tossed around by the guys was going to send the bastard straight to Skeeter's to check her out.

"When we get back to town, I want you to head out and hit the salvage yards over in Ash Flat," I said. "Nose around and see if they've had anyone showing up with used copper in the last few months. You don't find anything, check out that big one over by Ravenden. And don't call the sum'bitches. I want you on site letting them know who's asking."

"Thought you'd already checked all the salvage and scrap places within a hundred miles of us?"

"And now I want them checked again. You got a problem with that?"

"Nope." He gave me a shit-eatin' grin.

Fuck. The one time I wanted Wade to pitch a fit, so I could throw a punch, he decided to get agreeable.

CHAPTER FIVE

Kelli

"How'd you ever find your way to Skeeter's?" Zane set two glasses on the polished surface of the bar. She was on the working side, and I plopped my butt on one of the wooden stools across from her. I watched as she reached under the counter and pulled out a dark bottle with no label on it. Tipping it, she poured a clear liquid into one of the heavy tumblers.

We were the last two souls out front. Charlie was in the back tallying up the night's take. A soft glow from a single pendant hanging above us was the only illumination in the deserted room.

The last thing I was interested in was answering a bunch of questions. But it was a minor miracle that the feisty brunette had been able to hold back this long before digging into my past. In an attempt to put off the interrogation, I placed a hand over the top of the empty glass.

"Thanks, but nothing for me. Really need to head back to the motel. I'm beat."

Watching the last customer stagger out the door a few minutes after closing had been mind-numbingly beautiful. A sad observation, considering it was only the fourth night on the job. A bed and oblivion were the only things I was interested in. Feet were whimpering and my arms and back were screaming, *why are you doing this to us?*

Carrying trays loaded with drinks while dodging groping hands made for one grueling workout. Turned out dropping my pricey health club membership wasn't going to be such a big deal after all. My biceps, triceps, quadriceps—I'm talking *all* my 'ceps—had never been worked this hard at a gym. Brain surgery was beginning to look easier in comparison. Over the last few days, I'd developed a whole new respect for women who worked in taverns.

"Aww, come on. Share a drink with me. Consider this an atta-girl for sticking it out for more than one night. You're a freaking natural. Surprised the hell out of me, considering how prissy you looked when you first showed up." She set the squatty, half-full tumbler in front of me and jerked the empty one out from under my hand. She flashed a smirk before splashing some of the liquor in the empty glass for herself.

"Girl, I about pissed my pants at the look on your face that first night. When you realized you had to wear my Salvation Army rejects, your nose did this wrinkle thing and your eyes got this glazed look. But damn if you didn't keep smiling. You made those rags look like a million bucks." She picked up her glass and held it aloft in a toast.

I knew Zane loved to tease, and she probably really had thought my reaction was funny. Probably. Hopefully. That didn't stop me from feeling terrible for letting her see my disgust that day. I settled back on the barstool. If she wanted to talk, I'd stay and talk.

Picking up the heavy tumbler, I sniffed the colorless liquid. No noxious fumes burned the lining of my nose, so I figured it was safe to drink. Out of the corner of my eye, I saw Zane roll hers. Afraid I might have offended my new friend, I tossed back a much larger swallow than was strictly ladylike. Hell's molten fire landed on my tongue and scorched a path down my throat. Deep, racking coughs had me leaning across the bar as I braced myself against the wood. Pretty sure I was about to deliver a lung.

Zane reached across and pounded on my back. "Damn girl! That ain't water. I'd have givin' you a warning to sip it if I'd known you were gonna chug it. Burns a little bit, don't it?"

When I was able to form a sentence, I wheezed out, "What *is* that?"

"Another one of those things you're not supposed to ask questions about." She gave an exaggerated wink. "It's getting harder and harder for Sawyer to get his hands on the really good stuff. Give it a chance and don't guzzle it next time." She let a much smaller measure of liquid slide down her own throat then hummed in appreciation.

While I wiped tears from my cheeks with the back of my hands, I nodded in silent agreement to keep mum about the mystery liquor. The list of things not to ask about was growing.

On the first night I'd worked, she'd mentioned the three rooms out back, whimsically called "furnished apartments." They'd been number one on the list of things to turn a blind eye to. My private speculation on their use was confirmed after one night of watching couples wander over to talk to Charlie or one of the bouncers. The discussion always ended with a key being passed and the couple heading for the dimly lit hallway at the back of the building. It didn't take a genius to figure out they weren't going back there to play tiddlywinks.

"You were about to tell me how you ended up working here." Zane ran a finger around the rim of her drink.

"It's a long story and not much fun."

"Give me the short version. It doesn't have to be fun. Not all stories are." Her voice softened.

"The short version..." The words faded as I wondered how much of the past to reveal to satisfy Zane's curiosity. Giving a mental shrug, I decided that if she wanted a story, I could give her a doozy. I hadn't planned on keeping why I was there a secret forever. So what if the story was humiliating? That just made it more interesting for the listener.

"You know what?" I dredged up a smile for my newest bestie then carefully sipped more of the liquid fire. Huh, didn't burn nearly as bad, and it was setting up nice, warm fuzzies in my tummy.

"What?"

"On second thought, it's a really funny story. One big joke, and it was all on me."

"Wait." Zane threw her hands up as if she was going to physically stop any more words from spilling out of my mouth. "Why do I get the feeling you're about to rip a big ol' scab off a major hurt?"

"Maybe because it's the only way to get to the truth." I shrugged. No bitterness this time, just a nice, numb blank space.

"But you have to promise me something." Leaning in closer, I dropped my voice to a stage whisper. "You can't tell your boyfriend or anyone else."

She leaned toward me and, in the same stage whisper, said, "Not a problem. I don't have a boyfriend—yet."

"What about Sawyer? I got the feeling you two had

something special." I dropped the whisper and tipped my head sideways in surprise. That made me start sliding in that direction, so I jerked back to a more or less upright position.

"That would be a big *hell no*." She rolled her eyes.

"But you talked him into hiring me. He must have some feelings for you. Sawyer doesn't strike me as the kind of guy that lets just anyone dictate to him." Why was I trying to insist they had something going on? I should be relieved. Every time my thoughts drifted to him, I gave myself a lecture to stop being a creeper because he belonged to Zane.

"Puh-lease!" She rolled her eyes. "I may have pushed for him to hire you, but if he really didn't want you here, nothing I said would have changed his mind. He saved my ass when I was younger and gave me a job when I needed it, but that's about as *special* as it gets between us. Just because he let me put my two cents in doesn't mean diddly-squat. You should have figured out by now that it's hard to shut me up."

Zane flashed a big grin at me. "You being here has nothing to do with me, other than he knows I'm a pain in the ass if I don't get my way when I want something."

Having seen her in action, I believed she had a point.

"Okay, then. Guess it's story time." I slapped my hands on the bar and shot her a big grin.

After my big build-up, I just sat there and stared off into the darkest part of the room. This was going to be harder than I thought. Heaving a sigh, I twisted a loose strand of hair around my index finger. "Now I know why stories start with 'once upon a time.' You have to tell the juicy parts of the past so your audience can understand the now parts."

"Hey, I'm good with however you want to start." Zane

settled into a more comfortable position as she leaned on her elbows and propped her chin in one hand.

Pulling my gaze back to her, I began, "I guess you could say I ended up at Skeeter's by following in my momma's footsteps."

Zane cocked her head and gave me a skeptical look. "Say what? From the way you talk, to the way you dress, it's pretty clear you come from money. I ain't never seen a waitress make enough to afford a daughter classy as you."

"If that waitress marries a rich man old enough to be her daddy then she can raise her daughter any way she wants with his money." You just had to be more interested in that money than who you hurt.

"Your momma married some old rich dude and your daddy is a millionaire? Was she able to make everyone forget where she came from?" Zane stared at me as if my answers could change her world.

"Real life isn't quite so tidy. When you lie and cheat to get a rich husband, you don't actually deserve a fairytale ending. Unfortunately, it's usually the ones lied to who end up paying."

"Are you paying for your momma's lies?" Zane frowned.

"Me and others. Best part? I didn't realize what a lie my life was until a few months ago."

"What happened?" Zane reached for my glass, splashed more of the "good stuff" in before refilling her own.

The numb feeling was fading, so a fortifying sip was just what I needed to help ease the story. "Jackson Radcliff married my momma when I was around two years old. Momma not only managed to hook a very rich, very old man, but she talked him into adopting me. The adoption was never a secret, and he insisted that I called him Jackson.

In second grade, I'd desperately wanted to be like all the other boys and girls. I'd wanted a daddy, not a Jackson. During art, I'd drawn a picture of a man holding a child's hand. I'd even given the man grey hair so there was no mistaking who I was drawing. Extra care was given to form the perfect letters in *Daddy*. It took more courage than I had to simply start calling him Daddy. I'd been positive he'd understand when I presented him with the picture. He'd taken one look, torn the paper in half, and handed the pieces back to me. Lesson learned without a word being spoken.

My voice went flat. "He died a little over six months ago."

Zane immediately launched into exclamations of sympathy, but I talked over her to drown her out. I neither wanted nor needed her condolences. "By the time he passed, the two of us didn't share a whole lot of good feelings. Not that we ever had. I found out just how little he thought of me the day the lawyer came to the house."

I snorted, thinking about that day. Snorted? Time to cut back on the liquor. "The reading of the will was a real show. It could have been something out of the movies, with the lawyer coming to the house to inform us of Jackson's last wishes."

Jackson's brother, sister-in-law, two nephews, and their wives had been all smiles. Momma declared them to be horribly vulgar to me later. But they had a right to the smiles, as it turned out.

"Before the lawyer got down to business with the will, he handed me a file. As he passed it over, he told me it was the only item left to me by Jackson. He'd been instructed to inform me that it was the last help I would ever receive from the Radcliff family." I'd actually felt sorry for the man at the time. He'd looked uncomfortable as he carried out Jackson's final instructions.

"He said it contained information that might help me find my biological father, should I be interested. Which was a bit confusing, since I'd grown up believing that my real daddy had died before I was born." Confused didn't come close to covering what I'd felt sitting in that room, hearing those words. I'd turned to Momma, expecting her to somehow fix everything. But as I watched the blood drain from Momma's face, I'd known she wouldn't be fixing anything.

"Son of a bitch! Why would a man, that'd been your daddy for all those years, do that to you? I don't care if you called him Daddy or Jack-ass-son. The bastard took you as his own and should have been a daddy to you." Zane jerked to rigid attention.

I couldn't help laughing at Zane's outrage. It felt good to have my foul-mouthed friend so furious on my behalf.

"Sure, it hurt having the lawyer pull a skeleton out and rattle bones in front of the gathered vultures. But later, it was actually sort of...I don't know...freeing. It felt right that I hadn't called him Daddy all those years when I had a real one out there somewhere."

"Did your momma fess up to lying?" Zane narrowed her eyes.

"Momma was too busy throwing a hissy fit to admit anything. After the lawyer dropped the Daddy File on me, he proceeded to tear the doodles out of Momma's plans for the future. Come to find out she hadn't been the only one keeping secrets. The mansion, all of the businesses, a lot of the money—shoot, just about everything she thought Jackson owned—was tied up in a Radcliff family trust. After he died, the administration of the trust passed to his younger brother. She was put on a monthly allowance, and it was a *whole* lot less than what she was used to spending."

While Momma wailed over how she'd been cheated, I'd gone through the only thing Jackson left me. There hadn't been a lot in the Daddy File other than directions to a town called Copper Ridge, and the only name in the file wasn't my dad's, but a bar called Skeeter's. A short handwritten note stated that my momma used to work at Skeeter's, and if I wanted to learn more, it was up to her to tell me.

"I tried to talk to Momma a few weeks after the meeting with the lawyer and it turned ugly. She was furious Jackson told me about her working at Skeeter's and my father being a whole lot more alive than he was dead. She refused to tell me anything about my real father. Said if I insisted on looking for him, it would be without her help. As far as she was concerned, the past was dead and buried and she wanted it to stay that way. She told me to stick to the plan and I'd be better off than chasing after some broke hick mechanic just so I could call him daddy."

"Your momma's *plan*—what was it?" Zane sounded suspicious, angry, which struck me as odd, but a lot of things Zane said and did seemed odd. It was part of her charm.

"Momma had been grooming me ever since I was a teeny-tiny girl"—I hovered my hand a short distance above the floor—"to marry a rich man."

"And you went along with it?" Zane scrunched up her face as if she'd gotten a whiff of a rotten egg. "I understand having a goal in life. I've got one. Had it for years. What I can't understand is letting someone else make goals and plans for you." She then murmured, "Especially if it's your mom."

"Momma's a lot like you—a force of nature. It doesn't

matter what others say or think; you get to rolling and you're this big ol' tsunami—nothing can stand against you." I grinned at my new friend to lessen any sting Zane might feel.

"Besides, the plan was fun for me growing up. Cheerleading, dance classes, pageants, riding lessons. You name it, Momma put me in it. Once I went to college, it didn't matter what classes I took as long as I made it into the right sorority." If I came off being *that* spoiled rich girl, I wasn't going to apologize. I'd enjoyed growing up the way I had.

"What about control? Didn't you ever want to be the one in control of your life?"

"I never even knew what real control was until I quit my job, broke up with the family-approved fiancé, and defied Momma by moving to Copper Ridge to look for my daddy."

"Wait! You were engaged? How the hell are you just now mentioning that?" Zane slapped the bar, eyes bugged.

She had a good point. How had Bradley become such a non-issue that he didn't rate top billing in my life story? I'd thought he was perfect at one time. He was good-looking, successful, and his family and the Radcliffs were old friends. Momma had been thrilled, and for once Jackson had approved of something that involved me.

Having no real answer, I shrugged. "Guess that shows just how much *not* in love I was. Besides, when Bradley learned I'd been cut out of the Radcliff money, his affections noticeably cooled. He had this way of looking at me as if he'd been cheated. We were both relieved when I gave the ring back. Momma took it way harder than I did."

Zane stared into her empty glass for so long that I couldn't help wondering what was going on in her head. An awkward feeling of having overshared personal drama had me tapping my scarlet nails on the polished wood surface of the bar. "Okay then, it's late. We probably should—"

"So, what's the next step? How are we gonna find your daddy?" Zane's matter-of-fact questions threw me. Events over the last few months had taught me that when things got rough, so-called friends disappeared faster than Jimmy Choos during a half-price sale at the boutique.

"It's taken me over six months to even make the move to try and find out who my father is. I don't really have any plans beyond asking Lonnie about the time Momma worked here. Stands to reason he'd know who my father is. I want to find out who he is and what's going on in his life first. It would be wrong to just show up on his doorstep. What if he doesn't want me messing with his life?"

Standing, I lifted my glass and tossed back the tiny amount left in the bottom. More than ready to call an end to the night, I rounded the bar to wash my glass before drying and putting it back in the stack. Zane gave a token protest, but she was as beat as me. She didn't put up much of a fight when I grabbed her glass and gave it the same treatment.

As we made our way to the office to gather our purses, Zane slipped an arm around my waist and bumped hips with me. "You don't have to do this alone, you know."

"No, I didn't know, but I do now." I gave a little hip bump of my own in a show of gratitude.

CHAPTER SIX

Kelli

"Now, ain't you a pretty sight to start off my night." Lonnie flashed me a smile as he walked in the back door.

If me being in his kitchen came as a surprise, he didn't let on. He sure didn't let it slow him down. He headed straight for the cooler where the vegetables were kept. Moments later, he was back and had everything lined up on the stainless-steel table with surgical precision. Tomatoes, onions, lettuce, each waiting its turn under his knife, nothing bagged or precut here. Only when he was settled into a rhythm of slicing did he ask, "Whatcha doing showing up so early, girlie?"

Zane had warned me that Lonnie was a fanatic when it came to his kitchen and time schedule. The warning hadn't been necessary. I'd been trying to talk to him all week and he always said the same thing: "You're gonna have to catch me earlier in the day iffin' you're wantin' to talk, girlie."

Problem was, he never came in early, and the moment

he stepped into the kitchen it was like watching a video on fast forward. The man was a choreographed whirlwind of activity. I suspected he'd been doing the same routine for so many years that muscle memory alone would have gotten him through the night even if he was half dead.

"Lonnie, remember when we first met? You said you'd share stories with me about the past?" I leaned a hip against the steel table, doing my best to look casual.

"You're gonna have to—"

"Don't tell me to catch you earlier in the day. You just walked in the door."

He chuckled as he said, "Was *gonna* say, you need to give me some settling time, girlie—I just walked in the door. Toby will be here in thirty or so and I'll have more time to talk."

The last thing I wanted was for the weekend helper, Toby, to show up and hear our discussion. I dropped the *just killing time* attitude. "I'm not here to slow you down, Lonnie. Give me something to do, and I'll help you prep for the dinner crowd. I have some important questions about people who used to work here."

He stopped chopping long enough to level a look at me before he said, "Girlie, you said you were wantin' to hear stories about the old days. Don't recall you wantin' to ask questions about people that used to work here."

Zane had predicted Lonnie might get *lockjaw*, as she put it, when questioned. Employees of Sawyer's were never eager to share information with strangers. That the questions were about someone who used to work at Skeeter's made it even worse. Zane had pushed to be there when I asked if he remembered my momma. Not wanting anyone else to hear what he might have to say, I'd steadfastly refused her offer.

I found myself scrambling to keep him from shutting

me down. "It wasn't really a fib saying I wanted to hear your stories. I do. I just might not have told you the whole truth."

"And what's the whole truth?" He dropped his knife on the table and gave me his full attention.

Taking a deep breath, I rushed my explanation, hoping it wouldn't sound so bad if I got it out fast. "I'm not as much of a stranger as you think. My momma used to work here around twenty-seven years ago, when I was a baby. She would've had a boyfriend at the time, and he's the one I'm hoping you have information on. I think he's my father."

"What do you mean you *think* he's your daddy? You don't know who your daddy is?" Lonnie appeared to soften.

I walked over to nudge him aside with my shoulder, then grabbed his knife and ran the sharp blade through the thin skin of a tomato. I concentrated on each slide of the razor-sharp blade with an intensity normally reserved for major surgery. It gave me a good excuse to not face him while I shared the small amount of information I had.

"Momma left the area with a man from Little Rock when I was a baby. They got married and he adopted me. Up until a few months ago, I thought my real father had died before I was born. I asked Momma about all of this, but she's not willing to tell me who my biological father is." The breath I took had a hitch in it. "I'm hoping you'll help me figure out who he is."

The silence in the room was broken only by the sound of the knife contacting the cutting board after each slice. I took a peek to see what Lonnie was doing. I found him studying my features with a diligence absent when we'd first been introduced. He caught me looking and asked, "What's your momma's family name?"

"Hutley. Her full name is Denise Rena Hutley Radcliff."
Fine tremors had me placing the knife back on the table to
keep from slicing one of my fingers. The tremors weren't
confined to my hands, but I hoped the shakiness of my legs
wasn't as obvious.

"Well I'll be dipped in doo-doo! You're Denise Hutley's
little Kelli! Why the hell didn't you say so, girlie, when you
first showed up?" Lonnie grabbed me by the shoulders and
pulled me in for a bear hug.

Relief was my initial reaction to Lonnie's memory of
Momma, closely followed by worry. Months earlier, when
I'd seriously started thinking about trying to find my dad,
it'd been one of those abstract ideas—*wouldn't it be cool to
know who my real father is?* Now that there was a very real
possibility of finding out, doubt that I was doing the right
thing slapped me in the face.

Lonnie stepped back but didn't release my shoulders.
"Let me get a good look at you." He studied my face as if
trying to connect it with a memory. "You've got your
momma's eyes. Hard to forget eyes on a woman carrying
that color of green." He squinted and turned his head sideways. "But the rest of you is pure Emmett. Just like your
brother, excepting for the eyes. His are blue, same as y'all's
daddy."

The wonder of hearing my father's name for the first
time was lost the moment Lonnie said the word *brother*.
Brother? My brain refused to associate that word in any
shape or form to my life. Momma wouldn't have kept
something that important from me. The idea was ridiculous. That would've meant she'd left a child behind when
she'd run away from Copper Ridge. What kind of mother
would do that?

It wasn't that I had any illusions about Momma. She
was shallow and more than a little self-centered, but I had

no doubt that she loved me. She would have loved any child that belonged to her. No way could Momma have done what he was saying. Lonnie had Denise confused with someone else, and I refused to believe different.

I took a step back and Lonnie's hands fell away. The happiness on his face turned somber. "What's wrong, girlie?"

"You're remembering the wrong woman. My momma didn't have any other children. I'm an only child." I lifted my chin a notch, letting frost coat my words. I had no reason to be mad at Lonnie, but there it was.

Lonnie studied me silently, then, nodding as if coming to a decision, he moved back to the prep table. Reaching down to the open shelving underneath, he pulled out a long steel-framed contraption with shiny blades and plopped it in front of the pile of onions. He then strolled over to his collection of knives, selected one, came back to the table, and laid it next to the kitchen gadget.

As I watched, I kept telling myself this had been a waste of time. He was thinking about the wrong woman and that was that. Besides, it was probably for the best. It'd been a crazy idea to look for someone who'd never cared enough to search for me. It wasn't Lonnie's fault he was remembering things all wrong. I was asking him to remember something that'd happened twenty-seven years ago. After that length of time, anyone was bound to get confused.

"Thanks for trying to help, Lonnie. I'm going to head out front and get an early start on setting up for tonight." I infused extra warmth in both my smile and my voice.

"Hold up there, missy. You ever worked a mandolin before?" His no-nonsense tone let me know I wasn't going anywhere.

"Uh, no. But I've seen the cook use one before."

"The cook?" Lonnie shook his head. "Just get on over here, and I'll show you how it's done."

Not seeing a graceful way out of it, I moved back to the table. He was thorough in explaining how to use an instrument that had my fingers curling in fear. He sliced one onion to demonstrate, then stood by and watched as I tentatively went through the same motions.

"Just remember to use that finger guard, and you'll do fine." He took up where I'd left off slicing the tomatoes.

We worked in silence for several minutes. It wasn't until I'd relaxed into the rhythm of the mandolin that he started talking.

"I'd only been working here a year when she showed up. Some thought she was a little too big for her britches. But I suppose when you were as beautiful as she was, it was easy to start thinking you were better than most."

"Lonnie, I don't want to—"

"Hush now and listen. Just gonna tell one of those stories you were so eager to hear." He waited until I went back to working the mandolin.

"It was wintertime when she blowed through the doors here. We all knew she was too young, but ol' Skeeter hired her anyway 'cause a beautiful woman is always good for business. It was like watching bees swarm the only flower in a field on the days she worked. But she was picky when it came to men. They needed plenty of money and be willin' to spend it on her. Discouraged most fellers right fast, I can tell you. Everyone, that is, but Emmett Wilks. He had a face and a way with him that made the ladies fight for his attention." Lonnie shook his head as if the foolishness of women confounded him.

"Everything changed the day Emmett laid eyes on the new girl. From that time on, he was here every day after he got off work sweet-talkin' her. She done her best to ignore him 'cause the only thing he had in plenty was good looks. But it weren't no time before he had her moved into a tiny trailer parked on a piece of land outside of town. She kept working for a while, and he would still come in every day after work. Lordy, the way them two carried on, you'd-a thought they invented falling in love." He chuckled quietly with a faraway look in his eyes.

"This went on for about a year before she come to Louis to let him know she was quittin'. Some months later, they had a boy that was the spitting image of Emmett. Not many years after the boy, they had a baby girl."

He paused for so long that I was afraid he would stop. "Lonnie, what happened after they had the girl?" I asked.

He wouldn't look at me now. "Things changed. Denise showed up here after the baby was close to a year old asking for her old job back. Louis was more than happy to put her back on the payroll 'cause she was still a looker. If anything, she was even more beautiful with the added curves from bearing children. But there was a desperation about her when she came back. It was as if she was chasing after something she thought was missing in her life. Damn fool people oughta stop worrying about what they're missing and realize what the hell they've already got."

Once again, he stopped, but the break didn't last as long. "Back then we didn't get as many strangers in here as we do now. But one night, a group of city bigwigs came in flashing money. You would've thought they owned their own personal printin' press the way they was throwing it around. Bragged about everything from the fish they was catching to one-upping each other on who had the most money. But they weren't the only ones doing some fishing while they was here. Denise made it her business to get friendly with them."

Lonnie cut a look at me from under his shaggy

eyebrows then cleared his throat. "You don't need to know all the particulars, but she managed to hook one of the older ones. When her fancy man left to head back to the city, she up and disappeared, taking that baby girl with her."

The tears rolling down my face had nothing to do with the onion I was slicing. There was no way to deny his story was about my family. "Did Emmett ever look for me?"

Lonnie laid his knife down and took the step necessary to place a hand over mine. "Your daddy took Grady and left here a week after y'all were gone. They stayed away better than two weeks. When Emmett got back, he was a changed man. He never mentioned Denise or you again. He'd always been a hard worker, but after he come back from Little Rock, he attacked work like he was fightin' fire. It weren't long before he was working for himself. He put up a solid little house and built his own garage out by it. He done the best he could in a bad situation. Your daddy was a good man."

Hearing him praise Emmett had a bitterness spewing out of me that I didn't even realized had been festering. "If he was such a *good man*, explain how he could just give me up? What kind of father signs papers to give his daughter away to another man?"

"Your momma and daddy never got married, girlie. That limited his legal rights without him hiring some fancy lawyer. Nobody knows what happened when he went after y'all, but Emmett didn't have no money to fight your momma and her rich feller. He had Grady to think of, too. Who knows? Maybe he had to take what he could in order to not lose both of his children. But your daddy loved you, and don't you ever think different. Even when things was darkest between him and Denise, all it took to light that man up was to ask after you two kids. Lordy, his chest would swell up so big he'd near bust the buttons clean off his shirt with pride."

I nodded as if agreeing with him, but the actual believing came harder. Using my forearm, I mopped at the tears dripping off my chin. It wasn't very ladylike, but it was that or pull up the tail of my t-shirt and scrub. Lonnie solved the problem when he handed over a kitchen towel.

"I need to see him, Lonnie. There are so many questions only he can answer." When the words came out of my mouth was the moment I realized my decision had already been made.

"Aww, hell." Lonnie rubbed a leathered hand down his long face, pulling his frown deeper. "Child, your daddy passed, going on a year now. If you have questions, you'll have to ask your brother. But he might not have any answers for you, seeing as he wasn't much more than a baby himself when this all took place. I reckon he would've been somewhere around five or six years old at the time you and your momma left. Ask Zane to keep an eye out for Grady tonight. There's a good chance he'll show up, it being the start of the weekend and all."

It had taken me six months to make the move to search for my father. For what? To find out I was too late? A sadness filled my heart for a man I'd never known. How was I supposed to switch gears and introduce myself to a brother I'd just found out about? You were supposed to be able to trust your parents if nobody else in the world. Right? How would a brother feel having me show up as a reminder that his momma had chosen to keep me and left him behind? Would he resent me? I'd resent the heck out of him if the situation was reversed.

"Lonnie, can we *please* keep this between us? I need to figure this out, and I don't want Grady hearing about me until I do."

"Well, I reckon it ain't nobody else's business." He gave my hand one last pat. "But, girlie, we all need family. I remember one of the last times Emmett came by with you and your brother. That boy told everybody in the place how he was the big brother and you belonged to him. Grady let us know right quick it was his job to protect you. You just think on that while you're figuring things out."

CHAPTER SEVEN

Sawyer

I stood in Skeeter's entrance with three of my guys and scanned the crowd. Just because the first person I spotted was Kelli didn't mean I'd walked through the door looking for her. The table full of men she was yukking it up with was practically in the doorway.

I watched as her friendly smiles turned to a deer-in-the-headlights stare the moment she spotted me. The moment was just that, a moment. She was quick to smooth out her features and replace it with a cool smile. She did this head-toss thing as she turned her back on me. Oh yeah, complete rich-chick move. I held back a smile that would scare the shit out of most people who knew me. Someone should warn the princess those kinda moves just stirred the bastard in me.

After checking out the rest of the room, we headed deeper into the building. Wade following in my wake while the other two split off in a different direction. Kelli wasn't the only one I'd spotted. Grady was seated one table over from where she was still shooting the shit with some locals. It wasn't a complete surprise to see him, but he hadn't been around much the last few weeks. But then, we hadn't parted on the best of terms. I checked out who was sitting at the table with Grady and recognized the regular drinkin' and hell-raisin' buddies he ran around with. Whatever had Grady shitting bullets the other day, I didn't believe any of those men had any part of it. Fuckin' mysteries. Hated them.

I tipped my chin at Grady as I passed, and he nodded back. Looked like the dumbass wasn't going to ignore me, but if he had something to say, he could damn well make the trip back to my table. He'd made it clear he didn't want my help. If he'd changed his mind, he was going to have to come to me to do the asking.

Wade took the seat to my left as I claimed the chair that placed my back to the wall. The location of the table made it easy to keep an eye on the rest of the room without a lot of rubbernecking. Being at the back of the room, was about as private as you were going to get in this crowd. We'd barely settled in our seats before Zane was there bringing my usual double shot of whiskey.

"You decide to stop in and check up on your new employee in person instead of calling to old-lady gossip with me?" Zane loved to tease, and her favorite target was me. She'd ridden me pretty hard the other day when I'd called to question her about Kelli.

I ignored Zane's question as I lifted my glass and took a healthy swig. Studying her over the rim before setting the tumbler back on the table, I could tell something was off with her. She was trying to hide a buzz of anger behind her normal sass. If she'd had any worries about the newcomer, she would have already warned me when we talked the other day. Whatever had her pissed had nothing to do with Kelli.

"What's up, Zane? Problems?" If it wasn't Kelli putting that fire in her eye, my next guess was Zane's fucked-up family.

"Nothing I can't handle." She waved away my concerns. "As far as Kelli, you can relax. She's a kickass waitress." She gave me a tight smile, making it clear she wanted me to drop the questions and change the subject. "Just like me."

I watched her for a second longer before relaxing back in my chair. "Last thing we need is another one of you running around this place."

Wade barked out a laugh that earned him a narrow-eyed look from Zane. At her glare, he grabbed for her hand and gave her a sick, cow-eyed look that was as fake as every promise he'd ever made to a woman. "Now, Zane, sugar. You know I don't agree with him. Say the word and I'll take you away from all of this."

Zane pulled her hand back and wiped it on her shirt. "Men around here are such assholes that learning to act like me is the only way she'll survive this place."

She didn't even try to hide her relieved grin as she turned away to go wait on another table full of asshole men.

After Zane left, I found myself searching the crowd. My eyes settled on Kelli as she wiped down a table two rows over. I studied the woman I'd been wasting way too much time thinking about. Another damn mystery.

There hadn't been a chance to drop by Skeeter's lately. Basically, since I'd given Charlie the green light to hire her. One thing for damn sure: she wasn't the same woman who'd slammed through the door looking for a job. That one had been wearing fuck-me heels and an outfit better suited for a boardroom than a bar room.

Tonight, she presented a different picture in jeans that hugged her long legs. The denim material was tight enough to make a man have to adjust himself every time she moved across the damn floor. I'd lay money on them costing more than what she could earn in a week working here. Hell, maybe the whole month. But I couldn't fault the way they displayed one of the sweetest asses a man could ever hope to fill his hands with. Sadly, some kind of low-heeled, short boot had replaced those cock-teasing heels from our first meeting. The black tee she wore was snug enough to show off generous tits and short enough to leave a thin strip of skin exposed between the hem and the band of her jeans. Whenever she leaned over to place drinks, the smooth dip of skin in the small of her back played peekaboo with anyone watching. And there were plenty watching besides me.

Yeah, she'd done a good job dressing the part she played, but there was no hiding the elegance and grace in her movements. She walked across the bar as if strolling through a room at some swanky society gathering. It surprised me to see the easy way she had with customers. Laughing with some, wary of others. Either Zane really did have a calling for turning socialites into waitresses, or tea parties hosted a rougher crowd than I'd figured.

Zane hadn't been the only one I'd called to check up on Kelli. When I'd talked to Charlie, the man had grudgingly admitted she was doing better than expected. Said she did her job without complaint, and he hadn't caught her doing any snooping—so far. Charlie was a suspicious bastard, which made him the perfect manager for a business known to flip its finger at the law.

Zane had insisted Kelli didn't have any interest in the questionable sidelines that went on at Skeeter's. I wasn't sure how true that was. Zane had never lied to me before, but she'd never been so taken with a stranger before, either. She sure as hell had never worked so hard to convince me to hire someone obviously not suited. That girl had something up her sleeve, and somehow Kelli played into it.

Lately, half the fuckin' people I knew were acting crazier than a nest of outhouse rats. The destruction of stills that had managed to remain hidden for decades had the old moonshiners spooked. Then there was Grady, tied in knots over something he wasn't willing to talk about. And now Zane was hellbent on trying to prove how great Kelli was.

If asked, I would say I didn't want Kelli here, but that would be a lie. It cranked my ass trying to nail down why she got under my skin. It didn't take a genius to figure out why my dick was interested.

The day she'd walked in, I'd pegged her as lost. Then she'd asked for a job and threw my natural caution into overdrive. Whole time she'd been mouthing off that verbal résumé, I'd considered that she might have been placed at the bar to try and dig up dirt on me.

There was also the possibility she was after one of the other men, with less-than-sterling reps, who hung around the place. But I didn't buy it. She was too refined. Nothing about her whispered undercover fed or cop. If they were going to try something, they would've picked a woman who actually could've worked in a bar. Not someone who walked straight out of a Miss Manners book.

She damn sure wasn't anything I normally sniffed around. I wanted a woman who could handle the grittier side of life. God knew I stayed ass-deep in gritty most of the time. My women were brassy and bold, willing to get down in the dirt with me, whether it was to fight or fuck. The dirtier the better. But I wasn't big on denying myself when something came along I wanted. Kelli was well on the way to becoming something I wanted.

She was a looker with that long fall of blonde hair and those green eyes so brilliant they looked fake. Then there was that tiny cleft in the middle of her chin that begged to be nibbled. And it wasn't just her face or the body that tempted a man to break more than a few rules. She had fire under all her politeness. She drew a man in, made him ache to taste some of that honey that practically dripped from her full lips with every word she spoke. Any woman not tough enough to handle shit when it happened had no business being here. 'Cause if there was one thing you could count on, it was shit always happening.

The kind of men and women who hung out here weren't the bashful type. Put a beautiful woman in front of them and some of the men were going to make suggestions that could make a seasoned whore blush. Those kinds of situations weren't a problem for the women who worked here. They gave as good as they got. Hell, half of them considered their waitressing as more of a backup for slow nights. Helped pay the bills when they didn't have any offers to take a trip to one of the back rooms.

Just because Kelli wasn't interested in selling her goodies didn't mean there weren't going to be plenty of dickheads trying to change her mind. She wouldn't be able to handle things the way Zane did. That girl was a tough little shit. She had to be to survive in the family she came from. She had no problems telling someone to fuck off if they messed with her.

"Damn, Sawyer. You're about as much fun as a sore tooth tonight. What the hell you stewing about?" Wade tossed back the last of his whiskey. Before setting it down, he uncurled a finger from around the glass and pointed at a busty platinum blonde seated across the room. "Marilee's been shaking her titties in your direction since we got here and you ain't paid a bit of mind. If it was me, I'd be jumping all over that."

I'd been doing a good job ignoring the woman Wade was pointing out. I knew she'd been looking for any excuse to make her way to my table, and Wade's gesture was the opening she'd been waiting for. And fuckin' hell, she just shimmied out of her chair and started in our direction.

In the past, I'd found her over-the-top pursuit amusing, and had more than once taken her up on what she offered. She came about as close as any woman ever did to being something of a regular for me without there being any real commitment from either side. I knew for a fact she shared more than a laugh with several of the men in the bar, and it didn't bother me. But whenever I showed up, she would abandon whoever she was with in favor of me. Brassy and bold, what I normally wanted in a woman, was looking cheap and boring tonight.

"I should break that damn finger off and stick it up your ass." I dropped the thick tumbler back on the table hard enough to crack it.

"Whatcha oughta be doing is kissing my rosy-red ass for getting her to come on over." Wade didn't even blink at my threat. "You've been in a shitty mood for weeks and this last one's been the worst. Either you're on the rag or you need to get laid. Ain't never known you to have a dry spell when it came to women, but here comes a big ol' rain cloud." He pointed at the woman making her way over to us. "Do us all a favor and go get wet."

A middle finger was Wade's reward for being a buddy.

"Hey, Sawyer. How ya doin', sugar?" Marilee bent over to deliver her breathy greeting in my ear.

I shot Marilee a frigid glare that would've had a sane person turning around and heading right back in the direction they'd come from. But not Marilee. She was too confident in her overabundant charms to realize shit was about to get ugly.

A loud round of laughter caught my attention. It came from the floor section Kelli was working. Whatever was taking place at that table was a hell of a lot more interesting than the woman trying to polish my bicep with her double-D tits. Because I was trying to focus on what was happening on the other side of the room, I was a hell of a lot easier on her than I'd normally be. "Not tonight, Marilee."

Kelli stood by a table crowded with pussy-faced college boys. Most were strangers. One was all too familiar. Mason Webber, youngest son of Walter Webber, was an entitled bastard who thought Daddy's money made him bulletproof. Talk around town said he was making a career out of going to college he'd been enrolled for so long. From the looks of it, he'd hauled a bunch of buddies home for the weekend. They were eyeballing Kelli like a pack of coyotes slobbering over a fresh kill.

Marilee wasn't used to being ignored, and took my brush-off as a personal challenge.

"Aww, now what's up with acting all hard and cold, sugar?" Marilee bent over a little farther, making sure I had an unobstructed view down the front of her blouse, all the way to her barely covered nipples. "I hear wet heat applied to a hard head is a miracle cure for a cold-hearted man."

"Marilee, do you know what the difference is between being sexy and being slutty?" I bounced an emotionless glance from her tits back up to look her in the eye.

"No, sugar. What's the difference?" She grinned as if she'd won some kind of prize because I was finally paying attention to her.

"See, that's the problem with sluts. They don't know the

fuckin' difference." I stood abruptly. Marilee had to do some scrambling to keep from doing a face plant on the table when the arm she'd been leaning on so heavily was no longer there. As I stalked across the floor, I heard her shrilly calling me a few choice names that had nothing to do with sugar.

CHAPTER EIGHT

Kelli

I'D LEARNED that taking orders in a bar was never as simple as asking, "What will it be?" There were rituals to be observed, barroom etiquette to be carried out. Greetings were followed by "witty" one-liners and the obligatory laughs on my part. Only after these social niceties had taken place did the average customer get down to the business of ordering drinks.

The laughing stage of the rites were being observed when I noticed a couple of the guys glance toward the entrance. One look and they were scooting up in their chairs, directing their buddies' attention to the door with head jerks. Curious, I looked over to see who had grabbed their attention.

Four men in a loosely knit group were paused in what I called the vestibule. Zane had laughed at me for giving the doorway a fancy name. From the gentlemen's stance (I'm using the term gentlemen in the loosest sense of the word), and cold-eyed scrutiny of the interior, they might as well have been wearing matching vests with *You Don't Want None of This* embroidered on the backs. Okay, if they were willing to be matchy-matchy—which I bet never happened —they would have probably picked out something more to the point and vulgar.

As intimidating as each of the men were, one figure stood out from the rest. My new boss, Sawyer.

It was the first time I'd seen him since being hired. Over the last few days, I'd done a fair job of convincing myself that nerves had played a large part in making him seem more dangerous than he actually was. Wrong. If anything, he was more threatening than I remembered. Yet he drew me in, sparked an interest of the sort an employee shouldn't have for their employer. Then again, I had a feeling Skeeter's sexual harassment policy was vague to nonexistent.

I acknowledged him with a polite smile before making a point of turning back to my customers. There may have been a bit of a flounce when I turned my back on him. I wasn't normally a flouncer, but his stare was unnerving, and he was definitely staring at me. I felt a little better knowing I wasn't the only one having a crazy reaction to him. The men calling out their drinks weren't nearly as rowdy as when I'd first arrived at their table.

On my way to turn in tickets, I almost ran into two of Sawyer's companions. They were headed toward the pool tables and already talking smack to each other. Both men paused to let me pass in front of them. One of them executed an exaggerated hand sweep and murmured, "After you, darlin'." I supposed he could have been called charming if he didn't look like he ate road kill for breakfast.

After I'd passed them, I did a quick search of the room

for Sawyer. I located him, and a tagalong buddy, settling at a vacant table near the back. Nerves steadied when I realized he wasn't in my wait section.

They'd barely sat down before Zane showed up at their table with a couple of drinks. I felt my muscles tensing, but Zane didn't hang around talking long before moving off. I had a twinge of worry over what might have been said then immediately felt bad for not trusting Zane to keep our girl talk from last night private. Especially since I'd yet to share the results of mine and Lonnie's talk with her. I excused my lack of disclosure on the fact that she'd been late getting to work looking more than a little cranky. Beyond checking to make sure she was okay, we hadn't had a chance to talk privately since.

Knowing my boss was likely checking up on me presented a whole other layer of complication to a night that was already stressful enough. I did have a small hope that with him all the way at the back of the room, I could forget he was in the building. But it was hard to ignore someone who drilled holes in your back while you worked.

I was one of the few women trying to stay under Sawyer's radar ever since he walked in. All around the room lips were getting a fresh application of gloss and "the girls" were being plumped left and right. It was like watching the opening scene from a bad porno movie.

I'd just set a fresh drink down for an over-bleached blonde, but she was too busy eating Sawyer up with her eyes to notice. I had sour thoughts of offering a bar towel to catch the drool dripping off the woman's chin. Blondie had been letting another man buy her drinks all evening, but apparently he didn't measure up now that Sawyer was in the room.

When Blondie made her move, she didn't even say, "So long, sucker," before taking off in Sawyer's direction. I watched the abandoned suitor, curious to see how he handled being deserted. In the short time I'd been working here, more than one argument had been started over a woman. Tonight wasn't going to be one of those nights, however. Loser Boy took one look where Blondie was headed, slapped some money on the table, and made a beeline for the exit. Sawyer won by default.

Blondie moved with a loose hip swing guaranteed to draw attention. When she arrived at Sawyer's side, she leaned over, plastered those impressive breasts against his arm, and whispered in his ear. Clearly, they weren't strangers. Figured he'd go for the bimbo type. Not that I cared. Because I didn't. Nope.

"Kelli. You're up," Randy, one of the part-time bartenders, hollered at me. The sound of his impatient voice snapped me back to the job. I could feel a flush rising at having been caught standing and staring. I grabbed an empty tray, loaded it with a collection of mixed drinks and beers then headed out to make the rounds.

While delivering orders, I noticed the last empty six-top table in my section had been taken over by a group of men. Their trendy clothes and faddy haircuts marked them as not being the run-of-the-mill customers who frequented Skeeter's. They reminded me more of the kind of guys I used to run across in the trendier clubs in Little Rock. Had to be tourists. It wasn't unusual to hear the regulars grumble about the number of *damn city slickers* finding their way to Skeeter's nowadays.

After dropping off the empty tray, I headed in their direction. Once closer to the table, I got a bad feeling they were going to be a mixed bag of nothing but trouble. First impression said this was a group of five older college students about to use an underclassman for entertainment. The youngest one in the group struck me as a newly minted card-holding drinker just itching to try out his fake ID.

It wasn't hard to pick out the puppet master of the group. He was the largest of them, both physically and personality wise. With a glossy pretty-boy shine, he sprawled back in his chair with a wide-legged ease that made it clear he thought he owned the world.

The closest college was a good two hours' drive. The way all of them were whooping and carrying on, they must have used the drive to get their drunk on. Drunk and cocky were not a good combination in this place. Shelving my misgivings, I plastered on a welcoming smile.

"Hello. My name's Kelli and I'll be taking care of you this evening." My friendly greeting set off a round of hoots and shoulder punches. I suppressed a sigh.

First time Zane had heard me greet a customer that way she'd pulled me aside. She said I sounded like a high-class hooker and to knock it off. I really tried, but five years of providing *polite* customer service was hard to break. Sometimes the routine greeting slipped out. When it did, I'd discovered it best to pretend I didn't know pornographic thoughts were circling the table.

"Well, hellooo, Kelli." The one with the superior attitude did the talking. "I'm Mason Webber." He then paused as if that was supposed to mean something to me. When I gave him a blank stare, he frowned as if not sure how to handle my lack of reaction.

He recovered quickly, though, and hit me with a smarmy smile. "Looks like Charlie finally decided to add a little class to the *play* list." He drawled out his lame compliment while his eyes took an insulting tour of my figure.

A kick of surprise mingled with my disgust. Sounded as if he'd been to Skeeter's enough to know Charlie. The way he said "play list" made me think he also knew about the women who worked the back rooms. I could see he expected me to be flattered he'd placed me higher than the others on his personal caste scale.

I dropped the wattage on my smile and added a hint of frost to my voice. "Has everyone had time to decide what they want?"

From the way he tightened his lips, my lack of reaction to his backhanded compliment didn't set well with him. But he didn't push the issue. "Brought my boys here to celebrate our buddy's birthday. And I want to make sure Danny boy gets a special present." He winked at me as if we were together on making Danny's *special present* happen.

I turned my attention to the kid Mason backhanded with a hard slap to the middle of his thin chest. Danny blushed and swatted at the flurry of hand slaps the rest of the group flung his way. If it was his birthday, I had a feeling it was closer to his nineteenth than his twenty-first.

"Well, how fun for him and the rest of you." That bad feeling was getting stronger.

Mason smirked at me before saying, "We'll be wanting to order from the special menu, babe."

I wasn't stupid and knew what Mason was really asking for, but chose to pretend I didn't have a clue.

"Sorry, kitchen's closed. Drinks only from now until we shut the doors at one." I itched to ask for Danny's ID, but that sort of thing was supposed to be taken care of by one of the two bouncers usually found hanging out by the front door—if they felt inclined to ask. From what I'd observed, they never seemed overly worried if everyone drinking was legal or not.

Despite having taken a dislike to Mason, I felt sorry for the birthday guy. The kid just wanted to run with the big boys and was probably all excited they'd singled him out for a birthday road trip.

I decided to give them some sound advice, knowing they wouldn't take it. Mason had obviously promised his "boys," and Danny in particular, a walk on the wild side. "Look, fellas, there's a two-drink minimum per person if you're going to take up a table. If you're looking for food, you need to hurry on back into town. There's a new Chili's in Copper Ridge and they have a great bar. You'll have a lot more fun celebrating your friend's birthday there."

What I didn't say was that they were less likely to get into trouble in a tamer spot. A few of the bar's regulars were already giving the loud group the hairy eyeball.

"Wrong kind of menu, babe. Danny wants one of the 'special desserts' available here. And baby, you look all kinds of sweet." Mason ran a finger down the length of my arm while he talked.

This guy was seriously creeping me out. Maybe it was because he and his buddies could have come from my world of country clubs and polite conversation. But in their eyes, I wasn't an equal because I worked in a backwoods bar. They made me want to check to see if I had a price tag hanging off one of my boobs.

I moved to take a step back to prevent any more touchy-feely. Mason stopped my retreat by sliding a couple fingers in one of my jean's belt loops. He then jerked me forward to stand between his spread legs.

Anger replaced my friendly attempt at steering this group of Future Business Leaders away from trouble. I gave one more try at keeping the situation from getting out of control. "You need to take your hand off me right now. Neither me nor any of the other women who work here are on any kind of 'desserts' menu. Whoever told you that was having a joke at your expense. Since you're not happy with me as your waitress, I'll send one of our other servers over."

I didn't have a clue how it worked with the women and the back rooms and had no desire to find out. Whatever the rules, it didn't take a genius to figure out it wasn't a great idea to admit those women and back rooms existed. Not even if it was to someone who seemed to know a lot more about how this type of transaction worked than I did. By sending over one of the woman I'd seen take a man back, I'd pass the problem to someone who knew how to handle it.

"Look, I know the score, babe. I'll even put in a good word with Charlie for you. Tell him how you didn't go blabbing shit to some stranger." Mason tightened his legs, trapping me by more than just a finger in my belt loop.

Up to this point I'd been trying to avoid a scene that would catch Sawyer's attention. If I struggled now, as close as I was to his crotch, everyone was going to think I was giving Mason a lap dance.

"Come on, babe. You look classier than the rest of the *ladies* in here." The way he said "ladies" gave it a nasty ring. "How 'bout you and me take my virgin friend here to the back and put on a little show and tell for him?" Again, he backhanded the mortified Danny in the chest.

While I might not be as tough as some who worked here, I wasn't the same butter-wouldn't-melt-in-my-mouth debutante I'd been six months ago. Thanks to Zane's unique examples of customer relations and a week working at Skeeter's... well, let's just say I'd had a whole lot of the *polite* knocked out of me.

Wanting to be sure his friends heard, I spoke up nice and loud. "Sooo tempting." Waiting half a beat, I tapped a finger against my bottom lip as if considering the offer before adding, "But just like there's a two-drink minimum at the table, there's a one-hour minimum in the back rooms. You can't rent them by the minute. Sorry, you're out of luck."

The explosion of laughter wasn't limited to Danny and the rest of his buddies. Men at surrounding tables joined in. All the ridicule didn't set too well with Mason. He erupted from his chair so fast that it went flying backward. On the plus side, I wasn't trapped by his legs any longer, and he let go of my jeans. On the down side, he grabbed my upper arms in a bruising grip and jerked me up against his furious body.

"You stupid bitch! No fucking whore is gonna—"

He never finished his sentence.

CHAPTER NINE

Kelli

RESCUE DIDN'T COME without collecting a few extra bruises. Being ripped out of the hands of Mason set me free but sent me staggering backward, arms pin-wheeling in a crazy attempt to maintain balance. I came to a jarring halt only after my backside slammed into the edge of the table behind me. The force of the crash sent the drinks on the table flying in my direction, soaking my back in a wave of beer and whiskey. The men seated at the table were up and latched on to my arms to prevent me from joining the bottles and glasses on the floor.

"One more word, asshole, and the only thing you'll be sticking your dick in is a grave."

Sawyer must've heard enough of our conversation to figure out what Mason had come looking for. He had Mason's shirt balled up in a fist so tight that there had to be skin clamped with the material. After delivering his message, he tossed Mason backward with a flick of his wrist into the arms of his white-faced buddies.

The frozen silence from our little corner of the bar quickly spread through the rest of the room. It didn't last long. Sounds of chair legs being hastily scraped across the concrete floor was followed by a general exodus. Many for the exit, but just as many headed in our direction.

Zane pushed through the circle of bodies surrounding me, calling my name and asking repeatedly if I'd been hurt. My groan of frustration at having caused a scene didn't escape Sawyer's notice. He shot a question at Zane: "She marked up?"

Zane took his question way too seriously and began an upper-body exam that was more thorough than my last physical. She ignored assurances that I was fine. The only battle I won was when she wanted me to moon the entire room so she could check the damage to my hiney caused by the table I'd collided with. I was not dropping my pants.

Not until she was satisfied there was no major damage did Zane answer Sawyer. "Her arms are going to be bruised and painful as hell. Don't see anything else topside. She won't let me look at her ass, but she hit the edge of that table damn hard when he pushed her. That's gonna leave a mark." She ended her report with a vicious glare at my attacker.

"Now wait a damn minute! I didn't push that bit—"

Sawyer cut Mason off with a cold, flat voice. "You come into my place, put your fuckin' hands on one of my women, and think you're gonna walk out of here a fuckin' hero?"

I felt embarrassed to have caused a scene. I was the one who'd bragged about how well I could handle difficult customers. As big a jerk as Mason was, I felt like it would have never gotten to this point had I handled the situation right. Sawyer was taking me being *one of his women* way beyond backing up an employee.

I scanned the people left in the building to see if anyone was going to try and talk Sawyer down. One look at the excitement on the surrounding faces and I knew no one here was stopping anything. I had a terrible suspicion that murder might be a spectator sport for these people.

I didn't feel sorry for Mason, but I was worried for Sawyer. The rich always found a way to come out on top. Since no one else was willing to intervene, that pretty much left me.

"Sawyer, this needs to stop. I'm not one of your women, so don't act like this is personal. I'm the one he had the problem with, not you. I don't need your help to settle this." Nerves made me want to fidget. I managed to control the urge. Barely. It didn't help that the local crowd was itching for a brawl. They stared at me in confusion and there were a few complaints of *what the hell, lady?* My attempt to put a stop to any more violence didn't appear to be a popular idea.

Sawyer never took his eyes off his target when he spoke to me. "As long as you're one of my employees, you're mine. Some dick breath walks in here and lays a hand on you, it becomes personal."

"Does that mean if someone walks in here and hassles Charlie you're going to protect him?" That got a few chuckles out of the crowd. The way Charlie frowned let me know he didn't think my question was all that funny.

"Charlie isn't some sorority chick that knows fuck all about taking care of herself in a bar fight."

"There wasn't going to be a fight. Right?" I appealed to Mason, hoping he'd be smart enough to back off from a coldly furious Sawyer.

At my question, Mason's buddies started whispering

among themselves and to him. Hand gestures toward the exit made it plain they just wanted to get out of there. Mason showed no signs of admitting he was in over his head, though. Giving up on talking sense into him, the others started apologizing for any misunderstandings. Their explanations and excuses were loud in an attempt to drown out any words Mason tried to interject. Their efforts to worm their way out of trouble were doing more to calm the situation than anything I could have said.

"Fuckin' candy asses." Disgust curled Sawyer's lips. "You think just because you can drink and screw that makes you grown-ass men? Get out of my place, Mason. If you or any of your pussy friends ever come back, you won't walk out next time."

Mason pulled away from his much smarter companions and pointed a finger in the middle of Sawyer's chest. "Fuck you, Sawyer! You're a dead man."

I held my breath with the rest of the stunned witnesses. One look at Mason's white face showed that even he finally realized he'd gone too far. If the proverbial pin dropped at that moment, it would have sounded like an explosion when it hit the floor, the silence was that absolute.

The dead air was broken by a low chuckle. I watched, amazed as the chuckle grew into a full-blown laugh. I'd have sworn Sawyer had just heard the funniest joke in the world if I hadn't heard Mason's threat. At first, only one or two in the crowd joined in on the chuckles. It didn't take long before most of the room was laughing.

Everyone except Mason and his buddies.

They could have been cut from stone. That drunken high they'd been on when they'd first arrived was long gone. They'd been scared sober. The only one that didn't seem to realize the danger they were in was Mason. Fear had ruled for a moment, but with everyone laughing—at him again—that spark of sanity flickered out. Rage took over.

"Laugh it up, asshole. You think you're the big bad man around here? My family fucking *owns* this county. Just a matter of time before we own this fuckin' dive, too." Mason turned his crazy eyes on me before continuing, "That means you'll be one of *my* women then, bitch.

The last word had barely cleared his lips when a fist shot out and blood erupted from Mason's shattered nose. I hadn't even seen Sawyer move. Another lethal strike to Mason's jaw had his head snapping back, and his body followed in the perfect imitation of a felled tree. His friends didn't so much as twitch a pinky in an attempt to catch Mason. The resulting thud from his head bouncing off the floor had me wincing in sympathy. My instinctive response was to make sure he was still alive. Yeah, the thump was that scary. But Zane placed a hand on my shoulder and shook her head. Stopped from offering aid, I latched my eyes on Sawyer to see what he would do next.

If I hadn't been watching, I'd have missed the slight flick of his chin that had his men shuffling the crowd back to make a hole for the guys to shoot through. They didn't waste any time making good on their escape. They were in such a big rush that Sawyer had to call them back to collect Mason. I was relieved to see he was trying to raise his head. Two of his buddies pulled him to his feet, half supporting, half dragging him out the door.

It was over. The crowd who'd stayed inside milled around, slapped each other on the back, and dissected Sawyer's fist work as they made their way back to their tables. I could hear a few guffawing over how pants-pissing scared the city boys had been.

The ones who'd hung around outside began to make

their way back in, crowding the bar and shouting out drink orders. The band returned to the raised stage, tossing back beers and getting ready for their next set.

I felt like the only person in the building who didn't know what my role was now that the violence had passed. A lost feeling I didn't understand. It wasn't the first argument I'd seen between men while at a club. Egos and alcohol were the only ingredients needed to stir up most fights. Men mouthed off, made threats, and did a lot of posturing. In the end, would-be combatants were always more than willing to let friends pull them apart. Everyone went their separate ways secure in the knowledge that they would have kicked ass if not stopped.

But what went down with Mason had had a darker level of violence. Sawyer had been the epicenter of that darkness. He'd been brutal in my defense. I should have been repulsed. I wasn't. Talk about a primal reaction to having a man willing to fight for you.

Sawyer stood a short distance away with the three men who had arrived with him earlier. I watched as the two who'd been playing pool nodded in agreement to something he said and quickly left the bar. The one who'd been sitting at the table with him stayed behind, and they seemed to be having a serious discussion. Everyone else in the building was busy returning to the business of having fun. Well, everyone but the blonde who'd been hanging all over Sawyer. She was giving me a death glare. She made it clear she didn't appreciate having her evening with Sawyer interrupted.

"Your ass end and back are soaked. Why don't you call it a night and let me take you home? Crowd's smaller now; the rest of the girls can handle it until I get back." Zane was hovering. I appreciated her concern, but it only added to my emotional turmoil. How was everyone back to normal so quickly? I'd just had a huge reminder that this wasn't the world I'd grown up in.

"Miss, are you sure you're all right? You took a pretty hard fall into that table." The question came from one of the men I had waited on earlier.

Before I could reassure him, Zane cut in. "She's gonna be fine, Grady. I'm taking care of her. Go on back to your friends. I'll send someone over in a minute."

Zane's words finished tipping my world off its axis. Grady?

"Shit, Zane! Grab a chair, she's going down!"

It was the feel of a strong arm guiding me to a chair that let me know I was again providing a show for the customers. But even knowing I was causing another spectacle couldn't take away the wonder of staring into the blue eyes of my brother.

CHAPTER TEN

Kelli

"THAT'S IT, take deep, slow breaths. Soon as you're feeling up to it, I'm taking you home." Zane smoothed a hand across my back reassuringly. Both her and Grady had me anchored to a chair.

"Please, let me up. Everyone's staring." My words came out in a whisper. Why I bothered was a mystery to me. Most of the eyes and ears in the place were already trained on the three of us.

I felt like an idiot with Grady and Zane trying to push my head between my spread legs. How in the world did they even move that fast? One minute I was staring at a man Zane had called Grady, and the next I was pushed into a chair and staring at the floor. This whole wreck of an evening was just the cherry on the top of what had been a day of gut-wrenching surprises.

Zane took a step back, but Grady stuck close to help me

stand. Back in an upright position, I got a good look at my brother. He had to be? Didn't he?

"If you need to stay here and work, Zane, it won't be any trouble for me to take her home," Grady quickly offered.

I searched for similarities that could be pointed to as positive proof we shared the same blood. Features like his chin that had the same shallow indent, or how the sharp angles of his cheekbones matched mine. My hair would be the same dirty blonde as his if not for pricey salon visits. The resemblance was strong but not so obvious that I would've picked him out of a crowd and said, "That's my brother." I'd pretty much proved that by not recognizing him earlier. He was definitely handsome, which caused a surprising swell of pride.

I was staring. It was getting awkward.

"Thank you so much for your kindness, but there's no reason I can't take myself home, Mr....?" I was fishing for a name, again. But I had to be certain this wasn't just another man named Grady. For all I knew, that could be a popular name around here.

"Wilks, but call me Grady. If you're worried about me being a stranger, Zane here can tell you I'm just a big ol' pussycat." His grin was infectious. I appreciated his efforts to lighten the mood and found myself grinning back at him.

Zane's dry laugh pulled my attention to her. "Oh, Grady would get you home safe and sound, but I'd be more likely to call him a tomcat on the prowl for some pus—"

"Zane!" I shrieked at her. Anything to stop her from finishing that thought. Zane might not know this was my brother, but I did, and any reference to anything sexual was just creepy.

Grady grabbed his chest and staggered backward dramatically. "I'm hurt you'd say such a thing, Zane."

The spark of laughter in his eyes said she was probably more right than wrong. Another complication. It was going to be weird enough for him to discover a little sister had come looking for him. A nightmare if he was attracted and *then* found out he'd been hitting on that sister.

I was going to need to keep my distance until I'd figured out how to approach him about our sibling status. It was no longer a matter of *if* I would tell him. My mind had been made up the moment I realized my brother was standing right in front of me. Seeing him in the flesh was a whole different matter than an abstract idea that I had a brother out there somewhere. I wanted a chance—the one my momma had stolen—to be a sister.

"Look, I'm perfectly fine. Wet, but in no danger of injuring myself further. I'm going to go grab my things and head home." I was desperate for a tiny slice of normal to right the crazy my night had turned into.

Zane and Grady both started protesting.

SAWYER

"HOW MANY FUCKIN' men are going to have their hands on you tonight?" The minute I said it, I knew it was out of line. The words just popped out the moment I got close to their little group.

I'd turned and seen Grady with his arms wrapped around Kelli. He could have been the savior from the second coming the way she was staring at him. That look on her face sliced the shit out of the thin restraints holding my anger in check.

"Now wait a minute. She doesn't need you saying shi— eh, stuff like that." Grady was puffing up and calling me out for growling at the princess.

Too bad. My bar, my employee.

"What the hell's the matter with you, Sawyer? Grady's just trying to help." After Zane shot me a *what is your problem* look, she turned back to Kelli. "You really should let me take you home."

Kelli sent me a glare of her own before jumping into the renewed argument between Zane and Grady over who was driving her back to the motel.

"Everybody just shut the fuck up," I said. "Zane, go grab her shit out of the office and meet us outside at my truck. Grady, you have a problem with me, you know where to find me." Not giving anyone a chance to protest, I pushed past Grady to get to Kelli. Sliding an arm around her waist, I pulled her tight against my side then headed for the exit at a fast walk. I wasn't counting on her stunned silence lasting long. I managed to hustle her all the way to the gravel parking lot before she put on the brakes.

"What do you think you're doing?" Kelli tried to plant her feet, but I'd anticipated that move and kept plowing straight ahead, leaving her little choice other to than walk or be dragged.

"Thought I was pretty clear on what I was doing."

"Well, I didn't agree to go home with you."

"Wait to be asked, princess."

Kelli flushed at the way I'd twisted her words.

We were a few steps from my truck when I fished the keys out of my pocket and popped the locks. I was wondering where the hell Zane was when I spotted her rushing toward us.

I opened the passenger door and bundled Kelli inside. She may have gotten in, but she looked mad enough to hop right back out. Pointing a finger at her, I played my ace. "Stay in the truck or you're fired. You've cost me enough money tonight."

I couldn't care less about any lost revenue she may or may not have caused. But I was interested in seeing just how important this job was to her. She shot daggers at me before pulling on her prissy dignity like a suit of armor. She gave a sniff, then made a point of ignoring me, staring a hole through my windshield. I had my answer. She wanted the job pretty damn bad.

Zane was breathless by the time she made it to where I leaned against the open passenger door. I blocked Kelli just in case she changed her mind and tried to hop back out of my truck.

"Here." She thrust the purse at Kelli. "Sawyer's being an ass but you're safe with him. Call me tomorrow if you don't think you can make it in to work and I'll let Charlie know. If I don't hear from you, I'll run by and pick you up somewhere around a quarter after five. We're not scheduled till six, so that'll give you more time to rest. Don't worry about your car; ain't nobody stupid enough to bother it here."

I wasn't too sure how true that was, considering what had happened to BW's truck in this parking lot. Not that I was really worried the same thing would happen to Kelli's car. I figured it was safe enough as long as she didn't have a beef with Jase's wife, Char. I straightened out the grin tugging at my lips from the memory of Char and her spray paint.

Kelli gave Zane what I was starting to recognize as her princess smile. "Thank you sooo much. Unlike *some people*, who are forcing me to accept help, I appreciate everyth—"

I slapped the door shut, cutting off Kelli's prissy words. Had a feeling if I didn't, she'd spend the rest of the night finding ways to bitch about me. Zane sighed but didn't say anything. Wiggling a goodbye with her fingers at Kelli's furious features, she twisted on a heel to head back in to work.

"Don't be an ass to her, okay? I don't want you making her mad enough to quit."

I stalked her to the rear of the truck before asking, "And just why is that, Zane? Why is it important to keep her here?"

Zane waved an airy hand and kept walking as she talked. "I like working with her. No big deal. Everything doesn't have to have some deep hidden meaning, Sawyer."

Zane was already out of hearing when I did some bitching of my own. "Lately that's all the hell I've run into."

KELLI

"I'M STAYING at the Paradise Motor Inn. Room fourteen." I broke the silence first. Sawyer had neither lectured me on the way back to town nor questioned me. For all the attention he paid, he could've been the only one in the truck.

If he noticed he was being punished by my silent treatment, he hadn't let on. That's the problem with giving people you don't really know the silent treatment—instead of making them uncomfortable, you're the one who starts to feel self-conscious, and it just ends up being awkward instead of a lesson.

"Kinda below your standards, isn't it?"

Yep. No sign that Sawyer was relieved the silence had been broken. Just a snarky comment. Punishing silence? Big fail.

"Since you have no idea of my standards, that's a big assumption on your part."

"Princess, driving a BMW is a piss-poor way to hide the type of life you're used to living."

"Stop calling me princess. I don't like your new name for me any better than being tagged as a debutante. You don't know enough about me to be sticking labels on me. I'm not hiding anything. The car was a gift." Oh yeah, that didn't make me sound like an entitled brat. Not at all.

"Good to know you're not hiding. Means you can tell me what you're doing in Copper Ridge and why you're taking up space in my bar." No teasing now. His voice had the same hard, flat chill he'd used when talking to Mason.

"Taking up space?" I might have been angry over him forcing the drive back to the motel on me, but belittling how hard I worked made me furious. "If you paid more attention to business, you'd know I pull my weight. Ask Charlie if you don't believe me. Talk to Zane; she'll tell you I do more than 'take up space.'"

"I'm sure she would. Which is kinda strange, don't you think, considering she's never given two fucks about a debutante like you before. As a matter of fact, she's usually damn free with her opinion about them, and it ain't flattering. Which has me wondering: what makes you so special?"

"You're crazy. Zane's right, you're so paranoid about strangers you're willing to think the worst of anyone that's friendly to me. News flash, Sawyer, I don't care about your shady business dealings at Skeeter's. My reasons for working there are completely personal. Maybe you should spend more time at the bar if you're so worried." I was the crazy one. Last thing I wanted was him hanging around. He was too infuriating, too arrogant, and way too distracting.

"Why? Am I not paying enough attention to you, princess?"

"Don't flatter yourself. I'm not looking for your attention." Even as the words came out, the heat behind them was lukewarm at best.

He pulled to a stop in front of my unit with a jerk then pinned me to the seat with the sudden heat in his dark eyes.

"You sure? I think maybe you're getting bored with your little city boys. I think you want a man who leaves the lights on and doesn't ask permission to kiss more than those pretty lips. If you can handle sweat-slicked bodies and the taste of pussy on my tongue as it fucks your mouth, invite me in." His eyes burned into me before he exited the truck.

It would've been nice to say it was outrage that froze me in place—nice, but a lie. His crudely sensual words conjured up graphic pictures of him doing as promised. Pictures that should have had me blushing instead of soaking my panties. Sawyer was at my door and had it open before I'd banished the dark seduction of his words.

His look said he could read every dirty thought parading through my mind. I did nothing to stop him when he shifted me around on the seat, pulling me to the edge. He pushed his body between my legs, his hips keeping my thighs spread. Hooking a hand around the back of my neck, he pulled me toward him.

Shivers arrowed down my back in anticipation of the unknown, the expectation of an aggressive assault on my mouth. Reality was much more devastating. The first touch of his lips feathered across the fullness of mine. The unexpected gentleness had me parting them on a tiny gasp. He needed no further invitation to sink into the kiss, his tongue exploring deep into my mouth, the invasion slow and sweeping, inviting my tongue to dance with his in discovery. Fingers worked their way below the waistband of my jeans to tease with a promise of more.

The moan that escaped from my lips shamed me, but not so badly that I was willing to push him away. I buried my face in his neck and wrapped my arms around him.

"I'm coming in." His whisper was a devil's temptation. One I was eager to give in to. "We can fuck the curiosity out of each other." The deep growl of his voice hadn't changed, but his words were like a stinging slap to my face.

I stopped straining to get closer and moved my hands to his chest to push back enough to search his face. I didn't know whether to be relieved or insulted when he stepped back so quickly. "What do you mean curiosity?"

"I'm not your type any more than you're mine. That doesn't mean we can't enjoy reminding ourselves just how wrong we are for each other." The indifference in his voice sent a different kind of shiver down my spine.

"In other words, I'm just an itch you want to scratch because I'm different."

"Same deal for you, princess. I know your type." Sawyer took another step away and slid his hands in his back pockets.

It wasn't the same deal for me, though. Not exactly. I would agree his appeal had a lot to do with him being different from what I was used to. What he didn't realize, though, was that that was a good thing. The men I'd grown up around, and almost married, had all been entitled snobs. They worried about appearances and social standing more than they cared about the people they were supposed to love.

Sawyer might be crude and quick to violence, but he didn't care what anyone thought about him. I and everyone else would always know where they stood with him.

Unfortunately, he'd already decided that whatever we could have would never be anything more than sex. Not necessarily a bad thing. I had a feeling it would be amazing sex. I just wasn't sure I wanted to have mind-blowing sex with someone who called me princess and believed that was all there was to me, who knew "my type."

Without taking my eyes off him, I fumbled around on the seat behind me, searching for my purse. Feeling it under my hand, I grabbed it and clutched it to my stomach.

"Everything you think you know about me is wrong." Slamming the truck door after I'd hopped down from the seat did little to quiet the voice in my head. *Not everything he said is wrong, is it? Admit it—you're tempted. Despite how angry he makes you, despite his distrust, you are so tempted.*

"Does that mean you're not asking me to follow you through that door?"

"Curiosity may lead to a lot of things, but letting you follow me through that door isn't one of them."

I didn't hear his truck pull away until I was safely inside.

CHAPTER ELEVEN

Kelli

I CAREFULLY KEPT my face blank as I slid onto the thread-bare cloth seat of Zane's old Buick. I had to put some muscle into closing the door, as it fought me to stay open. It was like being in the middle of a tug of war and the door had the advantage. I did a mental fist pump when I won the battle.

The first time I'd seen the moving wreck Zane drove, I'd been shocked the heap even ran. The mismatched doors, the patches of peeling blue paint, and a large dent above the right rear wheel didn't instill a lot of confidence it would make it out of park.

I tried to appear causally interested as I did a slow scan of the interior. It was worn beyond the point of shabby. The roof of the car had none of the fabric left, and it looked like Zane had painted the bare metal black with a brush. Would it be polite to mention what a great job she'd done? Probably best to let it slide. Despite the decrepit condition of...well, everything...the interior was spotless.

The cleanliness shouldn't have really been a surprise. Zane was meticulous when it came to her appearance. She might wear bargain-basement clothes, but they were always clean and pressed. I suspected she lived hand to mouth and her car was just another clue as to how little money Zane had to get by on.

"It's safe to put your purse down. You're gonna bruise your boobs if you smash it against your chest any tighter." Zane's dry voice made me jump.

Afraid I'd hurt her feelings, I flung my Hermes bag on the seat beside me. It landed on its side and half the contents exploded from the wide mouth of the bag. I apologized as I chased tubes of lipstick and other life essentials around the floorboard and dug them out of the crack where the seatback met the bench cushion.

Zane sighed as she watched my frenzied scramble. "Relax. We both know you're seriously uncomfortable right now because you think I'm ashamed of my car. Well, I'm not. It gets me where I need to go and that's all I care about. Get over it and tell me what happened when Sawyer took you home last night. Was he an ass? He can be a butt-hole, but he can also be really helpful if trouble comes knocking."

"Don't let him scare you into running off." Zane wagged a finger back and forth between the two of us. "We make a great team."

I was relieved she was willing to ignore my car snobbery. "Yes, he was an ass, and no, I'm not quitting." I'd keep just how close I'd come to inviting him to spend the night to myself.

"Good, I was sweating it." She fanned a hand in front of her face. "The way you were acting last night had me thinking I'd show up this morning and have to bitch-shame you into staying."

I laughed at the face Zane made. Making me laugh was something Zane was very good at doing. She was also good at putting me at ease after I did or said something stupid. I felt foolish to doubt our friendship was genuine. Still… what Sawyer had said about Zane avoiding someone like me was going to eat at me until I asked, "He did say something last night that made me curious."

"What about?" Zane cut her eyes over to me then returned them to the road.

"This is going to sound so junior high, but he claimed I wasn't the kind of person you would normally make friends with. Said that you actually disliked former perky cheerleaders and sorority sisters." I laughed faintly as if the idea was ridiculous. Mostly, though, I felt like a needy preteen wanting her to deny what he'd said.

"Busted." Laughing, she shot a look over like we were sharing a joke.

I didn't see anything funny about Zane pretending to like me. It hurt.

"I see." My reply was so politely chilly that the tip of me tongue probably had frostbite.

"Brr, got cold in here, didn't it?" Zane shivered dramatically. "Look, when you first showed up, I pegged you as one of *them*. You know, a snob who thought she was better than me on account of my clothes and where I worked. Then you asked for a job and it all changed. I saw an opportunity to study one of you society type chicks up close and personal."

"How quaint. I'm an anthropological study for you." My momma would have been proud at the hint of disdain in my tone.

"Gonna pull out the big words, huh? Put the hayseed in

her place. That's okay, because if that mouthful means what I think it does, you're right. There's so much difference between how you and I were raised, we might as well have come from different planets. Here's the thing: I need to learn to live in the world you grew up in. So, yeah, I wanted you around hoping to pick up some pointers. It's just a bonus I like you. A lot. You're not like most rich bitches who think their shit don't stink."

If I was to be honest, I'd been no better at our first meeting. Hadn't I dismissed her as being unimportant because, *shock and horror,* she was just some uneducated hick who worked in a bar? And didn't that make me the snobby bitch Zane had thought I was?

"You had an agenda when you talked Charlie and Sawyer into hiring me?"

"We all have agendas. You came here looking for a father." She pointed a finger at me. "Agenda. Having you walk in and ask for a job was like a freaking present. Nobody passes up a present. My pushing the guys landed you the job; that makes me your present. See? Mutual gifts. Everybody wins." She looked very pleased with her explanation. Then her expression sobered. "Are we good?"

I didn't answer immediately. Both of us were guilty of making assumptions. Both of us had moved past those preconceived ideas and found a friend. "Yeah. We're good."

Zane blew lip-smacking kisses my way and had me laughing, again. The silence afterward had a comfortable vibe to it. Still, I couldn't help asking, "What would you have done if I hadn't gotten the job? You've said Sawyer didn't hire me on your account."

"Pfft, that's easy. I would have bitched Charlie out something awful, until he got tired of it and begged Sawyer to give you a job."

"All of that, just so you could keep me around." I shook

my head in wonder. "Thing I really don't understand is why do you want to be like me? There's nothing wrong with you."

"There is if I'm in love with a guy that comes from a rich family. I don't want him ashamed of me when we're around his parents and high-class friends. That means I need to start acting like a lady, and believe me, that's one thing my mom won't ever be accused of." Zane frowned when she mentioned her mom.

"I never thought there was a snowball's chance in hell of it ever working out," she continued. "We come from such different backgrounds. But then his brother married a moonshiner's granddaughter. That got me to thinking maybe it *could* happen. I just have to work at putting some shine on me, and that's where you come in." She sounded as if she really believed it was that simple.

"Zane, if this guy doesn't love you enough to appreciate how wonderful you are, then he's a jerk." I didn't know who she was talking about and already didn't like him.

"Oh, he doesn't love me, yet. But he will. I just have to convince him." She waved a hand in the air. "Now that you know I'm using you, you can be more helpful. Instead of me watching and trying to figure out how to act like a lady, you can just tell me how to make it happen."

I didn't think it was going to be as simple as Zane thought. "I'll help you however I can. You know that, right? But do you honestly think a man who would be ashamed of the way you are now is worth it?"

"I'm the one not worth the spit it's gonna take to make me shine." Zane's voice faded to a whisper. As if realizing how pitiful that sounded, she flashed a snarky grin at me. "What's the matter? Afraid you're not up to the job?"

I wanted to dig deeper, find out why she would say such a thing, but she clearly wasn't ready to confide in me.

Being there for her was the best I could do. "Are you kidding? You'll be too good for him and his whole highfalutin' family by the time I get through with you."

Zane kept a straight face as she said, "You bet your fuckin' ass I will," before busting out laughing. I joined in while secretly hoping I was around to support her when this crazy idea went all kinds of wrong.

"Okay, enough about my future plans," she said. "What's going on with you? Yesterday was wackadoodle and you never got the chance to tell me what Lonnie had to say about your mom. Did he remember her?"

So much had happened last night that I'd forgotten she was out of the loop. "He remembered her, all right. At first, I thought he was remembering the wrong woman. It took some to convince me, but what he had to say cleared up why Momma was so dead set on keeping me away from Copper Ridge." Anger washed through as I thought about the lies and years lost.

"What? You're killing me!" Zane bounced in her seat. "Did you find out who your dad is or not?"

Somehow, saying it out loud to another person made it more real. "Emmett Wilks."

The silence after my big announcement was unexpected. Watching her for a reaction was like watching an actress from a silent film. A parade of exaggerated emotions crossed her face while she considered what I'd said. Surprise was followed by sadness. Realization was quickly followed by shock, then, "Holy shit! Grady Wilks is your brother! That bitch kept your brother a secret from you. I'm sorry, I'm sorry... She's your momma and all, but... Holy shit, Kelli, you have a brother!"

Zane's outrage vindicated every horrible thought I'd had through the night about my momma. "I know, it's insane. How does a mother do that?" There was no answer to such a question, and I expected none.

"What do we do now?"

It was the same question she had asked when I'd told her I was looking for my father. Such unconditional support caused me to wonder how I'd been lucky enough to find a friend like Zane in such a short period.

I cleared my throat before answering, "I've got to figure out a way to break the news that I'm his sister—then the rest is up to him."

"Can't you just tell him? You know the longer you put it off, the harder it's gonna be. Treat it like a Band-Aid. Rip that sucker off. Hair and all." She reached over to pat my knee.

"Sure, I just sashay up to him and say, 'Hi, brother. I'm the child Momma chose when she ran out on you and Dad.' That's sure to be a conversation he's dying to have." Just the thought of it tied my stomach in knots. "If he shows up again tonight, am I supposed to tell him in the middle of the bar? Won't that be fun, having all those eyes and ears witnessing our family reunion? Not the way I pictured having this discussion with him."

"If he shows up, are you really going to be able to keep from telling him? If he was horrible, that'd be different. Believe me, I understand horrible brothers." Zane shrugged. "Grady's no angel—what man is? Still, he's a decent guy, one of the good ones. He deserves to know who you are. Haven't you spent enough time separated?"

"What Momma did wasn't fair to either one of us," I said. "Does that make it right for me to show up out of the blue wanting to become a part of his life? What if things are going perfect for him right now and my sudden appearance messes up everything for him? I'm not just trying to figure this out for me. I have to think about him, too." I suddenly felt weary to my bones. Last night, if I wasn't thinking about Grady, it was Sawyer blocking any chance of getting sleep. Both men were a problem. Both had the potential to break me.

"Zane, do you think we could drop this for a while? All I want is to get through work tonight without providing Skeeter's customers with another floor show. Mrs. Whatley stopped by my room today dropping plenty of hints that she wouldn't tolerate any hanky-panky business happening at her motel. She runs a respectable inn, you know," I said, mimicking Mrs. Whatley's high-pitched voice before frowning. "I'm guessing someone told her about the fight I started last night."

"What she runs is her mouth. I can't believe you're staying in that rat hole of hers." Zane pushed a strand of hair off her cheek with the back of her hand. I was grateful she was willing to turn our conversation in a new direction.

"I've had about as much of the Paradise Motor Inn as I can enjoy. Charlie doesn't have me scheduled to work Monday or Tuesday. That'll give me three days to look for somewhere more permanent to live. Any suggestions?"

"If my place wasn't so tiny, you could stay with me, but believe me, we'd end up killing each other having to share the bathroom. Sawyer has a few places he rents out. Want me to ask if he's got anything available?"

"I didn't realize he rented to the public," I replied cautiously.

Zane looked at me strangely, but what did she expect? The only rentals I knew Sawyer was involved with weren't exactly the kind of places I'd call home.

"Well yeah, of course he does, or I wouldn't have offered to ask him. If he doesn't show up tonight, I can give him a call tomorrow."

"Uhhh, these rentals... they're not anything like the rooms at Skeeter's he rents out, are they?" No way was I moving into a place owned by him if it was anything like the so-called *apartments* in the back of the bar.

"Holy shit! You think I'd set you up with a place in a cathouse?" The snort from Zane made it clear how stupid she found that notion.

"Those apartments were already there when Sawyer bought Skeeter's. The women that use those back rooms? That's on them. Sawyer don't run those women. Nobody does. Sure, he makes them pay for the room—he's not running a charity, after all—but you're not going to hear any of them complaining. Lot safer to do business in a place where a badass gets a look at their customer when they go up to the bar to rent a room. More important, the customer knows that badass is close by. Sawyer has plenty of legit businesses, too. He may own rough-ass bars, but they aren't the only things he owns. So, you want me to ask him about a place or not?"

Surprised by Zane's heated defense of Sawyer, I felt trapped. I wasn't sure having him as both boss and landlord was such a good idea, especially after that scene in his truck last night. Coming up with an excuse that wouldn't upset Zane further was beyond my abilities at the moment, so I gave in. "Okay, sure, why not. I was really hoping to find something fast, though."

"Not a problem. If he has anything, I'll get the keys and we'll go check them out tomorrow." Zane was happy again. That made one of us. I mentally crossed my fingers that he didn't have anything available.

Zane drove past all the trucks in the lot at Skeeter's, parking in the back. She looped her arm through mine once we were out of the car and heading for the rear door of the building. "Don't worry. We'll find you a place to live and you'll figure out the right time to tell Grady every-thing. It'll all work out." She gave my arm an encouraging squeeze.

The way things were stacking up, I was going to need all the encouragement I could muster, and I wasn't just thinking about my brother.

CHAPTER TWELVE

Kelli

ANY HOPES for an uneventful night were doomed by eight o'clock. In that short time, I managed to drop a tray fully loaded with drinks, slapped a customer for pinching my tush, and watched a woman slap *her* husband because he was flirting with me on their anniversary. Personally, I thought the guy deserved a slap for bringing his wife to Skeeter's to celebrate in the first place. When Grady walked in and took a seat at one of the tables in my section, I'd already resigned myself to accepting that the bar gods were against me.

When I looked over in Grady's direction, he smiled so sweetly that I didn't have the heart to ask Zane to take his order. Besides, she was right. It was time to rip through all the lies of the past and see if we could figure out how to be a brother and sister after all these years.

I greeted him with a smile. "Hi, Grady. I'm glad you

came back tonight. I didn't get to thank you properly last night for all your help."

He winked at me and drawled, "I wasn't sure how happy you'd be to see me. Sort of got the impression you belonged to Sawyer. Was I wrong?"

"Definitely wrong. I don't *belong* to anyone, and I'm not in the market for a boyfriend. Not that I don't like men, because I do, just not right now. Not saying I don't like you. You seem really great." I was babbling like an idiot. Blowing out a frustrated breath, I told him, "Before I say anything else stupid, would you mind meeting me outside? There's something I wanted to discuss with you. In private."

"You sure Sawyer got the message you ain't looking for a boyfriend? Looked like he was peeing a circle around you last night to keep other dogs away." His blue eyes were lit with laughter. In that moment, it was easy to picture how he'd have tormented me if we'd grown up together. It would have been wonderful.

"Just go on outside and wait for me. I'll protect you from the big bad dog if he shows up." He had me smiling when it should have been impossible. I wanted to hang on to this moment of teasing. After I told him who I was, he might never want to see me again.

"With an invitation like that, how can I refuse?" He stood and meandered toward the exit, tossing jokes back and forth with friends, and I smiled with them, even though I had no idea what was being said. Grady—my *brother*—seemed to be on good terms with just about everyone in the bar.

I scanned the crowded floor for Zane. When I spotted her across the room, it was easy to tell she'd been watching the exchange between Grady and I. She was fairly bouncing on the balls of her feet with excitement. She'd already figured out what was about to happen and gave me two thumbs up.

Charlie nodded when I told him I was taking a break. "Sounds like a damn fine idea. When you come back, try something different. Like not screwing anything else up tonight."

No sense in telling him it would all depend on how the talk went with my brother.

* * *

KELLI

"OVER HERE," Grady called out softly. He'd been watching for me to exit the building.

I paused at hearing his voice. This was it. Twisting on a heel, I headed in the direction he'd called from. The weak light by the entrance didn't extend all the way to the end of the porch. His voice was all I had for guidance. My eyes adjusted to the darkness and I was able to pick him out from the other shadows. The fall night was cool, but it was nerves that had goosebumps chasing up and down my arms.

"Thanks for agreeing to meet me out here. I know it must have sounded strange, since we don't really know each other." If I wasn't careful, my runaway mouth was going to start babbling again. I stepped off the end of the porch into the filmy light provided by the three-quarter moon and a million stars. Not stopping at his side, I wandered around the corner and further down the side of the building, away from the entrance. I didn't want any new arrivals, or departing customers, witnessing my confession.

Grady followed, not saying anything until I came to a halt. "What's up, Kelli? You gave me fair warning you weren't looking for a man. That makes me think you might need a friend." He leaned against the side of the building, bending a knee as he braced a foot against its rough exterior. "Darlin', it's pretty clear you don't belong in a place like this. Are you in some kind of trouble?"

"No, not in any trouble." I had hoped inspiration would strike with the perfect words when I needed them. Nope, not happening. Inspiration was a fickled witch and left me hanging. Taking a deep breath, I just opened my mouth and hoped for the best. "As for me not belonging here, maybe I don't, but I want to." It was impossible to control the quiver in my voice. Grady moved away from the wall, reaching out as if to pull me into a hug. I stepped back, afraid that if he touched me, the rest of my words would never find a way out.

"I came to Copper Ridge because I was looking for my father. That didn't work out so well, but I did find someone just as important. Someone I had no idea even existed. It's not like I expected any of this. You need to know that this is as big a shock to me as to you. I'd didn't come here to hurt…"

Grady closed the gap and reached for me again. This time he didn't go for the hug, but reached out with a hand and took possession of mine. "I'm trying to follow, but you're losing me on this winding trail you're taking. Best to keep it straightforward when dealing with a simple-minded man."

His gentle teasing helped to steady me. "I came to Copper Ridge to find my father, but instead, I found you. My brother."

He didn't just drop my hand but flung it away from him. He tripped over his own feet trying to back away from me. "Whoa…that's a *hell* of a long way from simple."

It was my turn to follow him. More like chase. "Wait, wait! Look, I didn't believe it either when Lonnie first told me, but the facts all added up."

I was counting on him believing my bizarre claim because it came from a man he'd known his whole life. "He said he remembered me as a baby, knew your dad…our dad, Emmett. He worked with Momma years ago right here at Skeeter's."

The words tumbled over each other in my rush to make him stop and listen. "Lonnie's the one who told me about you and explained how Emmett passed last year. He talked abou—"

"Hold up. Just hold up a damn minute." Terse words. He held his hands out, palms up, warning me not to come any closer. He was no longer trying to escape, but his body fairly vibrated with tension. "Lonnie's the one who told you this shit?"

Afraid to say anything that would put him on the run again, I just nodded. Then, worried he'd not seen the movement in the darkness, spoke up, "Yes."

"How old are you?"

"Twenty-seven."

"What's your full name?"

"Kelli Louisa Radcliff."

"Where'd you move here from?"

"Little Rock."

The one question I thought would have been his first ended up being his last: "What's your mom's name?" His voice took on a rougher edge.

"Denise Hutley Radcliff."

Grady went silent. I figured he was fact-checking my

answers against what he remembered of the sister he'd lost so long ago. When he did finally start talking again, the number of *fucks* coming out of his mouth let me know he wasn't liking how the facts were lining up. I remembered how careful he'd been with his words the previous night. Guess he no longer cared to be polite around me.

"This *momma* of yours." He sneered the word like it was the filthiest curse he knew. "She never said, 'Hey, Kelli, did I ever tell you about your big brother? You should check him out sometime.'"

This was all wrong. I'd messed up the telling and didn't know how to fix it without making Momma out to be some narcissistic bitch. Oh, wait, she was. Had a feeling it wouldn't be a big surprise to him.

"I get it," I said. "Last thing you ever expected was some stranger showing up claiming to be your sister. A brother wasn't even on my radar when I moved here looking for my dad. But I'm willing to explore what it means to have a brother. Don't you think we've lost enough years being separated without going into the how or why? I'm not standing here asking why you never came to find me."

Grady paced off three steps one way then back the other. He repeated the same pattern over and over while he pinched the bridge of his nose. After what felt like days, he came to a stop in front of me, studying my face as intently as I'd searched his the night before. I wondered just how well he could make out my features in the dark. When he finally spoke, the bitterness had been replaced with suspicion. "What now? You came looking for Dad and he's gone. What do you expect from me?"

"Well, I'm not asking to move in or looking for money if that's what you're worried about." Anxiety had me getting snarky. Afraid the next step would be breaking down in tears, I raised my voice in frustration.

"All I'm asking is for you to just give us a chance to get to know one another. You weren't having a problem offering to be friends before finding out you were my brother. Forget I'm your sister. Let's just work on being friends if that makes it easier for you."

The yelling got a hand slapped over my mouth. Grady searched the parking lot for witnesses to our first fight as brother and sister. I realized it was seriously messed up that a yelling match with my brother made me want to smile.

"Shhh, don't be screaming," he said. "Folks will be running out here thinking I'm killing you. We don't need to be broadcasting you're my sister in a parking lot where just anybody can hear." As if just realizing he was touching me, he jerked his hand away like I had the plague. That hurt.

"I don't *care* who knows. Is that a problem for you?" I leaned forward, hands fisted on my hips

"Dammit! Yes, it's a problem! A big problem! You can't be going around telling people I'm your brother." The vehemence of his demand shocked me.

"What do you mean I can't tell people? What's the big deal? Lonnie already knew you had a sister. I'm sure there's plenty of others who remember it, too."

"People forget. You left so long ago, no one around these parts has thought about you in years. I don't want them suddenly remembering I have a sister. I sure as hell don't want them knowing you're right here. What are you doing working at Skeeter's, anyway? This is a damn nightmare." He was back to pinching the bridge of his nose.

"Did *you* forget? Is that why you don't want anyone else to be reminded? What? You want me to disappear again and not mess up your tidy, perfect life?" I was in danger of cutting the palm of my hands with my fingernails.

Grady went motionless. A low, ugly laugh that went on and on was the only answer he gave. When he finally stopped, he pointed a finger at me. "Listen, you don't know anything about my life. We're going to keep it that way until I say different. I want a promise. Right here. Right now. You don't tell anybody else about this. And you need to make damn sure anyone you've already told keeps their mouths shut."

"Give me one good reason why?" I narrowed my eyes.

"Because if you don't, there is no way in hell we'll ever get the chance to know each other."

I believed he meant every word that came out of his mouth, which was the only reason I agreed to the promise.

Grady twisted away from me and stormed off around the side of the building. I followed at a much slower pace, trying to figure out where everything had gone horribly wrong.

Rounding the corner, I saw Sawyer standing in the light of the porch, staring in the direction Grady was making tracks. Some small noise must have given away my presence, because Sawyer pivoted, spearing me with a look. His frown drew his eyebrows down, and then he shifted to watch Grady's retreating figure, then back to me. Great. Could the night get any worse?

"What the fuck were you doing back there with Grady?" The harsh timbre of his voice poked at my snarled emotions.

"If a day ever comes that it's any of your business? That's the day I'll tell you. Until then, I suggest you mind your own." Lifting my chin, I returned his glare, daring him to push me for an answer.

"You're confused, princess." His tight-lipped smile gave him a predatory look. "I decide what I want to make my business. If I decide it's you, you'll fucking learn what that means." He moved away from the door, heading back to the dark parking lot.

The stupid man left me standing there frustrated and aching for a hair-pulling fight.

CHAPTER THIRTEEN

Kelli

THE TIP of my nose brushed the surface of the tiny mirror. I carefully examined the makeup around my eyes, searching for flaws in my attempt to camouflage another sleepless night. The sole fixture in the windowless bathroom might have made a decent nightlight, but that was about it. On second thought, any self-respecting nightlight would be insulted at the comparison. I could only hope I hadn't ended up emulating Taylor Momsen.

My sleepless night was thanks to my newfound brother. I'd tossed half the night trying to figure out what difference it made if others knew I was his sister. His final threat, before he walked away, was enough to ensure I'd follow his demands. Spending the day with Zane was the perfect way to keep me from driving myself crazy thinking about it.

A heavy knock on the room's door signaled Zane's arrival. Giving one last glance at the dim reflection of my face, I yelled, "Door's unlocked. Come on in. I'll be ready in a sec." Great, Zane asked for help learning proper etiquette and here I was, having a screamversation through a closed door. I heard the door open then close with a bit of a bang.

Stepping out of the bathroom, I paused in front of the adjacent closet. I pulled out a denim jacket that was every bit as distressed and expensive as the ragged jeans I had on. It cost a lot of money to dress poor on the side of Little Rock I came from. Keeping my voice raised, I called out, "Sorry about all the boxes. Let's hope we find a place today so I can finally unpack."

It wasn't until I had both arms pushed through the sleeves that I moved around the corner to smile at my friend. I didn't quite manage to swallow the yelp of alarm as I recognized the man standing in the middle of the room.

It was the first time I'd seen Sawyer since *the Kiss*. In my mind, time would forever be marked BTK or ATK. The trick would be to keep him from realizing the impact the original TK had on me.

"What the fuck do you think you're doing leaving the door unlocked? This ain't Mayberry. Keep your damn door locked."

"It was open because I was expecting Zane. I'm not stupid." Except when it came to him. Filthy words and surly orders weren't supposed to be appealing. I was beginning to think I had this perverse draw to men whose only mission in life was to make me miserable.

"Well, smart girl, do I look like Zane?"

I could have told him he looked like a lot better reason to have a sleepless night than worrying about my brother. But I had a little more self-respect than that. Barely.

Ignoring his question, I asked one of my own. "What are you doing here, Sawyer?"

"Zane called, said you needed a place to live. Makes helluva lot more sense for me to haul you around to check out what's available than her doing it." He blew off helping find me a place to live as if it was no big thing.

Shock at his offhand explanation froze me in place. Was he for real? Zane wouldn't pass me off to Sawyer.

He wandered over to the stack of boxes lining the wall. "Looks like you're planning on hanging around Copper Ridge for a while."

Before I realized what he intended, he flipped one of the loose flaps on the boxes open. The contents had him tilting his head sideways for a better view.

Knowing what he was studying so intently had my stomach twisting in knots. Intending to block his view, I darted forward to slap the cover closed. One of his large hands shot up, stopping me short. He could easily hold me off, and I wasn't willing to engage in a childish struggle. I watched helplessly as his free hand disappeared inside the container then emerged with a confection of siren-red lace and strings tangled between his fingers. A wicked smirk lifted the edge of his lips as he rolled the silky material between rough fingers.

"Surprising." The growl in his voice made me want to squirm.

If his intent was to embarrass me, I refused to let him see it was working. I would... I would... Well, I'd watch silently and pretend I wasn't melting into a puddle to join the other questionable stains on the carpet.

"Just because Zane called you doesn't expla—" I was cut off mid-snark by Miranda Lambert belting out "Just Like You." Zane's idea of a joke when she personalized her ringtone on my cell. I hurried over to the bedside table to grab my phone. Just the girl I wanted to talk to.

"Zane, did you send Sawyer?" I did my best to follow

Zane's apologetic explanations but was finding it difficult to concentrate on what she was saying. Sawyer was making it impossible.

I watched as his hand plunged back into the box. This time he pulled out one of my favorite satin corsets in a delicate peach shade. The garment dangled by its narrow straps from two of his blunt fingers. With the sexy little number held in the air between us, he did that head-tilting thing again. Only this time it was me he had his sights locked on. He *wanted* me to know he was picturing me in its waist-cinching, boob-lifting embrace. And the first real smile I'd ever seen from him spread across his face.

There was an all-out war going on between my brain and my body. Brain urged me to dash across the room and rip the snippet of material away from him. Body was trapped watching him lift one intimate piece after another and holding them up against the backdrop of me. I felt like a life-size version of a paper doll.

I had no clue when the conversation on my cell ended. One minute Zane was explaining why it was better for Sawyer to show me rentals, and the next I was holding a silent phone pressed against my ear.

"Zane clear things up?" He watched me with that smirk still tilting the corners of his lips.

It was hard to be mad with my friend. Zane really believed Sawyer was a terrific guy and probably thought this was a great idea. What puzzled me was why he would stand in for her. I was going to fix that right now and offer him a way out. "You don't have to do this. I can wait until Zane is free to take me."

"It'd be fuckin' rude to reject my offer and hurt my feelings. You don't want to be fuckin' rude, do you, princess?" He was teasing, and I wasn't sure how to respond. From the moment he'd walked through the door, it had felt like having a wolf show up with a tennis ball clinched in his sharp teeth, wanting to play fetch. I found myself wanting to reach out and take the ball, knowing there was a very real possibility I'd end up losing a finger or two.

"You seem comfortable with rude," I said. "Pretty sure your feelings are safe." Needing to break his hold, I dropped the cell back on the dresser and picked up one of the hand-knotted hair ties littering the scarred top. I finger-combed my hair into a high ponytail and busied myself with securing it.

While I made busywork for my hands, he eyed the outfit I had on. "You gonna be warm enough in that getup?"

I just *knew* his question had nothing to do with my jeans and jacket. He was picturing me in the same type of delicate feminine intimate he was smoothing his thumb back and forth across. Lord have mercy…he was petting the damn thing.

"I've got long johns on." Let him picture that.

An appreciative chuckle left his lips as he dropped the sexy garment back into the box. He moved on to the next open carton as if he had every right to inspect its contents. I no longer cared. He'd already had his hand in the one guaranteed to cause me maximum discomfort.

I had no reason to be ashamed; lots of women enjoyed sexy undergarments. It shouldn't matter if my obsession with them was just a little more excessive than most. Maybe if he continued to rummage through the open boxes, he'd find the one with my tampons. Wouldn't that be a treat?

I sighed and asked, "Warm enough for what? Why do I need to dress warm?"

"You ask a lot of questions for someone piss-poor at answering them." Sawyer abandoned his snooping.

"And you're such an open book." I shook my head.

"What I am is direct. Say what I mean, take what I want, and protect what's mine." The list sounded suspiciously close to a threat. He dropped the smile and became all business. "Now are you going to be warm enough in that getup on my bike?"

"As in a motorcycle?" Never having been on one before, the thought both terrified and thrilled. Mostly thrilled.

"No, I was planning on wheeling you around on the handlebars of my ten-speed while we looked at rentals."

"Cute." I rolled my eyes. It actually was pretty funny. Something I never expected from Mr. Badassery. Shoot, this whole conversation wasn't anything I would've expected from him.

"Princess, I haven't been cute since I was three." As if suddenly tired of teasing me, he said, "We're wasting daylight. If you want to find a place to live, your ass better be following mine when I walk out the door." He didn't wait for an answer, just left the door wide open as he exited the room.

I wasn't about to miss my chance to ride something Momma had always demanded I not go near. I grabbed my bag and dumped the contents on the bed. Snagging only the essentials, I stuffed them in the pockets of my jacket.

Afraid I'd taken too long, I rushed out of the motel room to find Sawyer leaning against a beautiful machine, waiting for me. The bike was the same one that had been parked in front of Skeeter's the first day I'd pulled into the parking lot. He held a black helmet in his fist. When I got close, he stood and pointed at my head. "You're gonna have to do something different with your hair." He held up the helmet as explanation.

"Right." I grabbed the holder at the base of my pony and gave it a quick tug. Hair tumbled in a wild fall around my shoulders and down my back. Again, I finger-combed the mass, but this time I fashioned the strands into a loose braid that fell down the length of my spine.

I was worried the entire time I fussed with my hair, afraid he would get tired of waiting. But he now seemed to be in no hurry despite his earlier claim of time being wasted. Soon as the braid was completed, I reached for the helmet. He ignored my outstretched hand and lowered the headgear in place. His knuckles brushed against the underside of my jaw as he adjusted the strap.

To distract from his nearness, I asked, "Where's yours?"

"Brain buckets are for pussies and chicks."

That took my mind off his touch. "Are you kidding me? You just called it a brain bucket. That shows you know how important it is to protect your head. Riding without a helmet is criminally negligent." How could he be so careless with his life? Why did I care?

"Princess, you're bitchin' about one of the few laws I haven't broken. Arkansas agrees with me and says I don't have to wear a helmet. Now, climb your ass up on the bike and let's get the hell out of here." He moved to the motorcycle and slung a leg across its leather seat. Once he was settled, his stare challenged me.

I wanted to go church lady all over him. Wanted to tell him to stick his orders where the sun didn't shine. But I *wanted* on that darn bike more. A movement out of the corner of my eye gave me the excuse needed to break our staring contest. Mrs. Whatley stood in front of the office door, pretending to polish the glass. No doubt she was straining to hear every word spoken between Sawyer and I. It was the motivation I needed to remember just how badly I wanted to move out of the Paradise Motor Inn.

Walking over to the motorcycle, I asked in the most

sickeningly sweet voice I could muster, "How do I climb on without breaking... something?"

Sawyer didn't answer me. He was staring at Mrs. Whatley. Nodding in her direction, he asked, "You been having any problems with her?"

I glanced back at the old gossip and shrugged. "She's just hoping for something juicy to spread. Having you show up probably made her day. It'll give her an excuse to remind me, again, that she runs a respectable business. She claims to be worried about the kind of hooligans I associate with at your less-than-respectable business. It'll break her heart when I finally move. She won't have near as much to share with her quilting club."

He turned his eyes to my face, searching for something. Whatever he saw must have satisfied him. He pointed to the foot peg. "Pretend you're mounting a horse and that's your stirrup. You have another one on the other side. Same as with a stirrup, you'll use it to mount, dismount, and for balance. Understand?"

It surprised me how patient he was being. The instructions were clinical, highlighting the seriousness of paying attention to his directions. Having him explain it in terms I was familiar with was a relief, boosting my confidence. All those fancy equestrian lessons were going to pay off in a way I could have never imagined.

After he swung a muscled thigh across the bike, he motioned me closer. "Your turn."

He had both feet on the ground and the bike was still on its stand. Moving next to him, I placed a hand on the leather seat behind him and went to step on the peg. It was awkward, and I was doing a horrible job of trying to throw a leg across in one fluid motion.

"Put your hands on my shoulders. It'll give you better balance."

I shifted my hands to his shoulders and immediately felt more centered as I easily mounted the bike. That all evaporated when one of his large hands wrapped around my thigh. He slid me forward until his butt was pressed against my center and my legs were cradling him. "Put your arms around my waist and don't try any fancy leaning shit on the curves. Glue your tits to my back and let your body follow mine."

If he'd hadn't sounded detached as he talked me into position, I would've been suspicious of all the close contact. Apparently, I was the only one having trouble remembering he was instructing me on how to ride double on a motorcycle.

Not until satisfied I was balanced, with a secure hold, did he straighten the bike and kick the stand up. My heart was about to beat out of my chest. It was a tossup on whether it was from excitement or being coiled around Sawyer. The guttural roar of the engine was much louder than expected, making me cling even tighter to him. He pulled away slowly from the walkway and eased out onto the road. By the time he blew past the city limits sign, I was laughing in sheer joy at the wildness of the experience. My laugher must have been the signal Sawyer had been waiting for, because he grabbed another gear and turned the beast loose.

CHAPTER FOURTEEN

Kelli

BY THE TIME Sawyer slowed to a stop, I was ready to admit to having fallen in love with the monster machine I sat on. Mommas had good reasons to demand their daughters stay away from motorcycles and the bad boys who rode them. Both were irresistible once sampled.

No momma in her right mind would want her daughter around a man capable of controlling that much power between his legs. I was pretty sure I'd had a mini-orgasm as we rocketed down the highway, and it wasn't just from the pulse of the bike. If I smoked, I'd light one up. I now understood what my more adventurous girlfriends had meant when they called motorcycles the world's largest vibrators.

Using his shoulders for balance, I stood on the foot pegs before dismounting. With my feet back on solid ground, my legs were shaky from the adrenaline rush of my first bike ride. Right. Just the bike ride.

I pulled off the helmet and handed it to Sawyer while avoiding eye contact. If he was smirking, I would die. He took it silently and hung it from the handlebar by its chin strap.

Embarrassed or not, like an addict, I couldn't wait to climb back on and twine my body back around his. Hanging on to Sawyer added a whole other layer to the experience. Our bodies moving in sync. Every twist and turn amplifying the bunching and stretching of muscle against muscle separated by the thinnest of denim barriers. His butt tucked tight into the apex of my thighs was the most erotic foreplay a woman could ever experience.

Wrapped as I had been around his body, my hands got plenty of playtime with Sawyer's muscle-corded torso. Each lean into a curve became an excuse to readjust my hold. An excuse to subtly explore the ridges and valleys that made up his abs. And oh lordy, the intoxicating masculine scent of his skin had surrounded me, seducing me not with some expensive cologne but the honest smells of soap and sweat and man.

"What do you think?" Sawyer asked as he swung off the bike. His words shifted my attention to him. He raked a hand through his dark hair, doing little to tame what the wind had styled. It was the kind of hair a woman could run her hands through and not be afraid of having her palms come away slicked with some fancy hair gel.

"Hellooo, anybody home, princess? I asked what you thought."

My voice a full octave higher than normal, I stuttered, "N-nothing. Standing here waiting on you and not thinking about anything." I was terrified he'd read my face and figure out what I'd been thinking.

He raised an eyebrow, his smile saying I was busted. But he didn't call bullshit on my *nothing* or the reason for my flustered state. He jerked a thumb back over his shoulder. "You taking a look inside?"

Of course. The rental he'd brought me to see. *Please let him think I'm just an idiot. That will be so much better than the truth.* I glanced in the direction he indicated and saw we were parked in front of a long row of rustic cabins. From where I stood, each one appeared slightly different than the one beside it.

The one we were parked in front of was last in line, giving it a smidge more privacy than the rest. Painted a pale yellow with white trim and shutters, it had clapboard siding and a charming porch. The two windows flanking the front door were decked out with flower boxes. Both boxes overflowed with late summer blossoms and early fall blooms.

The one thing all of the cabins had in common was the killer view of the lake at their back doors. This definitely wasn't the trailer park I'd pictured him owning. He'd brought me to an upscale lakeside resort, and I couldn't keep the skepticism out of my voice when I asked, "You own all of these?"

"Yeah. And not a single whore in any of 'em." He offered me a lopsided grin.

I was going to *kill* Zane.

I ignored his wicked smile. "Renting a room at a resort wasn't what I had in mind. Didn't Zane explain I was looking for a long-term rental?"

Shrugging, he began walking toward the quaint cabin, digging in a front pocket for a key. "This gives you options. Do a month-to-month for now. If you're still here when summer comes around, we can discuss what you want to do then."

What he said made sense. So why did I want to argue and convince him I was going to stay? What if my brother decided he didn't want me anywhere near him? Sawyer was right about one thing: I had a lot of questions and no answers.

After following him through the door, I stopped just inside the entrance. The rustic charm from the outside continued on the inside. The living room and kitchen were open to each other, giving the interior the appearance of being more spacious than it was. The decor was perfect for a vacation rental, overlooking a lake. So what if its white-washed walls had a few too many plaques with cutesy *Life is Better at the Lake*-type sayings for my taste? It had a homey touch reinforced by the comfy, overstuffed furniture.

I was happy to see its knickknacks were of the shabby chic variety that conveyed a feminine touch. No stuffed fish with lures dangling from their lips were tacked up on the walls. It definitely had a feminine touch without going overboard.

I crossed over to the door that led to the bedroom. Again, the shiplap walls were whitewashed and continued the theme of shabby chic. The bed was a queen with a metal headboard and a quilt rail at the bottom. It boasted a mattress that made me want to weep at its softness when I sat on the edge of it.

The en suite was small, no bathtub, which was a shame, but it was clean, functional, and bright. Yay for the bright. I could see my reflection in the generous mirror without using a flashlight.

When I came out of the bedroom, Sawyer was poking around in the kitchen. Opening cabinets, pulling out drawers. "I was told there was enough shit in here to get by if you wanted to cook. Seems you have most everything you'd need."

"Haven't you ever been in here?" I watched him as he continued to open doors.

"Drop by one or two times a year to check on the property." He stopped his investigation and faced me. "Have a manager to take care of the day-to-day. He's the one you'll deal with if you take the place."

He abandoned the kitchen to head to the room I'd just left. I stared after him, a frown on my face. Trailing him into the bedroom, I found it empty but heard him going through the vanity in the bathroom. I waited by the bed for him to finish his inspection.

Running a hand over the softly colored quilt, I thought the place was perfect for me. No reason to ask if he had anything else I could view, which made me curious about what else he did own.

The contrast between Skeeter's and this resort was as mind-blowing as the difference between a wart-nosed hag and Julia Roberts. Zane had claimed he had other businesses that were legit. I hadn't thought Zane was lying— exactly—but I hadn't realized how nice those other businesses would be.

While the kinds of places he chose to own weren't any of my concern, it was... I kept coming back to the word *puzzling*. I should be grateful he owned something I wouldn't be afraid to live in. But why *did* he own something I'd be comfortable calling home for the short term?

"Problem?"

Startled, I turned from scowling at the bed to find him closer than I'd expected. For a big man, he moved quietly. A couple more steps and I'd be trapped between him and the bed. I took a sidestep, planning on easing around him. "No. No problem. Everything is lovely."

He mirrored my evasive action, keeping me trapped. He

stepped even closer. "If you don't want the cabin, say so. I've got a couple other places I can take you to check out."

His offer made me forget about escaping and brought my frown back. Why would a man who had legal options to earn money choose to skirt the law with places like Skeeter's?

"What's going on in that head of yours?" He studied me so intently it was as if he was trying to see inside my head.

How he lived and made money wasn't my business. Mustering a toothy smile, I told him, "You walked in on me making a mental list of the things I'd need when I moved in here." I was such a liar. "I love this cabin. When can I sign the papers?"

"Bull. Shit." He stepped forward. I retreated, the back of my knees hitting the bed. "How about you tell me what the hell's really going on, princess? 'Cause you can't lie worth a shit."

"Do you have to be so crude all the time?"

"That's it, isn't it? You had me pigeonholed. I'm supposed to be the crude sum'bitch who owns dives and gambling houses, safely hidden away from decent folks. Then you see this place, shiny, semi-fancy. A place a family with a little money can come and do wholesome family shit. And you wonder, what's going on? Crude bastards shouldn't own places where decent, wholesome people can go.

"You expected a countrified slum lord with a rundown trailer park. Didn't you, princess?" He didn't raise his voice. He wasn't angry. He sounded amused more than anything. At me. Maybe at himself.

I flushed. I *had* expected a trailer park. I *was* shocked he owned this resort. But it wasn't for the reasons he thought.

I threw my arms out. "I don't understand you. I don't understand this." I pointed to the spot where we stood.

"This is safe. You don't have to wonder if the next stranger through the door is going to start a fight, pull a gun, or haul you away to prison. If you have safe, why do you need dangerous?"

"Safe is boring. Safe is a lie. How did your safe world treat you, princess?" He lifted my braid and gave it a gentle tug. "When you left *safe*, did you leave it kicking and screaming or did you willingly leave it for the dangerous?"

"We're not talking about me. Remember?" I didn't want him to continue. He was too close to the truth.

"Bet you've been warned your whole life to stay away from motorcycles, 'cause they're fuckin' dangerous. You'd been taught to fear the men riding them, 'cause they're fuckin' dangerous." The gravelly rumble of his words had me swaying closer when I felt him tugging on my braid again. "But princess, you ate that shit up today."

"I don't want to talk about me." My breathy demand sounded worse than weak.

"The sharp edge of doing something dangerous sliced you raw. Left you open. And so fucking alive." He pulled the tie at the end of my hair free and loosened the mass, one soft tug after another. "Safety wasn't what you wanted when you bound your body to mine on the back of my bike."

"I was just doing what you told me to do. You said to lean on you. Hang on tight to keep from falling. I did all of that to be safe." I really was a terrible liar.

"Did I tell you walk your nails across my stomach and sink them into my chest? To drive me nuts with your tits? I've probably got scorch marks on my back from you rubbing them back and forth. Did I tell you to squirm your pussy into me so hard I was ready to beg you to unbutton my jeans and wrap your hand around my cock?" He gripped my hair. Pulled my head back. Forced me to meet his burning stare. "Safe had nothing to do with that ride, princess."

When had "princess" stopped being a taunt and become a caress? I wanted to close my eyes. Block him from seeing the hunger in them. But I couldn't.

Sawyer pulled me into him as he leaned into me. A rough cheek pressed against the softness of mine. His warm breath tickled my ear as he whispered, "I'm not fucking safe."

CHAPTER FIFTEEN

Kelli

I SHUDDERED AT HIS WORDS. I knew what he was telling me. Knew he was waiting to see if I was a coward as well as a liar.

Despite his truth about not being safe, if I asked he would step back. We would walk out to his bike; I would climb on behind him and curl around his body. Then every move he had just described would be played out again, by me. That was my truth.

Not willing to give myself a chance to change my mind, I turned as much as his tight grip on my hair allowed. I pressed a soft kiss against his stubble-shadowed cheek. His fingers relaxed, giving me the freedom needed to continue pressing kisses until I reached the corner of his mouth.

Sawyer let his hands drift down my body to settle on my hips. His fingers dug in so tightly they were in danger of leaving bruises, but he made no move to dominate. It was up to me to make the choice to be with him.

I shifted until my breast pressed into his chest, pushing my hips into his. After nipping the perfection of his bottom lip, I soothed it with a feathering stroke of my tongue. The teasing bite broke the restraints Sawyer had placed on himself.

He took control of my mouth, and it was dark and feral and a grinding heat with none of the gentle seduction of our first kiss. The taste of him promised the wild and untamed. A large hand moved to grip the back of my neck, holding me captive. His other kneaded the lushness of my ass. The ache between my legs that had started out as a tingling awareness had morphed into a raging, consuming need.

I wrenched my mouth from his, sucking in great gulps of air. I'd forgotten to breathe. Denied my lips, he moved the assault to the sensitive skin behind the curve of my ear. He whispered raunchy, filthy words of what he was going to do to me. Heat blossomed in my cheeks. No one had ever said those kinds of things to me before. I was in serious danger of spontaneous combustion. Everything had turned into a need. I needed to be naked. I needed him to be naked.

I went wild in that need. He praised my wildness as he helped me remove his shirt. He encouraged me to be ferocious in my demands. He pushed my jacket down my arms than had my tee up and tossed over his shoulder. He growled at the sight of my breasts displayed in black silk and lace. He lifted the weight of them in his palms, teasing the diamond points of my nipples with his thumbs. When that wasn't enough, he worked the lace cups down, anchoring them under the fullness of my breast, giving him access to take turns sucking and biting the dusty, rose-colored buds. I appreciated his appreciation, but the tugging pressure led to wanting so much more from him.

I got busy working on the snap and zip of his jeans. I whimpered in frustration when he grasped my arms and set me away from him. My displeasure was forgotten when the hands that pushed me back stripped off his jeans in one smooth motion. I didn't have time to get more than a glimpse at what his clothes had hidden before his hands were at the waistband of my jeans. They made quick work of unfastening and peeling the soft denim down my legs, leaving them pooled around my half boots.

He knelt at my feet and one of his large hands landed in the middle of my stomach. With a wicked grin, he gave a shove. I squealed in surprise, falling backward onto the bed. Legs draped over the edge, I raised my torso and braced with my elbows so I could watch, watch the play of muscle in his wide chest as he pulled off my boots and finished stripping off my jeans.

When I was left in nothing but a triangle of black lace, held in place by bows at my hips, he sat back on his heels. His eyes burned with a heat that had nothing to do with anger as he stared at that minuscule scrap of cloth. He clasped my knees and spread my legs wider. I was back to fighting for each breath, but I couldn't take my eyes off him, wanting, no, needing to see what he was going to do to me.

He smoothed a path up the sensitized skin of my thighs, the coarse texture of his hands raising goosebumps. Shifting his palms under my ass, he slid me closer to the edge of the bed. His shoulders edged my legs impossibly wider as he settled between them. His fingers traced heated circles at the lacy edges of silk. His thumb wandered onto the surface of my mound and smoothed back and forth over the lace.

As I watched, I thought, *Dear God, he's petting it the same way he did those panties earlier in my room. Has he been imagining doing this, then?*

Sawyer glanced up, captured my stare, and gave me a slow wink. "I've been going crazy all day wondering what the hell you had on under your clothes." He slipped his fingers up to toy with the bows at my hips. "It's like a fuckin' present waiting for me to unwrap and play with what's inside."

He jerked on the dangling strings and exposed my bare mound. "Fuuuuck, baby. A pussy this pretty deserves all the fancy shit you pamper it with. It's a damn shame you've been wasting this on city boys. You're about to get pissed, honey, 'cause you're going to learn just how boring your safe life has been."

His gravelly groan and playful words were worth every minute of torture to have smooth lady-parts. I had always wondered in the past why I bothered. Finally, I had an answer. And when he leaned over and ran his tongue up the center, every thought narrowed down to one: *ohmygodohmygodohmygod*. I closed my eyes in pleasure.

"Open your eyes, princess."

He had moved back, his heated eyes staring into mine as they fluttered open. He reached up and pressed two fingers against my lips. I didn't know what he wanted.

"Suck," he ordered.

I was still confused, but as he pressed harder against my lips, I opened my mouth and let him push them in. I swirled my tongue around his large digits. It was unbelievably erotic to suck on his fingers while he watched with that hooded gaze of his. When he removed them, it was so abrupt that my lips made a popping sound.

"Hell, princess. You're going to make me blow my load like a damn teenager." He growled the words.

I didn't have time to wonder if I'd been doing something wrong before the real reason he'd wanted me to suck on his fingers was explained, by actions, not words. He used his now-slick fingers to part the folds on either side of my clit. He teased the sensitive area without actually ever touching the quivering bundle of nerves. Building the tension but never letting me free-fall over the edge. When he angled forward and buried his tongue in my pussy in one swift move, my arms turned to mush and I fell back on the bed. But the relief I craved didn't come. Sawyer was keeping me on the edge of insanity

"Please, Sawyer, please." I was begging and didn't care.

He raised his head at my pleading, making me want to scream in frustration. He wasn't supposed to stop the pleasure. He was supposed to stop the torture and let me come.

"When you come, it's going to be on my cock." His gravelly voice sounded raw.

"Then get your fuckin' cock in me! Now!"

He roared with laughter. "When you think about what you said, you're gonna be so fuckin' embarrassed later, princess."

He reached for his jeans and pulled out a condom tucked inside a pocket. He stood, and my greedy eyes devoured the sight of him stroking the condom down the length of his hard shaft. He crawled on the bed, straddling me. Bracing with one arm, he used the other to shift me farther up the bed. Again, he took over the space between my spread legs, this time with his thick thighs, then he was there, the broad head of his dick pressing into my entrance, and it was heaven.

I groaned at the feel of him pushing into my wetness, his beautiful cock creating a delicious stretch that was just on the edge of pain but wholly in the realm of pleasure. He was going so slowly that I was amazed at his control, but grateful for it. It'd been a long time between the ex-fiancé and now. Because of Sawyer's restraint, each advance elicited a puff of pleasure from my lips. Each retreat built the anticipation for the next advance. By the time he was balls deep, we were both sweating and panting.

His forearms kept the full weight of his body from crushing me. He rested his forehead against mine as he strained to hold still. "So fuckin' good."

"Yessss," I breathed out, but was already missing the ebb and flow of his body. I lifted my legs and locked my ankles in the small of his back. Pressing with my heels, I arched my pelvis, urging him to move.

Sawyer huffed out a guttural laugh. "My greedy princess."

I froze at hearing him call me his. He didn't give me time to decide how I felt about the claiming. He began a rhythmic rocking that sucked me into a deep well of dark sensation. My fingernails dug into his back. That peak I'd wanted to hurtle over was back, and so much sharper. The tortured grimace of pained pleasure on his face let me know he was right there with me. He rested all of his weight on one arm and slid the other between our bodies. My feel-good button turned into an exploding fireworks stand at his touch. His magic fingers were the final boost that sent me plunging over the edge of endless sensation. Tiny screams of completion escaped from my constricted throat.

Not until my release did Sawyer allow himself to finally join me in the chaos. Listening to him cuss his way through ejecting into my body set me off again, my powerful contractions doing their best to milk his cock dry. He stayed buried in my warmth until the last contraction faded away. He rolled to lie beside me, but didn't let go of our connection completely. He had his hip pressed against mine and a hand resting on my heaving stomach as I fought to slow my breathing to something more normal.

It could have been minutes or seconds later when I heard him groan as he forced himself to roll off the bed. He headed into the bathroom, and that was my signal to start scrambling to get dressed.

I wasn't going to lie there like a needy female giving him the chance to order me to get my clothes on. I already had my jeans and long-sleeved tee back on and was pulling on my boots when he walked back into the room. I lifted my head when I heard him enter, and stared at him. His body was beautiful, and for a little while it had been mine.

He paused in the doorway and studied me. "What? No after-sex snuggle?"

"I didn't figure you for a cuddler."

"I didn't figure you for a screamer. But..." He spread his hands and shrugged.

"I'm not." My protest didn't have much steam behind it. Honesty made me add, "Usually."

If he expected me to duck my head while he walked around the room naked, well, that wasn't going to happen. My eyes followed as he retrieved his jeans from the floor and pulled them on commando. I noticed he had to adjust himself carefully before pulling up the zipper. There was some satisfaction in knowing that having my eyes on his body had him semi-hard. Not until he closed the snap did I go back to stomping my foot into the other boot.

Sex had always been enjoyable with my ex, but never earth-shattering. There were definitely cracks in my world right now. If Sawyer had set out to prove *safe* was boring, he could hang a banner: *Mission Accomplished.*

I'd thought I'd known what I was agreeing to. Sex. No safety net included. Sawyer had made it plain the other night he wasn't in it for the long haul. I'd wanted him badly enough today to agree to those terms. I wasn't going to cry foul now just because I wanted more. From the looks of what he'd stuffed in his pants, Sawyer wanted more, too. Too bad we wanted different kinds of *more*.

Pushing it to the back of my mind, I searched for the hair tie Sawyer had removed. Spying it on the floor, I retrieved it and braided my hair while he finished getting dressed. He seemed surprised I watched him while he moved around the room naked. He probably expected me to have buyer's remorse, but I wasn't a hypocrite.

I might be red in the face over some of the things I'd said to him—okay, screamed—but I'd reveled in the things we'd done to each other. I certainly wasn't going to deny myself the opportunity to ogle his beautiful naked body.

By the time I shrugged into my jacket, he had already walked out of the bedroom without waiting to see if I was ready to leave. *Snuggle? My patootie*, I thought, trailing after him. If he was worried I was going to be clingy, he was in for another surprise.

"You didn't say before we got sidetracked. When can I move in?" I passed straight through the living area and out the front door. He could follow me for a change.

Follow me he did, and if the scowl on his face was any indicator, he wasn't happy about something.

"Is that what you're calling what we did? Getting sidetracked?"

I smiled at him. "It was a very nice way to get sidetracked."

"Nice? Is that what you were being when you screamed at me to stick my cock in you?" Now Sawyer was smiling.

I narrowed my eyes at him. He was not going to shake me. "That's exactly what I was being. Now, take me back to the motel. I need a shower."

If he thought I couldn't wait to get the smell of him off

my body, so much the better. I marched over to the bike and jerked the helmet off the handlebars. It was on my head and fastened before he had completed his slow saunter to my side. My arms were crossed, and I was tapping a foot impatiently.

When Sawyer finally stood in front of me, he reached out a hand and chucked me under the chin. "Now there's my princess."

I wanted to slap his hand away but refused to play his game. He was infuriating, and this was the second time he'd called me his, when both of us knew he had no intentions of keeping me.

CHAPTER SIXTEEN

Kelli

"I WANTED to go back to the motel." My hands rested on Sawyer's shoulders as I studied the old two-story farmhouse we were parked in front of. A deep covered porch wrapped all the way around the white building, and a large semi-detached garage was connected to the porch by a covered breezeway. The yard surrounding the house was a well-maintained expanse of grass, devoid of flower beds or shrubs.

Not the sort of place I would've pictured him living. It was too domesticated and family-friendly—descriptions I didn't believe would ever apply to Sawyer.

It hadn't been until we were already here that he'd informed me—not asked—that we would be switching to his truck before picking up Zane for some kind of party. He'd been vague on the reason for the party and why it was necessary I attend with the two of them. Since he didn't strike me as a social kind of guy, my curiosity was piqued.

"You wanted a shower. My house has three. The door's open; go pick one. Now move your ass so I can grab the truck." He hitched a thumb in the direction of the garage.

"And what exactly am I supposed to do about makeup and clean clothes?" Never in my life had I attended an event not picture-perfect.

"It's a fucking bonfire at night. Who the hell is going to care if you painted your face or not? You don't need that shit anyway."

He'd gotten dangerously close to a compliment. I fought the urge to smile. "I'm not moving until you tell me why I have to attend this party."

"Fuck." Sawyer ran a hand through his tangled hair. "One of my damn men mentioned to Zane I was coming to this damn party tonight. She's been bitching at me to take her to one, so I'm taking her."

"That's actually nice of you. But it doesn't explain why you want me to go."

"I'm not being fuckin' nice. There's a good chance she'll end up getting pissed or her damn feelings hurt. I can't be babysitting her all night. The two of you are tight, so hang out and keep her out of trouble. If you're through with this interrogation shit, get off my bike and go take your shower. We're leaving in fifteen minutes, and I don't care if I have to drag your wet ass out of the shower and toss you naked in the truck." The look he shot me over his shoulder said he meant business.

His explanation didn't really explain anything, and yet it felt major that he'd given me any kind of one. I might have hoped he would admit he wanted to spend more time with me, but *almost* calling me beautiful made up for it. Besides, if Zane needed me, I'd be there.

"Fine. And thanks for the warning. I'll be locking the door to whichever bathroom I choose."

"Telling a man you're going to lock a door is as good as an invitation." The growl of the engine cut off any more comments as he rolled toward the garage.

* * *

KELLI

ZANE CAME BOUNCING out of her small trailer the moment we pulled up. Her home was small but scrupulously maintained on the outside. Two tiny pots of mums, one yellow, one white, decorated a corner of her small porch. An equally tiny pumpkin sat between the flowers. For some reason, seeing her attempt at decorating for the season had me swallowing a lump in my throat. She didn't have a lot of money, but she did what she could to make things beautiful.

I stepped out of Sawyer's truck as soon as she reached its side. She'd opened the door and claimed the back seat before I could switch places. Having no choice, I climbed back in the front.

We'd barely gotten on the road when Zane pushed into the space between Sawyer and me. She drummed her hands on the console she was leaning over. "So, you and Sawyer are friends now, huh?"

Good question. Too bad I didn't have a clue what we were. Sawyer and I both just sat there silently while she looked back and forth between us.

"Okaaay." I wasn't sure Zane could have dragged that out any longer. At last, she moved on to a different question. "This your first bonfire?"

My mouth was open to answer, but Sawyer cut me off. "She's not talking about the ones you jumped around waving your pom-poms at in high school."

Why had I ever thought Sawyer was the silent, broody type?

"This won't be my first outdoor party, but it will be the first where a fire is the main attraction," I said. Depending on how the evening went, having a large fire to push Sawyer into might come in handy.

"You'll love it," she said. "The Rydan brothers are putting it together, and they always do it up big. They're your kind of people. You'll fit right in."

The way she said "your kind of people" made me believe Zane was the one worried about fitting in. I was guessing her mysterious future boyfriend would be there, since she claimed my kind of people was also his. It also killed the small hope I had of Grady being here tonight. "Have you been to many of their parties?"

"No."

One-word answers were not Zane. I looked at Sawyer, trying to gauge what was going on, but he'd reverted to his stoic norm. The only clue to his thoughts was the muscle twitching in his cheek.

"Why not?" When I asked the question, I could feel the tension stretching from the back seat.

"Never been invited." Her offhand I-don't-give-a-shit tone was a huge red flag. As if she'd realized she was trying too hard to sound indifferent, her next words were bubblier. "I've always wanted to go to one of their parties. Sawyer gets invited all the time on account of Jase Rydan being his best friend. He never goes, though. You could have knocked me over with a feather when I heard he was this time. I mentioned to him how much I'd like to go, and he said I could tag along."

I glanced over to see if he would out her for nagging

him into bringing her. He remained quiet, but that twitch in his cheek might have been working a little harder.

"It about surprised the water outta me when you showed up with him. Guess you all got friendly when you were house-hunting."

Sawyer snorted, cutting off anything else she had to say on the subject. Zane paused and did the back-and-forth thing again between Sawyer and me. I could only pray the heat crawling up my cheeks didn't mean they were turning red.

"Okaaay. I figured he brought you along on account of us being friends." She waggled her eyebrows at me. "But maybe I figured wrong."

She would be waiting a long time if she expected me to add anything.

When I remained quiet, she said, "I don't really care why he brought you. I'm just glad he did. It's gonna be great!"

"Yeah, great." My enthusiasm was as fake as hers sounded hopeful. Even as nervous as Zane struck me, she was excited about this party. I also believed it had to do with one of the Rydan brothers.

Hearing Sawyer mumble, "Yeah, fucking great," put the seal of doom on the whole evening.

Time for a change of subject. I mentioned the cute little cabin I'd rented on the lake, and in typical Zane fashion, she took charge of the moving arrangements. She tried to rope Sawyer into helping us, and I didn't have the heart to protest. For the first time since climbing in the truck, she was acting like herself. Turned out I didn't need to worry about Sawyer showing up to help the next day. He shot her plans down in short order, claimed he had business to take care of. By the time she had the move all worked out, we were nearing the site of the bonfire.

Despite my misgivings about the party, when I saw the flames of a huge fire in the distance, a primitive stirring of excitement had me sitting forward in anticipation. Moths weren't the only living things programed to flock to flames when darkness fell.

The evening was at that twilight stage between the sun having just dipped below the horizon and the world being pitch black. It was still light enough to appreciate the beauty of the field we were driving across, and the surrounding wooded hills. I spotted several pieces of heavy equipment parked at the perimeter of the field, the kind I imagined would be used to rip trees out of the ground and build roads. I felt a tug of sadness at the thought of this beautiful setting being developed.

The closer we got to where everyone was parked, the louder a rhythmic beat, heavy on the bass, got. By the time I could make out figures in front of the biggest bonfire I'd ever seen, Sawyer was braking beside another pickup on steroids. What was it with men and trucks the size of battleships?

"Holy shit, Kelli! They've got a band out here in the middle of nowhere!" Zane had been using language suitable for polite company since she'd gotten in the truck. We'd been working on her not cussing as part of her goal to be more ladylike. It was a relief to hear her start spewing curse words. She shouldn't have to pretend to be someone she wasn't.

Sawyer appeared at our sides as soon as Zane and I hopped out of his truck. He moved between us as we picked our way over the rough ground. If one of us stumbled, he was quick to wrap a strong hand around our arm to steady us. A gentlemanly gesture I didn't expect. No, that wasn't true. He'd shown me several different sides of him today, and some of them were pretty spectacular.

The three of us paused on the edge of the action. I'd been to more than my fair share of extravagant affairs, but the size of that fire was beyond anything I could've imagined. The huge pile of burning trees was larger than most houses. There were a few people standing around talking; some sat on bales of hay that had been scattered around the perimeter of the fire. Many were taking advantage of the band and dancing in front of the flames.

The epic blaze wasn't the only claim to party greatness. Set off to the side was a long table made out of sawhorses and rough boards loaded with platters of food. Coolers sat beside the table, and people were helping themselves to beers from them. On the other side of the coolers was another sawhorse table loaded with mason jars filled with a clear liquid. That particular table would have been declared the winner in a popularity contest. I couldn't see them, but I could certainly hear an above-average band banging out country rock in the background.

Zane had said these were my kind of people. That made me wonder what she thought happened at the country club where I had spent so much of my time. First with Momma and Jackson as I was growing up. Then with Bradley and his friends after we became engaged. It was easier for me to picture Zane being one of the people dancing around the flames than my ex or any of his pretentious cronies. They'd never pull the stick out of their butts long enough to cut loose the way these people were doing.

"About time you showed up at one of my wife's parties."

"You should be grateful he's stayed away. He's threatened more than once to run off with her."

The deep drawls, which sounded so much alike, had me swiveling my head in the direction of the speakers. The men doing the talking were as tall and hard-bodied as Sawyer, but that was where the resemblance ended.

Sawyer had the dangerously sexy vibe locked down. These men were more civilized in their appeal. Not soft. Just less likely to shoot first and... Well, just shoot first. Both had the tanned skin of men who spent hours working in the sun. One appeared to be younger than the other, but there was no mistaking they were related. These had to be the Rydan brothers. From the smile stretching ear to ear on Zane's face, the non-married one played a major role in her dreams for the future.

All three men were doing chin tips at each other—the tough-guy version of shaking hands. I edged away from the trio to give me a better angle to watch their exchange. I was curious. I hadn't seen Sawyer around a lot of people in a close exchange, but I could tell these men were on the short list of people he trusted.

My movement caused the younger Rydan to turn his eyes on me. His smile was slow and appreciative, and I instinctively smiled back. Had I really thought these men were civilized? That smile was pure wickedness with a promise of fun. Sawyer narrowed his eyes at our silent exchange. As if feeling the death glare coming from Sawyer, he shifted his gaze to Zane, and this time the smile was the type a grownup gave to a favorite youngster.

"Hey, Zanie Mae. Surprised to see you here, kiddo, but glad you came." He walked to where she stood, reached over, and—holy humiliation—tousled her hair. Oh, he seemed genuinely happy to see her, just not in the way a woman wanted a hot and sexy man to look at her.

"Who's your new friend? You know we'll be standing around all night if we wait on Sawyer to introduce anyone."

I held my breath, waiting for her to rip into him. If not for calling her Zanie Mae, for making her feel like a kid crashing a grownup party. It didn't happen. Her smile faltered, but she didn't lose it. That was when I knew for sure this was the one she'd built big plans around. I understood why Sawyer hadn't wanted to bring her tonight. This man was going to break Zane's heart.

"Hey, Evan," she said. "This is my friend Kelli. We work together at Skeeter's. Kelli, this is Evan Rydan, and that's his brother Jase." She tossed a thumb in the direction of the other Rydan without taking her eyes off Evan.

Jase shifted to see who had caught his brother's attention. "Zane, good to see you. Enjoy yourself tonight." He offered me a polite hello from where he stood.

Returning his polite smile, I said, "Pleased to meet you." Very civilized—if I ignored the way he studied me as if I were some mythical creature only read about in books.

Evan wasn't the reserved type. He crossed over to stand in front of me and took my hand. He didn't give it a shake, just held it as he said, "It's a true pleasure to meet you, Kelli. I had no idea Sawyer had women as beautiful as you working for him. This beat-up ol' cowboy would have been stopping by Skeeter's more often."

He was charming, and not the oily, slick kind that made you want to wash your hand when he let it go. He was the most dangerous kind of flirt. Sincere in his admiration and confident enough to be self-deprecating about his own worth. The faintly cocky smile said he wasn't opposed to ripping the thin film of civility to shreds in the name of having a good time.

His comment about not knowing *beautiful women worked at Skeeter's* wasn't lost on Zane. It was what finally made the smile drop from her face. Hurt flashed in her eyes as they met mine.

I pulled my hand from Evan and started to reach out to her, but she gave a small, violent shake of her head. I understood what she was quietly signaling, and dropped my arm to my side. If I comforted her right now, Evan would realize he'd hurt her feelings.

Zane wasn't the only one to lose a smile at Evan's not-so-subtle flirting. Sawyer's eyes had gone flat. He reached out, snagged my hand, and pulled me back to his side. Away from Evan. "Save your bullshit for someone interested in it, Rydan."

With that one sentence, the mood went from festive to edgy. I didn't understand what was going on, and glanced over at Zane to see if she had any idea what had just happened. She was wide-eyed and just shrugged at me.

Jase frowned and stared from me to Sawyer—there was a lot of that going around tonight—as if trying to work out an equation that just didn't add up. Evan was the only one left with a smile on his face, but it had gone from friendly to puzzled.

An explosion of color and laughter slammed into the side of Evan's body, causing him to stagger backward. One of the most beautiful and vibrant woman I'd ever seen had her arms wrapped around his neck and was snuggling into his side. "Me, me! You can rub your bullshit all over me, cowboy."

Evan draped his arms around the blonde and clasped his hands in the small of her back. He laughed at her enthusiasm. "Whoa, careful there, hellcat."

"Sawyer, I don't know what that look is about, but if you plan on killing my brother-in-law, please wait until after the party. I spent too much time on this shindig to have you blow it up five minutes after getting here." This came from a woman, with stunning red hair, as she joined our group.

The redhead crossed over to Jase and wrapped her arms around his waist. He slid an arm across her shoulders, pulled her against his chest, and planted a kiss in the middle of her forehead. The move was smooth and automatic. You just knew it was something this couple had done so many times that it came as naturally as breathing.

The arrival of the stunning blonde and the scarlet beauty shattered the tension for everyone except Zane. Her eyes narrowed on the woman hanging off Evan. The hurt was gone, but I didn't like what was taking its place. I was afraid my babysitting job had just gotten a lot harder.

CHAPTER SEVENTEEN

Sawyer

"HELL, Char, I wasn't going to fuck up your shiny new brother-in-law." I'd definitely been about to fuck Evan up. Just for smiling and holding Kelli's hand. That smile she sent back said she enjoyed the attention he was throwing her way. I needed to get that smile out of my head or he'd find himself with a fist in his face.

Evan wasn't the type to poach another man's woman. He'd just never seen me get pissed over a little flirting. Probably surprised the hell out of him when I got heated. Well, that made two of us, buddy.

The blonde bombshell had picked the perfect time to claim Evan as her own. I hated it for Zane's sake, but I'd known when I brought her here there were better than even odds she would get hurt. Kelli thought I was being a nice guy bringing Zane to this party. She was wrong. I was the worst kind of asshole. I'd figured out a long time ago that Zane thought she was in love with Evan. Bringing her tonight was never going to have a good outcome. Maybe it was time she figured that out for herself.

"Oooh, who's the pretty boy, Char?"

The woman hanging off Evan batted her lashes at me. Fucking batted her lashes.

I would have written her off as an airhead, but there was something about her and the way she smiled at me. It was as if she invited me to laugh at how ridiculous we all were. I began to think her well-timed arrival wasn't as random as she played it off. I was willing to bet her calling me a "pretty boy" was also a calculated move on her part. It certainly had Evan throwing his head back with laughter.

It was interesting he didn't seem to mind her eyeballing me. Any other time, I would've been eyeballing her right back. The woman was hot. She just didn't give me the itch. Not the same way the woman who was digging her fingernails into the back of my hand did.

"Everybody, this is my friend and business partner from New York, Brianna Townsend," Char said. "She's a burden I took on in college and she is firmly strapped to my back. Bri, turn loose of Evan long enough to meet everyone." Char grinned at Bri with affection.

I knew Jase's wife made fancy jewelry; I just hadn't known she had a partner. I'd say she'd gotten hooked with a rich one. Bombshell had *privileged* and *spoiled* written in gold on her. Copper Ridge was a long way from New York. I wasn't sure two women could come any more different than those two.

"Bitch, you know you love me." Bri untangled herself from Evan, but she didn't move far from his side. I almost told her she didn't have to protect him from me. My urge to rearrange his face had passed.

Char turned a friendly smile on Zane. "We've never met before, but I believe I went to school with one of your brothers. I'm Jase's wife, Char. I've seen you a few times at Skeeter's and believe I've heard Evan call you Zanie Mae. What a great name."

"Nobody calls me that," Zane narrowed her eyes. "I answer to Zane or not at all."

Shit. Kelli would earn her babysitting money tonight. Zane was gearing up to put on a shit show. Time to get done what I'd come for then get her the hell out of here. If that meant I had to help these people figure out who was who, fine. I'd do it my way.

Holding up Kelli's hand, I said, "This is Kelli."

Using our joined hands, I pointed at Zane. "If you want to keep the peace, you'll call that one Zane."

I didn't bother giving my name. Bri was the only person here who didn't know me, and she'd damn well heard Char say my name; no need for me to repeat it. From the grin I got from the bombshell, she knew I was all out of politeness. Yeah, she wasn't anywhere near as ditsy as she was playing.

Rounding on Jase, I asked, "Now can we have that meeting that was so important I had to come out here?"

Jase wasn't stupid, either. He knew shit was about to get real if we didn't bust this group up. He'd been boss at his construction company for so long that giving orders was second nature and didn't hesitate to organize our group. "Evan is going with us. Zane, why don't you and Kelli go check out the food and grab something to drink. Colin's here and brought some of Char's family special recipe." He motioned to the table with all the mason jars.

I'd noticed Colin when we first got here, and planned on having a talk with him. So far, his moonshine sites had remained hidden, and I'd like to keep it that way. I also wanted to ask him to help keep an eye on Zane. She'd known him for years. She might feel less like an outsider knowing there was at least one other person here she was comfortable with.

"I suggest you visit him first. It's going fast." Jase made a move to leave, but stopped in his tracks when Evan started quarreling with him.

"What the hell, Jase?" Evan finally lost his smile. "Zanie Mae's just a kid. Don't be sending her over there."

"Fuck you, Evan! I'm not a kid." Zane balled up a fist and rabbit-punched him in the middle of his chest. Hard. "I busted out of my training bra years ago. You might not have noticed, but plenty of other men have."

"What the hell, Zanie Mae?" Evan flinched as he rubbed the spot her fist had just connected with.

Perfect. Evan just opened the curtains on Zane's shit show.

"And in case you forgot, I'm a Dockins. I've been able to drink your ass under the table since I was twelve." Zane had her fists balled down by her sides.

A headache started beating double time behind my eyes. In what fucked-up world had I thought it'd be a good idea to bring Zane tonight? And why had I thought Kelli might find some of my friends weren't so different from hers? I watched as she moved around me to stand beside Zane, and she wasn't the only one. Char and Bri were flanking her, too, in some crazy *sister backing sister* kind of shit. All four women were glaring at Evan.

"Evan, I've never had a problem with you, but you are stomping the hell out of my give-a-fuck right now," I said. "Either the three of us go somewhere to discuss the deal, or I'm packing up my women and getting out of here."

Jase slapped his brother on the back. "This has to be a personal best for you, brother. Four women ready to kill you in less than an hour. Let's go while you're still able to walk."

Evan resisted following Jase for a beat. I knew where he was coming from. He and Zane had one hell of a stare-down going on. He didn't want to be the first to look away, but he finally gave in and trailed after us.

"This would've been a hell of a lot easier if you played golf." Jase glanced over at me.

"I don't chase a fucking ball around with a stick. You should be embarrassed to admit you do."

"If you did, we could have discussed this over a civilized game. Instead, we're out here in front of a fire big enough the Forest Service planes are doing flyovers."

"Since I'd already agreed to come to your office, why the hell was it so important I come out here tonight?"

Evan had caught up with us. "I can answer that one. My brother was getting tired of Char chewing his ass because you never come to any of their get-togethers."

We'd reached Jase's truck by now. He reached over the side of the bed and grabbed three beers out of a cooler.

"That true?" I frowned at Jase.

He just nodded as he passed one of the bottles off to me then handed the other to Evan.

"Hell, Jase, I went to your fucking wedding." I twisted the top off the one he handed me and flicked the cap into the bed.

"Yeah, and disappeared right afterward with one of my cousins. You didn't even hang around for cake. Women notice shit like that." Jase's bottle cap followed mine.

"Why the hell does she care if I come to her parties or not?" I took a long pull on the beer. Despite the chill of the fall night, the icy bite of the beer was damn good.

"Because, asshole, she's grateful to you for saving her life and she's been trying to come up with ways to show you ever since. This bonfire shindig was her idea. Been planning it for weeks. She thought you might come to a party if there was a chance it could end up in a drunken brawl. She figured if that wasn't a big enough lure to get you here, talking about the damn plans for the golf course and clubhouse would. So we stay out here long enough to make her believe her plan worked." He killed the bottle in his hand. After dropping the empty in the cooler, he fished around in the ice for a new one. Evan and I did the same.

When all the caps stopped pinging around the bed of his truck, Jase held his bottle in the air and proclaimed, "Women."

Praise or curse? Guessed it depended on which one of us you asked.

"Talking about women," Evan lifted an eyebrow. "What's up with you and Kelli? Since when do you get bent over a little friendly flirting?" He draped an arm on the edge of the truck bed.

If he was waiting for me to share how I felt about Kelli, he was shit out of luck. "Change the subject or shut up. We ain't braiding each other's hair and talking about feelings. I don't know about you, but the last time I took a piss, it was still through a dick."

Evan and Jase both started laughing. We finished up another round, and this time Evan pulled out a new long-neck for each of us. As he handed mine off to me, he said, "Fair enough."

"What's going on with these moonshiners being put out of business?" Jase propped a heel against the bumper. He'd taken me at my word and changed the subject. "Char's worried about Colin. He's been telling us you've lost four sources for your moonshine. Any clue who's behind it?"

"Not yet," I said. "They're fucking ghosts. They take the copper, but none of that shit is showing up at any of the scrap places. It doesn't make any sense. There's not enough shiners left around that they have to fight each other for customers. You know as well as I do it's just a matter of time before there won't be anyone left making the stuff. It's a dying business. They sure as hell aren't in competition with that meth shit people are cooking in their barns nowadays."

"How's that affect the people you supply to?" Jase knew my family's history and probably had a fair idea of the long reach of my distribution network because of that history. What he really wanted to know was what I planned to do when the shine ran out.

"It's simple supply and demand right now. They're willing to pay more for the smaller supply. When the supply's no longer there, the legit joints will likely try and find another source. If they don't, they don't. It's not like the past, when they depended on it. They only stock the bootlegger shine for special customers as it is. It won't break them to lose it. The ones that run like rats when they see the cops will move on to harder shit. It's not a big deal to my bottom line. Don't worry. I'll still have plenty of money to put into your fancy-ass golf course."

"What if there was another option?" Jase eyed me.

"For the shine? Don't tell me Char is ditching the jewelry gig and taking up where her granddaddy left off?" I wouldn't put it past the little hell-raiser. She was on her best behavior tonight, from what I'd seen, but that woman had plenty of wild in her.

"Hell no. But she is worried about Colin. He's the closest thing to a brother she's got other than the dumbass I've been stuck with all my life." Jase waved in Evan's direction with his bottle.

Evan pulled his eyes away from whatever was holding his attention by the fire to join our conversation. "Fuck you very much, brother."

"It's something I've been working on for her," Jase

continued. "You know about those journals handed down through the generations of her family. Turns out there's more than just shine recipes in them. Seems at one time or other, they've tried their hand at wine, beer, brandy, you name it. She hates the idea of all of that family history being lost. Colin worked with her gramps from the time he was a kid, learning everything there's to know about making shine."

"Shit, you know there's no way for Colin to continue making shine in the woods if he wants to go big," I said. "I'll run whatever he makes, but he *will* be caught at some point." What the hell was Jase thinking? If Char was worried about Colin, this was not the way to protect him. Helping him expand his small operation was fast-tracking him straight to prison.

"Not if he's running a legal still." Jase met my gaze with a serious expression. "I've been working on it for Char for a while now. It's been a pain in the ass, but I'm about finished cutting through the red tape to open a legalized distillery. Charlotte wants Colin to use her family recipes to keep the tradition alive. She thought you'd be great as one of our distributors. You have contacts all over the state, and they'd still be getting the same shine they sold before, only legal."

"You're taking all the fun out of it, but everyone I supply now will definitely be interested. You go legal, there'll be a few more I know that'll want in on it." I'd have to shift from smuggling to a legal distribution operation. It would be some work, but in the long run, it would simplify things for me in a lot of ways. Make more money, too. Knowing Jase, he wouldn't be happy with some rinky-dink distillery. He'd see that it grew into something big. This was a chance for me to get in on the ground floor of some-thing with huge potential.

I shot him a smile. "Slick move on your part, roping me in and using my contacts to make sure your new company has a readymade source of customers."

He laughed and pointed a finger at me. "Colin's not the only one Charlotte's worried about."

"You and that wife of yours ain't gonna be happy until you have me toeing the fuckin' line in everything I do."

"Hell, you're already mostly respectable nowadays. You've got your finger in more businesses around the county than I do." He straightened from his slouch. "Talking about business, this isn't any of mine, but showing up with a woman in tow isn't your style. This Kelli must mean something to you, and she doesn't strike me as the type to put up with an outlaw. If you want to hang on to her, you might have to hang up your black hat."

"All woman like outlaws. For a while." That was the most he was getting out of me. I tossed my last empty in the cooler and held the lid while he did the same. Evan shook his head. He'd been nursing his last one, too busy trying to keep track of the girls to do much drinking. Not exactly a bad idea.

"I need to go check on the women I brought," I said. "Ain't no telling what Zane's tore up by now." Having seen the fire in her eyes when we left I was betting we'd find Zane drunk. If Evan was so damn worried about her drinking, he should have kept his mouth shut. Him making a big fucking deal out of it was the same as double-daring her.

At the mention of Zane, Evan threw a frown at his brother. "I can't believe you encouraged her to get drunk." Evan's normal easygoing attitude disappeared.

"I didn't encourage her to get drunk," Jase fired back at him. "You're the one that made an ass out of yourself calling her a kid. If she's drunk, it's because you pissed her off."

"You need to leave Zane alone," I leveled a cool look at him. "You know the kind of shit situation she comes from. You dropping in Skeeter's, being nice to her, is fucking with her head. You're making her think things that ain't gonna happen." Zane wouldn't thank me for telling Evan that if she ever found out.

"Wait a minute," Evan protested. "I'm nice to her *because* of her family. You're the one that hired a kid still in high school to work in a bar. If anything is messing with her head, it's all the damn men that don't care how old she is." Evan had gone stiff, his shoulders pulled back.

"Zane's never had a chance to be a kid. And you don't know shit about why she's at the bar." I stood taller and studied him. I had let him know Zane was sweet on him. But no way in hell would I ever tell the whole story of why she'd started working at Skeeter's when she was just a teen.

"Back off, Evan," Jase warned. "Sawyer's right. She lit up when she saw you. You're not doing her any favors being too nice. You embarrassed her in front of everyone calling her a kid. Especially calling her a kid when you've got a woman like Bri hanging all over you." Jase gave his brother a hard look.

"You know Bri was just being Bri," Evan shrugged a shoulder. "That didn't mean anything. You two don't know what the hell you're talking about. Zanie and I have been friends since she started working at Skeeter's. She knows that's all it is."

Evan killed the beer he'd been nursing and didn't bother putting it in the cooler. He just tossed it in the back of the pickup and turned to stalk back to the party. He might not have liked what Jase and I told him, but when he walked away, that frown said he was thinking things over.

CHAPTER EIGHTEEN

Kelli

"Stupid men. Well, one stupid man in particular."

Zane's eyes met mine and then we both shifted to stare at Bri. She stood with hands on hips, glaring at the backs of the men as they walked off. Char stood beside her, mirroring her stance and glare. When the guys were out of sight, they both turned to us. Or, rather, to Zane.

Bri reached out a hand to Zane but let it drop when it was rejected. "How ignorant does a man have to be to look at you and not see a beautiful woman? I'd kill him for treating me like a child. I mean, he's a friend and all, but a stupid friend. And not the benefits kind of friend, if you're worried. But holy heatwave, I bet the benefits would be amazing. Have you looked at his ass?" She used the hand Zane had rejected to fan her face.

"Bri! You're making it worse. You're letting your crazy show." Char shook her head at her friend.

"She's crazy all right if she thinks I give a damn what

Evan thinks of me. She can share all the benefits with him she wants. It won't mean a thing to me." Zane made a point of addressing Char. I wasn't sure if it was a positive sign that she was ignoring Bri or not. If she was ignoring her, she wasn't throwing punches.

"I know it looked bad, going full tackle on Evan," Bri pushed on trying to explain to Zane, "but we were close enough to hear and see what was going on before we came over. Tackling Evan was the only thing I could think of to keep her boyfriend from ripping his head off." Bri hitched a thumb in my direction.

"Wait a minute! Sawyer's not my boyfriend; he's my boss." My protest pulled the attention away from Zane. All three of them stared at me with various expressions of disbelief.

"Helllooo! Your current non-boyfriend was ready to kill her future boyfriend over flirting with you." Bri threw up her hands. "If I had an all-day-orgasm kind of guy eating me up with his eyes, I'd be waving the white panties."

"Shut up, Bri." Char sighed. "Zane, Kelli, I apologize for my deranged friend. I can't control her. All I can offer is that she means no harm. You probably won't believe me, but she can be nice around strangers. Too bad it's usually the ones she doesn't care for and it's that bitchy kind of nice. The good news is that if she's showing her crazy, she's already decided she likes you."

Zane's shoulder shrug made me believe that having Bri like her wasn't high on her wish list.

"Zane, if you say Evan is nothing to you, well, I believe you," Char continued. "He was an asshole for treating you like a kid. I can only guess it's because he's known you a while. Sometimes, when a man knew you as a child, he doesn't always realize you've grown up. That doesn't excuse him, but maybe you'll understand why he said what he did better.

"And Kelli, if you say Sawyer's not your boyfriend…" She rolled her eyes. "Hell, none of us believe that."

Bri and Zane both nodded. That Zane was willing to agree with Bri on anything was progress. To maintain that fragile peace, I was willing to bite my tongue.

When I didn't say anything, Char continued, "I need a drink. I hope you'll both take the chance to know us and share a drink with us. I've never been good at making friends, but I'd like to add you both to the list."

I waited for Zane to make the decision. There was a lot to like about Char, and Bri was the kind of friend everyone needed to make you look sane. If I stayed in Copper Ridge, life would be a lot more interesting having a circle of friends that included them in it. But I would back Zane on whether we had that drink or not.

"Did your man say Colin had made your family's special recipe?" Zane asked cautiously.

"Sure did," Char answered with pride.

"Hot damn, bitches! This is gonna be fun!" Bri punched the air with a fist.

* * *

KELLI

"Just kill me." Zane was holding her head as she tried to roll from her side to her back. She couldn't complete the move because of the pillows piled behind her.

Sawyer and I had brought her back to my motel room after leaving the bonfire. I'd been afraid to take her home and leave her alone. She'd been unconscious when he carried her in and dropped her on the bed.

The pillows behind her back had been my idea. They were to keep her on her side. I'd been terrified she'd throw up and choke to death on her vomit if she was lying on her back. In an optimistic move, I'd placed the wastebasket on the floor beside her. The plan was for her to use it if the urge to hurl struck. I will be eternally grateful it wasn't put to the test.

After watching her flail an arm behind her, trying to push the pillows out of the way, I took pity and moved them. Once the obstruction was gone, she melted back into the mattress. She slid an arm across her eyes to block the only sunbeam to find its way through a crack in the curtains. Other than that bit of movement, she could have been a corpse. Her pasty skin and lank hair wasn't a good look.

I set a water bottle on the bedside table with a couple of pain pills. It was hard to be mad at Zane for the drunken rampage she'd gone on last night. A girl could only take so much humiliation from the guy she thought she was in love with.

It was equally difficult to blame Evan. Zane was the one with the fantasies of the wonderful life they'd have together. The poor guy was clueless he'd broken her heart last night. Thing was, he didn't just break it. He tore that tender organ out, stomped it in the ground, and fed it to the dogs. He'd treated her like a little kid, flirted with me, and then wrapped his arms around another woman. Yeah, not a great night for Zane.

"Sit up a minute," I encouraged her. "You need to get these pills in you, and some water. I couldn't get you to drink any last night. You kept saying something about how

the shine was cut with water, so you didn't need any extra."
I rolled my eyes at the memory.

Zane did a lot of dramatic groaning, but she sat up, took the pills, and drank the entire bottle of water before melting back into the mattress. I could imagine this same scene being played out between Char and Bri—Bri being the one who could pass for the walking dead.

Last night, by the second red Solo cup of moonshine, Bri and Zane were thick as thieves. Char and I had sat back and let them bond. By the fourth—or was it the fifth?—they were holding each other's hair as they threw up simultaneously in the bushes together. Char got a picture of that one on her phone. If the friendship lasted, I needed to see if I could get a copy of that.

Unfortunately, they seemed to catch a second wind after expelling a lot of the alcohol along with the contents of their stomachs. I sort of blamed Char for what happened next. She was joking around when she warned the girls not to fall into the fire with their wild dance moves. Claimed they'd blow up, considering all the shine they'd been drinking. Somehow that transitioned into them filling their mouths with whiskey and spitting it at the fire to see if it would explode. Every time one of them reached the fire and flames shot into the air, they screamed in triumph. They drew quite a crowd. We were trying to convince them that was a terrible waste of whiskey when the guys showed up.

Sawyer gave me a what-the-hell-look, which said I sucked as a babysitter. Jase seemed to be more realistic in his expectations of Char's abilities to control her friend, and just grinned.

Evan was the one that confused me. Sawyer and Jase stayed back, willing to let Char and me handle the girls. Not Evan. He didn't exactly push me out of the way, but he did get in Zane's face and yelled at her for putting herself in danger. Pretty sure he didn't expect her to spray a mouthful of whiskey in his face while he was in the middle of his lecture.

"Kelli?" The weak voice tugged at my heart.

"What, sweetie?" I brushed a hand across her forehead.

"Did I make a fool of myself in front of Evan?" If her voice was weak before, it was barely a whisper now.

"No, honey. Now go back to sleep and let the pills work." I patted her shoulder, the only comfort I could offer besides the lie I'd just told.

"I know you're lying, but thank you for taking care of me." She was fading fast.

"That's what friends do." I wasn't even sure she heard me; she was already snoring before I finished speaking.

I surveyed the room, taking in the suitcases and scattered boxes. There weren't many. After all, I'd managed to haul everything here in my SUV. You can pack a lot of clothes and shoes in a SUV, and that was all I'd brought.

Zane needed to sleep off her drunk. I needed to repack everything scattered around the room. If I started now, by the time she woke up, I'd be packed and have the car loaded—well, mostly loaded. The front seat would need to be left empty, so Zane would have a place to sit.

Spending the day with her would give us plenty of time to hash and rehash every possible reason why Grady wanted to hide I was his sister. When I'd told Zane how angry he'd gotten over me showing up, she'd been ready to storm to his house and demand an explanation. I'd begged her to give Grady the time he'd asked for. She'd given in, but her comments about asshole brothers hadn't exactly been gracious.

All the boxes and suitcases had been filled and I'd finished clearing the bathroom of everything of mine. The only things left out were what Zane would need for a shower. A soft knock on the door had me hustling to get to it before the noise woke Zane. It was probably Mrs. Whatley dropping by to make sure I didn't run off with any of her lovely decor that was last popular in the seventies. I wasn't expecting to see Sawyer on the other side. Slipping out, I softly closed the door behind me and leaned against it.

"What are you doing here? You told Zane you had business to take care of today." I kept my voice low. The door wasn't any better at keeping sound out than the walls were.

"That was before she tried to pickle her liver at the bonfire." Sawyer leaned a muscled forearm against the door next to my head. His scent surrounded me and the heat from his body reached out to mine. "I got to thinking she wouldn't be much help today. She still sleeping?"

I had to clear my throat—twice—before I could answer him. "Yes, she is. I don't have much to haul out to the cabin. I plan on loading the car; that way we'll be ready to leave soon as she wakes up."

"I could help you take a load out there now." He flicked a piece of hair off my cheek, then smoothed a line across my forehead with his knuckle. I jerked, knocking the back of my head against the door.

"What are you doing?" My whisper was sounding more strangled.

"Offering to help move you out to the cabin." He leaned in and brushed his nose against my neck. "You smell so damn good."

"I'm not talking about offering to help me move, and you know it. I'm asking what you're doing right now. Here. With me." His answer was important. More than I wanted it to be.

"I'm trying to convince you it's a damn good idea for

me to help haul your shit out to the cabin. Not just to get your shit out to the cabin—so we can fuck. Zane killed any chance of that happening last night." He started nibbling on my jaw line.

"But what about the business you needed to take care of?" I tilted my chin up to make it easier for him to reach. Anyone could walk or drive by and see us making out against the door to my room. There was a good chance Mrs. Whatley was getting an eye full from her office.

I didn't care.

"I can cancel. Serve Jase right for dragging me out to that damn bonfire." He placed his other arm on the door, effectively trapping me between his two arms. He pushed his hips into mine, and I couldn't control the whimper that escaped my lips. I remembered in detail how talented he was with that hard length pressing into my stomach.

Before I could answer him, the door swung open behind me. If not for Sawyer's quick reflexes, we would have landed on the floor. Zane stood there with the door-knob in her hand, glaring at us.

"What the fuck, Zanie Mae?" Sawyer growled at her.

"Yeah, Sawyer. What the fuck?" she gave him the stink-eye. "These doors are thin as paper, and I'm trying to sleep while you're out here humping her against it. I got tired of listening to you try and talk her into going to the cabin to screw."

She gave him an evil smile. "Well, I'm awake now, sucker. That means you can haul me back to my place on your way to your meeting with Jase. I'll drive back here, and Kelli and I will handle the moving, so say your good-byes, lover boy."

CHAPTER NINETEEN

Sawyer

"WE'VE ALREADY STARTED the groundwork. I'm sure you noticed the heavy equipment last night on the way to the party." Jase stood in front of the draft table where plans for the golf course and clubhouse lay.

"The idea is to not disturb the land any more than necessary. We're hoping to keep it as natural as possible. The clubhouse with attached pro shop and restaurant will be located at the front of the property, and the road in will be limited to that area. The golf course will be laid out across the back. Any questions?"

"Didn't realize you knew a damn thing about building a golf course." I watched as Jase pointed out the different areas as he talked about them. As far as I was concerned, this meeting had been a waste of time. The only reason I was investing a chunk of capital in this venture was because Jase had come to me and asked. He was one of the very few people I trusted one hundred percent. And the man knew how to make money.

"I don't. That's why I've hired one of the best in the business to design and oversee that part of the construction. The clubhouse and the rest of the builds will be my designs. If you want to see the blueprints, I'll pull them out." Jase headed for a mahogany cabinet across the room.

"Not today. If you designed them then they're fine with me. I'll check them out later." I'd keep tabs on the project, but I trusted Jase enough to not micromanage everything.

He'd earned my trust years ago. He'd lied for me back when we were kids to keep me out of the law's hands, and I'd killed for him to save Char's life. We'd lost touch when he moved away to become a big-shot architect, but we'd reconnected because of Char when he moved back. I'd planned on keeping clear of him when he returned after a ten-year absence. He and Char had made that impossible. He was more of a brother to me than mine had ever been.

At my refusal to check out the plans, he made a detour and stopped in front of a different wall of cabinets. He pulled open a door and grabbed a couple of beers from a well-hidden fridge. As he passed, he handed off one, but didn't stop until he reached a seating area. He waved at a leather chair that sat across from the one he'd claimed.

I lowered into a seat that was damn comfortable. There wasn't a whole lot of sleep happening last night, and not because I had company. It was from wanting a certain woman in my bed.

"If you'd pulled a bottle of wine out of your fancy-pants fridge, I would've pulled my damn money from the project." I grinned at Jase.

Jase laughed. "I know my audience. The wine's in there, but I save it for my fancy-pants clients. If Kelli had shown up with you today, I imagine she'd have appreciated a glass."

"Why the hell would I have brought Kelli with me?" I'd have blown off this meeting for her, but I sure as hell wouldn't have brought her. Damn Zane had screwed any chance of talking Kelli into heading out to the lake house for a quick fuck. I'd seen the flare of interest in Kelli's green eyes. She'd been on the verge of giving in right before Zane dumped cold water on the plans.

"For the same reason you took her to the party last night. And the same reason you about took Evan's head off for flirting with her." Jase cut me a look before lifting his bottle. "I've never seen you do that before. You like the woman."

"I like women. All kinds of women. I've lost count of all the women I've liked the hell out of." And right now, I needed to go find Kelli and like the hell out of her.

"I'm not talking about all the women you've screwed. I'm talking about seeing you with a woman that would be a hell of a lot more comfortable in this fancy-pants country club we're building than she'll ever be at Skeeter's." His gaze met mine, and his plainly said, *Cut the bullshit*. "What are you doing, Sawyer? Kelli's not some Marilee or Connie. If she lets an asshole"—he tipped his chin at me—"in her bed, it's because she has feelings for him. You hurt her and she's through."

"Why do you care if Kelli gets hurt or not? You just met the woman last night." How was I supposed to tell him what the hell I was doing when I didn't know?

"I don't. Well, I do. Hate to see any good woman get hurt, and it's easy to see Kelli's a good woman. But I do care whether you screw up a chance to have that good woman in your life. Charlotte likes her, and you know she doesn't have a lot of women friends." He kept his eyes on me. Waiting.

Fuck it. "She won't stay."

"What the hell are you talking about?" He leaned over, resting his forearms on his knees, his stare intense.

"You say she doesn't belong at Skeeter's. Well, I do. Despite your attempts to make me a decent, law-abiding citizen that shit ain't gonna stick." I wanted to jump out of the chair and pace, but I forced myself to stay seated. "She's interested now, but at some point, the shine will wear off and the shit will show through. When it does, she'll go back to where she came from."

"Bullshit. You're not giving her a chance." He dismissed my worry with a grunt, stood up, and headed back to the fridge.

I followed his lead and got to my feet.

When he opened the fridge and looked at me, I shook my head. He closed it without taking anything out. "Listen, I'm telling you not to blow it. We both know you'll never be lily white. But you were already switching most of the money your family has made through the years to legal businesses. Way before Charlotte and I roped you into the country club or talked about starting a distribution company. I'm through preaching. Wanna go grab a bite to eat over at the Cozy Kitchen?"

"Naw, I've got to meet up with Wade out at Skeeter's." Time to let my men know the major shift in my ten-year business plan. Jase would harass the shit out of me if he knew I even had a plan. Whether Kelli worked into those plans depended a lot on if I chose to make adjustments to my businesses. Make moves she'd approve of. Jase was right: I'd already started making those adjustments before she showed up at Skeeter's. Keeping her around to see how things played out added incentive to keep to the plan.

"Good. I'll call my wife and have her meet me; she'll be a hell of a lot easier to look at while I'm eating than you. Besides, she's probably about to bust a gut wanting to know if I delivered the sermon." Jase gave a dry laugh.

"What was said was private." Oh, hell no. I didn't want him telling anyone what I'd told him. Especially not Char.

"Save your death stare for someone else. She wouldn't ask, and I sure as hell wouldn't tell." Jase snorted as he held the door to his office open for me to exit.

I bumped fists with him before walking out the door. It was as close to an apology as he was going to get.

* * *

Sawyer

"Did Clay find anything when you took him out to what's left of Harlen's still?" I studied Wade as I leaned back in an old wooden chair, pushed away from an equally beat-up table. For the first time since buying the bar I took a hard look at its furnishing. Everything in the building had probably been bought by Skeeter Louis when he first opened the bar.

I'd been using the building as my makeshift office since I'd bought the place. It was early afternoon, and Skeeter's wasn't open yet, so the three of us had the place to ourselves. Charlie was hanging at the bar. In the past, it'd been fine meeting with my people here before Skeeter's opened. In reality, I'd outgrown doing business that way more than a year ago. Maybe it was time to think about getting a real office. A suit would be next if I wasn't careful. Naw, not in this lifetime, but a comfortable chair wouldn't be so bad.

"Not much," Wade replied. "He didn't think they came in the same way you and I walked in. Figures they followed the creek through the hollow to where Harlen was set up. Found some boot tracks where they crossed the creek. Pretty sure there was only two guys." Wade took a sip of the beer he'd grabbed when he first showed up. "That was it. Don't think they knew an exact location, just a general area to search along the creek."

"Someone knew enough to send them in the right direction. That's a damn long creek bed." It'd be a miracle if we found anyone who'd seen anything the night of the destruction. The location was remote, it was late when it happened, and there were a million places to hide a truck.

"We'll keep looking for the copper. With it being the end of the cooking season, that's about all we can do. In the spring, we'll set up some kind of security. If there's anyone left interested in making moonshine. Right now, we need to go through orders and decide who gets what of our remaining supplies."

"I told you losing that last still would cut into the bottom line," Wade complained. "We were already having to cut everyone's delivery by half. You said yourself it's the end of the season. We ain't gonna pick up more shine anywhere else. What the hell are me and the boys supposed to tell everyone?" Wade hunched over the table, flattening his hands on its surface.

"I'll be making some of the deliveries this time. Gonna pull Vernon and Willis in to help me." I rubbed a finger along a long scar in the wooden tabletop. It might be time to upgrade some of the furniture. Kelli would like that. Nothing fancy, though. The regulars would hate any kind of change.

"What the hell for?" Wade sat straighter in his chair.

"Need to let bar owners and retailers know we'll be able

to supply all the shine they want when cooking season starts back up in the spring. And from now on they'll have a steady supply during the cold months, too." It was going to take a few days to visit all my customers, even with Vernon and Willis splitting the list with me.

"You've found a new source?" Wade frowned.

"Not a new one. An old one that's going legal, if you can believe it. I need to start setting up customers for it." Drumming a thumb on the table, I scanned the interior of the bar.

Jase would shit his pants if I made my office look just like this. I almost smiled thinking about it. The urge didn't last long. Kelli would call it a thug's den and turn her pretty little nose up at it. Not that I gave a fuck. There was a good chance she'd never stick around long enough to see it anyway.

"What the hell are you talking about? Since when did they legalize homemade moonshine?" Wade shot me a grin. He thought I was messing with him.

"Jase and Char are opening a distillery. They're gonna start making some of her granddaddy's shine recipes again. Legal this time. I'm gonna handle the distribution through my contacts."

What if Jase was right and I gave Kelli a chance to fit in here? She might get a kick out of picking shit out for an office. Hell, I didn't plan on spending any more time in it than I had to anyway. She'd just have to understand there'd be no suits for me, and no damn wine in a hidden fridge for fancy-pants. That shit wasn't happening.

"What're you gonna do about the buyers that sold it on the sly? Are you meeting with them, too?" Wade started peeling the label off the beer bottle.

"I'm leaving them to you. You'll need to let them know this is the last of it. If they don't have a liquor license, I'm cutting them loose. Hell, most of them have already switched to selling a harder high than moonshine ever gave a person." I suspected more than a few were making their own product, and it had nothing to do with liquor.

The frown was back on Wade's face. "That why you went to Jase's office today? Getting this all set up?"

"Small part of the reason. Getting the distribution business up and running is on me." Shouldn't be too big a hassle. I was ahead of the game, already having liquor licenses for the different bars I owned. That put me in the system, and I knew a few people who could help grease the wheels. "Other part had to do with me going into partnership with Jase and Evan on a country club/golf course thing they're building."

"Shit, Sawyer, what the hell's got into you?" Wade's voice was loud enough to attract Charlie's attention. He sent a curious glance in Wade's direction, then went back to his own business.

"How come you're deciding to get all legal and shit? We've got a good thing going here. Nobody messes with you or your people. Why you gotta go screw it all up? You don't need the legal shit. You've got contacts all over this damn state. We could use them to make *real* money, if you'd just listen to my ideas. But you shut me down every damn time I try to talk to you about them."

The half-assed attention I'd been paying to Wade and this meeting vanished. He had my full attention.

"Fucking hell, Wade. You're not my damn wife. What made you think I would start running future business plans by you?" Shifting my dealing out of the dark into the light of day would never be a popular idea with Wade. He enjoyed playing the bad man on my dime.

"Were you ever gonna let me manage any of your operations? The moonshine routes are out because *you're going legal,*" he said sourly. "You give Vernon and Willis control over the poker houses. You let them do any damn thing they want. The rest of the guys are just happy to have any kind of a damn job. They'll do whatever the hell you tell them. But me..." He jumped to his feet, pacing in front of the table. Hot eyes met mine and he banged a fist against his chest. "I want more than just to follow orders. *We* could be partners in one hell of a money producing operation. It's all worked out. I can deliver it to you.

"Damn it! In less than two weeks, you've changed your whole life. I've known you for years. Worked for you *for years*. Kept every dirty secret. For. Years. And now I don't even recognize you." His hands clenched at his sides.

I pushed my chair back and rose to my feet, taking my time. A coldness that went to the bone had settled over me. At my movement, Wade came to an abrupt stop. Even though his face was red with anger and his body was stiff in defiance, fear skittered around the edges of his eyes.

"You have a problem with the way I run my business, then you walk out that fucking door. Right now." I spoke so low that he had to lean forward to catch my words. "Go execute this fucking plan of yours. But if it involves a single one of my contacts I will hunt you down. Me. Not Vernon. Not Willis. Me. And you sure as shit will recognize me then."

He met my stare for five seconds longer than I would have thought possible. But his shoulders finally slumped, and he sounded weary when he said, "I'm not going anywhere. Because in the end, I'm just as trapped as everyone else that works for you and has nothing else to fall back on."

CHAPTER TWENTY

Kelli

"THAT'S THE LAST OF IT." I crossed the back patio, where Zane was sprawled in a cheerful red Adirondack chair. I passed her a sandwich and then one of the cans I'd been juggling.

Claiming the matching seat beside her, I settled back with my sandwich and the other pop. The bag of chips I'd carried out under my arm dropped into my lap as soon as I sat down. Snagging the top of the bag, I ripped it open and offered it to Zane. She grabbed a handful and passed it back to me. We both started eating like it was our job.

Zane came up for air first. "This cabin is the shit." Sighing in appreciation, she gazed out over the lake. Upending her soda, she took a long drink, let out a loud, watery burp then swiped the back of a hand across her mouth.

"Our etiquette lessons are really paying off for you," I deadpanned.

She laughed and shrugged. "You were right. I was stupid to try and be someone I'm not."

"I didn't say you were stupid. I said you shouldn't have to turn into someone else to make a man love you." This change of heart on her part had everything to do with seeing Bri with Evan last night.

"You can't make someone love you, either people fit, or they don't." Before taking a dainty sip of her pop she extended a pinky and grinned at me.

"Have you decided you and Evan don't fit?" I asked cautiously.

"Not like him and Bri do. They make sense. We don't." Zane tried to sound as if the idea didn't bother her. She didn't do a very good job.

"Bri told you last night she wasn't interested in him that way," I pointed out.

"Bri's a crazy bitch, but she's not crazy enough to turn down anything Evan might offer her."

"I thought you liked her? That you bonded with her over trying to burn your faces off with the whole spitting whiskey in the fire?"

"Yeah, she's a lot of fun." She sighed at the memory. At least, I was guessing she remembered some of what the two of them had gotten up to.

She suddenly sat up straighter, as if remembering something that brightened her day. "Too bad she lives in New York City."

Kicking a puppy wouldn't have made me feel any worse than what I was about to tell her. "Actually, she's thinking about moving here. Char was telling me it was pretty much a sure thing. Char's really excited. I think the four of us could have a lot of fun together."

"Yeah, a lot of fun." Her agreement rang hollow.

Shaking off her gloom, she arched an eyebrow and asked, "So, you and Sawyer. More than friends, huh?"

"Aren't you the one that just said people either fit or they didn't? What in the world would make you believe the two of us would fit any better than you and Evan?" My acting skills were on par with Zane's. Lousy.

"Oh, I don't know. Maybe because you're boning Sawyer and I can't even get Evan to toss me one." She grinned.

"It's just sex. He's made it plain that's all it'll ever be, and I'm fine with that." Did I mention I was a lousy actress?

"All shits and giggles aside, I've never seen him treat another woman the way he does you. You don't realize how weird it was to see you sitting in the truck with him last night. Sawyer doesn't date. Ever. He goes somewhere alone and hooks up. He's done *a lot* of hooking up. Marilee is as close to a regular as he's ever had, but he's different with you. Now, *she's* just sex. You? I don't think so." She shook her head.

"Is Marilee the blonde who was rubbing all over him at Skeeter's the night of the fight?" I picked at the chip crumbs on my shirt, keeping my head down.

"That's her. She was mad as an ol' wet hen when he left with you. Tried to act like it was no big thing; believe me, it was to her." Zane gave an evil laugh. "She went home with Wade that night. If she was trying to make Sawyer jealous, she's dumber than that big-ass hairdo she thinks is so sexy. She's one of those dogs that'll hunt with anybody that wants to head to the woods. Everybody knows it, including Sawyer."

"What does that even mean?" Sometimes Zane lost me with her country-isms.

"She's a whore, and not the working kind." She snorted as if the answer was obvious.

"There's a difference?" This should be interesting.

"Of course there is. There's the kind screws a man without trying to screw up his life; it's just a job to them. They do a service and get paid for it. Then you got the kind that's like Marilee. She'll sleep with anyone she can use in some way or other. She'll go after some other woman's man just to prove she can get him then after she's got them all broke up she moves on to the next one. She wants Sawyer because he's got money. She don't really care about him. Not the way you could if you let yourself."

"I think you got it right when you said you can't make somebody love you. Sometimes you take what you can get and hope that's enough." Now I was the one who sounded glum.

We both sat quietly, lost in our thoughts. After a short time, she slapped her hands on the armrest of her chair and announced, "Hey, gotta run. I promised to deal at the Dog House tonight."

She pulled up out of the chair, and I followed suit. We passed through the back door, stopped off in the kitchen to dump our trash, and then moved into the living room.

"I didn't know you worked anywhere else. What's the Dog House?" I frowned at my friend. What kind of dealing was she talking about?

"It's the nickname for one of the poker houses Vernon manages for Sawyer." This time when she smiled, it was genuine. "A lot of the guys that play there are married. They're the ones that started calling it that. I fill in some-times if one of the regular dealers needs to take off. It's good money, but I wouldn't want to do it all the time. Some of those guys are real assholes."

"Will you get into trouble with Sawyer for telling me about this?" I remembered all of the things I wasn't supposed to ask questions about. This sounded like one of them.

"You already know enough dirt to nail him to the wall if you wanted. What's one more thing?" She gave me a sly smile. "Besides, I figure he's nailed you enough times by now you're not interested in burning his ass."

"You're a mess." I shook my head at her foolishness.

"I've got to get out of here or I'm gonna be late for work. I'll be there Tuesday night, too, so I probably won't see you till Wednesday back at Skeeter's. Call if something comes up with Grady and you need me. I'm there if you want someone to kick his ass." She was reaching for the knob when the door swung in.

Sawyer stood in the opening and my stupid heart stuttered. One look and every word he'd said when he pressed me against that motel door this morning came back.

"On your way out?" He stepped away from the opening so he wasn't blocking Zane's path.

"Don't sound so sad," Zane teased. She gave me a final wave and headed out the door.

Silence was a third person in the room after her departure. He didn't seem to be bothered by it; I was paralyzed. The relief was real when he started talking.

"Did you get settled in?"

Something was off. His words were casual enough; the hint of savageness on his face wasn't.

"Yes, Zane was a huge help. All unpacked and put away. I started a list of things I'll need to buy now I've got a permanent place to live. We stopped at the grocery store on the way here and picked up a few necessities. Lots more to get, though." It was better when I was paralyzed. My mouth wasn't vomiting words.

Sawyer captured my eyes with his serious ones as he stalked across the room to stand in front of me. He stood so close that his breath feathered across my cheek. "Are you afraid of me, Kelli?"

It was the first time I could remember him using my name. For some reason, it made me think that whatever either one of us said from this point on was important—as in life-changing important.

"No. You've never given me any reason to be afraid of you. Why would you even ask such a question?"

"I'm not the type of man mommas like seeing their little girls bring home." He removed a thread of hair from between my fidgeting fingers. I hadn't even been aware I'd been twisting it. He rubbed the silkiness between his own before tucking it behind my ear. "Especially mommas like yours."

"We're in luck, then. Mine told me that if I left not to plan on coming back. Besides, she has lousy taste in men. Think I'll pick out my next mistake all by myself."

I shivered as his finger lightly traced the shell of my ear. And it didn't stop there. He trailed the rough tip of it down my neck to trace across my collarbone to the edge of my shoulder and back to the shallow valley at the base of my throat. He pressed the calloused pad into that hollow, measuring the frantic drumming of my heart's runaway beats.

"I'm worse than a mistake. I'm a bomb primed to blow your comfortable life to hell." He moved both hands to cradle my face. His eyes bored into mine as if he were trying to force me to acknowledge some great truth. "I want you, but you need to know I'm not offering happily-ever-after here. Hell, I can't promise happy-while-we're-together. The only promise I can make is to not be with other women as long as we're together. That's more than I've offered any woman. You get tired of roughing it? Run back to the city? I won't come after you."

"How do you know I'm not the one who's going to blow your complicated life to hell?" I whispered.

"Fuck, princess. You already have." He pressed his forehead to mine and sighed. "I sure as hell wouldn't have chosen someone like you as my first serious try at sticking with one woman. No matter what all the suitcases and boxes say about your intentions, I give it a fifty-fifty chance of you staying. So, damn straight you've torn the shit out of my complicated life."

"Where do we go from here?" I wanted to argue with him about me leaving, but he was right. It was too soon to say I'd stay for Sawyer. We were too new and he wasn't asking.

He drew back and his gaze dropped to my lips. The tension in the room shifted, the seriousness still there, just overlaid with a sensual edge. One of his hands drifted to tangle in the back of my hair, pulling, stretching my neck. I leaned back into his hold. He leaned over me and ran a tongue from collarbone to jaw. He nipped, then soothed the sting with a kiss. "Your skin tastes so good. Almost as sweet as that bare pussy of yours I've been waiting to taste again."

Heat flooded to my abdomen, and lower. But I wasn't completely lost to the fact I was sweaty from a day of packing and unpacking. I tried to twist away from his hold, but his hand gripped my hair tighter. He wasn't letting me go anywhere. "Let me grab a shower."

At the mention of a shower, he untangled his fingers from the strands of my hair. He took a step back, arms dropping to his sides, setting me completely free. "Good idea."

That was easier than expected, and a little insulting. Did I stink that bad? It was a struggle, but I managed to keep from sniffing my pits. I started backing toward the bedroom. "Okay then. I'll meet you in the bedroom... after. You know... I'm fresh."

I spun on a heel and fled. Worse—he let me.

With the bathroom door shut and water cascading from the shower head, I was fairly confident my muttered complaints wouldn't be heard in the bedroom. My soaping and scrubbing were extra aggressive, pinking my skin. "So, I stink, huh? Well, I'm human. I sweat. I don't glow, or dew, or any other euphemism a lady's supposed to use. I sweat!"

I stuck my head under the torrent of water to rinse the shampoo from the long lengths of my hair. Arms wrapped around me from behind and circled my waist, and I came out of the water sputtering and screaming.

"Holy shit, princess. Way to bust an eardrum."

Recognizing Sawyer's voice, and the amusement in it, did nothing to slow my galloping heart rate.

"My God, you almost gave me a heart attack. It's about to beat out of my chest." My scream must not have affected him too badly. He pulled my back against his chest and rested his chin on my shoulder.

"Let me check." One large hand slid up the slick skin of my wet body to grasp my left breast. His other hand spanned my lower torso until he was cupping my pussy to pull my butt firmly against a fully erect cock.

The wolf was back and wanted to play.

CHAPTER TWENTY-ONE

Kelli

"I BELIEVE you're supposed to place your fingers on a vein in my neck to check my pulse." My dry observation lost a lot of its sting when I wiggled my butt in his groin. The words might have come out a little breathy, too.

"I plan on placing my fingers all over your body before we're through." The hand on my left breast gave a firm squeeze then slipped underneath to cup its silken flesh. He brushed a thumb back and forth across the hardness of my nipple. Awareness shuddered down my spine to pool in my core. Two of the fingers gripping my pussy dipped inside, his thumb grazing my clit just soft enough to offer a tease. A low groan of disappointment whispered through my lips when they disappeared.

"Shhh, sweetheart, we've got all night." He settled his hands on my hips, turning me, pulling me almost out of the water. I flattened my aching breasts against his pecs. My breath hitched at the delicious heat radiating off his skin. He didn't play around—his mouth settled over mine, tongue thrusting deep. It was a dominant move that left no room for doubt that he was staking a claim.

When he broke the kiss, we were both gasping for air. It was gratifying to know I wasn't the only one affected by that kiss. This wasn't just about him showing how he could master my body. He was all in and not afraid to express it. He tunneled both hands into my hair, positioning my head at the perfect angle for him to plant tiny kisses along the length of my neck.

My hands landed on his shoulders, my restless fingers rubbing and kneading the bunched muscles straining with tension. I stepped back. I wanted to see. To explore. His body was magnificent and I wanted my hands on it. Sawyer resisted, but when I kept pushing at him, he allowed me some space. A question was in his gaze, a hard-ness lingering at the edges. "What's wrong, princess?"

"I want my fingers all over you, too. Please." At my plea, a softness stole over his face. He took my hands and placed them on his chest. I needed no other encouragement. My fingers curled in anticipation, nails sinking into his tanned pecs. I relaxed my hands and let one of my fingers feather its way to his nipple. I slowly traced the areola then flicked a long nail over the tight bud in the center. Sawyer hissed out a curse.

A secret smile curled the edge of my lips. Oh, this was going to be *so* much fun. I glanced up through my lashes to check his expression. He's eyes were mere slits; sexual tension had hollowed out his cheeks, making the angles in his face appear harsher. If I hadn't heard that lustful curse, I'd have thought he was about to murder someone.

Getting back to the business of paying the proper reverence to the amazing male figure in front of me, I leaned forward and caught a bead of water about to roll down the center of his chest with the tip of my tongue. Shifting to the side, I treated his other nipple to the same attention as the first, only this time I used my tongue to circle the areola before nipping the hard point in the center.

"Sonofabitch!"

Suddenly, an arm reached past me and the water shut off. "We're taking this shit to the bed."

The glass door to the shower was thrust open and steam billowed out to fill the bath. In seconds, he had us both centered on the bed, water still beading our bodies. He leaned against the headboard. I knelt between his legs.

"Whatever you want, princess." His voice was so gravelly it was more a growl than a human sound.

With him semi-reclined, he would be able to watch every touch, every kiss. It was exciting to know he was willing to turn his body over to me. I reached out with both hands and raked my nails the length of his torso, gliding through the ridges and valleys of his abs. I found and followed the faint trail of hair leading down past his taut stomach to an erection that looked painful in its fullness. An erection that almost touched his bellybutton.

A thrill of feminine power rushed through me. Me. I had done this, to a powerful and dangerous man, and he was going to let me do more. I wrapped a hand around the thick shaft. I would have been concerned at the size if Sawyer and I hadn't already proven we fit very well together. I marveled at the velvet texture of the skin covering the steel length. I squeezed as I pulled from the base to just under the broad head, pushed back down, then squeezed and pulled to just under the head again.

"Fucking hell, princess. There won't be enough left to do you any good if you don't hurry up and get your playing over with."

"Whatever I want. Remember?" My breathy tease had him throwing his hands over his head and gripping the ornate metal that made up the iron headboard. The muscles in his biceps were quivering, making me believe he was holding himself in check by a tiny, fraying thread.

I gave him a wicked smile in approval and heard him mutter to himself, "She's killing me."

Leaning over, I either added to his misery or gave him a measure of relief by licking across the top of his cock and gathering the pre-cum on the tip of my tongue. It was salty and musky and all man. At that first lick, the hard muscle jerked as if I'd tickled it. The movement caused me to squeeze harder as I pumped the length, causing more cussing. I focused on his face and he met my gaze with a heavy-lidded one.

Maintaining eye contact, I started at the base and dragged the flat of my tongue up the sensitive underside of his shaft. When I reached the flared edge, I swirled my tongue in a dance over the heated flesh. I watched Sawyer carefully to make sure I was pleasing him. From his white knuckles and the number of "fucks" coming out of his mouth, I'd say he was very pleased. So pleased that I settled into a rhythm that had his legs quivering. It was the shudders that signaled me it was time to end the torture. Posed over the head, I went deep, only stopping when my lips met my fingers wrapped around the base.

"About damn time." The growl made me giggle. And that giggle, while his cock was buried in my mouth, brought an end to him letting me do whatever I wanted.

Sawyer reached for my arms and dragged me up his body. I ended up straddling his hips, the swollen length of his cock nestled between the folds of my pussy. It was enough to make me want to do some cursing of my own.

"Raise up, princess."

It was impossible for me to resist sliding back and forth on his hardness. I was drenched, and coated the length of him in my juices. A moan of need rolled from my throat before I finally lifted myself off him. He had a condom ready, and the minute it was rolled on, he placed the head at my entrance, "Whatever you want *now*, princess."

A soft laugh spilled from my lips. He was giving control back to me. A surprise and a gift. Slowly lowering my body over his thickness was exquisite torture. When I was fully seated, I rested there, panting as if I'd just run a marathon. Bracing both hands on his chest, I began the slow withdrawal. He was on the edge of slipping out of me before I plunged back down. This time with force.

"Easy. I've got you." Sawyer moved his hands to my hips to steady me.

"Fast. Hard." They were the only words needed from me.

He didn't so much take over as help me to set the furious pace I needed. He pounded into me with a wildness I wanted. The wave was building and Sawyer was taking me higher with every thrust. I was willing to beg if it would take me over the crest. "Please. Sawyer, please."

He reached up, captured one of my bouncing breasts, and pinched my rock-hard nipple. That was the push needed to have me drowning in the sensations of giving my body over to something greater than me. My interior muscles clamped down on his cock, demanding to be filled with seed to complete the cycle this act of sexual frenzy had been created for in the first place. Sawyer roared, "Sonofabitch," his muscles clenching in reaction to his explosive release. He pumped into me once, twice, three times before his arms could hold me up no longer and he finally allowed me to collapse on his chest. Our bodies heaved in unison, and we sucked in great gulps of air. To move would have been impossible.

Only when we were no longer huffing did Sawyer say, "Princess, you need to roll off."

A nod and a sloppy flop to land on my back beside him was all I could manage.

He was doing better than me. He was able to climb off the bed. I did turn my head enough to watch his naked butt disappear into the bathroom. I was never going to be too tired to watch that show. A few minutes passed, and when he reappeared, he stood in the doorway and leaned against the jamb. He was spectacular in his nudity and completely comfortable with it.

"Is this progress that you didn't jump out of the bed the minute I left?"

"I live here now. I have nowhere to run. Besides, jumping would be impossible right now." Running from this man was the last thing I wanted to do.

He crossed the room and pulled back the covers. I scooched around enough to climb under them instead of lying on top. The chill in the room hadn't been noticeable until I was snuggled in the sheets. Sawyer climbed in behind me and pulled me into a spoon. The kind of heat his body threw off made the quilt unnecessary.

"Princess?"

"Hmm?"

"Don't expect me to be here in the morning." There was a hint of challenge in his tone.

"Okay."

The silence had a heaviness to it.

"I never spend the night." The challenge was gone, replaced with *reasonable guy voice.* The one they used when explaining something to a woman.

"Okay."

This time the silence didn't last as long.

"That's all you've got to say?" He wasn't happy but had nowhere to go with it. He'd started it, after all.

"No. Shut up and go to sleep or get up and leave. I'm tired. Goodnight." I buried my face, and the smile, in my pillow.

CHAPTER TWENTY-TWO

Kelli

TECHNICALLY, Sawyer could claim he didn't spend the entire night with me. We were asleep when he got a call that had him leaving my bed sometime around four in the morning.

A call at that hour would have had most people panicking, worried some disaster had taken place. If Sawyer was worried, he was a master at hiding it. He'd kissed me goodbye—total surprise—then told me he didn't know when he'd see me again. The way he said it didn't make it as final as the words implied. I understood he was a busy man.

Some of the business that took up his time was probably the type I didn't want to know anything about. Besides, I had business of my own he knew nothing about.

After he left, it'd taken me some time to fall back to sleep. At first, it'd been worry over where Sawyer and I were headed keeping me awake. I'd finally decided it would be heartache for me and business as usual for him. The only way I came out of this with any self-respect left was if I didn't fawn all over him. His ego, when it came to women, was already supersized. Sleep eventually claimed me, but it wasn't exactly restful.

When I crawled out of bed around nine, my thoughts weren't centered on what Sawyer was doing or where he was at. Now that I'd decided to accept what he was willing to share with me, my mind wouldn't let go of Grady's reaction to my return. His shock and denial had been anticipated. Insisting I not tell anyone we were brother and sister was understandable if he didn't believe it. But he did believe it. So why be so insistent that I not let anyone know about our relationship?

Having a whole day to do as I pleased, I convinced myself Zane had been right. I should go to his house and demand answers. The promise I'd made didn't specifically state that I wouldn't go see him, only that I wouldn't tell anyone he was my brother. After all, he owned a garage, I owned a car, and sometimes cars needed to be worked on. If while he checked out my car I managed to get him to explain why no one could know about us, well then, I could stop worrying.

First things first: I needed coffee and directions. Both would be easy to find at the Cozy Kitchen in the town square. After that, I needed to go shopping to pick up a few of the necessities on my list. There were plenty of small details that needed to be taken care of to make the move complete. Enough to keep me busy until late this afternoon. The plan was to show up right at closing time and hopefully catch him alone.

* * *

KELLI

DESPITE INSTRUCTIONS that included such gems as *hang a left at the old turkey barns, careful when you cross the creek,* and *them rocks can roll you right off the slab,* I managed to find both Grady's home and his garage.

He lived in a small white frame house with a tidy lawn, but there were none of the softer touches that showed a woman lived there. Things like flower beds and colorful pillows for the weathered rockers sitting on the porch were missing. They probably weren't even a passing thought for a man living alone.

It took me longer than I'd anticipated to run all the errands on my list. It was now past closing time as I climbed the steps to the porch and made my way to the front door. When my knocking went unanswered disappointment deflated me. There's nothing like psyching yourself up to do something then getting derailed. Standing in the shadow of the porch, I looked toward the only other place Grady might be if he was home at all.

I stared in the direction of the garage and had my suspicions confirmed when I saw my brother exit the building with another man. They came to a stop just outside and faced off against each other. Grady placed his hands on his hips, his stance broadcasting anger. The other man was yelling and shaking a fist in Grady's face. Looked like my brother had an unhappy customer. Before I could decide if I should try to help, Grady turned and stomped back into the garage.

The fist shaker kicked at the gravel before climbing into a big, shiny car. The car shook from the force of the door slamming shut, and gravel sprayed the side of the metal building as he gunned the engine when he took off.

I stayed rooted to the porch as the car fishtailed down the drive. I expected it to rocket past the house, and wasn't disappointed. What was a surprise was the brake lights flashing and the skidding of the vehicle as it shuddered to a stop. The car was thrown in reverse and came to a halt a short distance from the front of the house. The car was treated to another slamming door as the man exited it.

As he came toward me, I found myself backing away from the fury in his face. My vulnerability was hammered home as I remembered the isolation of the house. I calculated the distance to the garage and wasn't sure if Grady would even hear me scream should his crazy visitor decide to take out his anger on me.

He must have noticed that I watched him with a wary caution. He stopped at the bottom step and wiped a hand across his face; it was like he flipped a switch on his emotions. The anger disappeared, and an appreciative gleam took its place in his eyes.

"Hey, honey, you lost or a friend of Grady's?" A smarmy smile graced his too-round face.

Caution and instant dislike had me unwilling to answer anything this man might ask. Besides, I was getting just a little tired of everyone thinking I was lost all the time. "I'm not sure either one of those questions are any of your business."

"Don't go getting all prickly, hon. Grady and I are buds. Just making sure you're taken care of." He gave me one of those looks that made a woman feel like she needed a bath in acid afterward.

I didn't even try to hide my dislike. "Odd. Where I come from, friends don't normally yell and shake a fist in your face."

My words didn't seem to faze him. He just laughed and shrugged it off. "Even the best friends have a difference of opinion now and then. So, you're a friend, huh? What's your name, hon? I've not seen you around before. Strange Grady's never mentioned you. Now why would he be trying to hide a pretty thing like you from all his old friends?"

I wasn't sure what was going on between my brother and this man, but something was definitely off. Perhaps being rude hadn't been the right move, but I was flying blind here. I decided to switch tactics and share details. All lies, but he wouldn't know that. "That's because I'm not a friend. I'm here as a customer. We only met a couple days ago at my workplace. We got to talking, I found out he was a mechanic, my car needs work"—I spread my hands and blinked innocently—"so here I am."

"Wish my customers dressed as pretty as you when they came to see me." He ran his eyes the length of my body and smacked his lips. Disgusting.

"I didn't realize there was such a thing as appropriate garage wear when having your car checked out."

"Garage is that direction." He jerked his thumb over his shoulder, as if I couldn't see the big metal building behind him. "It's a little late in the day to be stopping if you're wanting to talk business." The smirk said he knew I was lying. That didn't surprise me. I'd been told more than once I was a lousy liar, but I was sticking to the story.

"He told me to come out to discuss the problem, and I'm running late. Being after business hours, I wasn't certain if he'd be here or at the garage. Now that I know he's not here, I'll drive to the garage." I didn't move, and neither did he.

"You didn't give me your name." His smile lost its friendly vibe.

"No, I didn't." I refused to turn away from his stare. We appeared to be at a stalemate. "You're making me nervous.

If you'd get in your car and leave, I would appreciate it. I don't have many days off, and I need to get my car checked out while I have the chance."

"Well, now, I surely didn't mean to scare you, hon. Why don't I follow you on back to the garage? Just to make sure Grady's able to help you. I wasn't aware he worked on foreign cars." He wasn't moving, and there was no way I was coming off this porch closer to him.

"That's kind of you, but not necessary. He's aware of the type of car I drive and said he'd take a look at it." The last thing I wanted was anyone in the garage when I saw Grady. Time to go back to being rude. Polite wasn't working to get rid of him.

"As I stated before, none of this is any of your business. If you don't leave right now, I'm calling 911 to report you for threatening me."

The stranger laughed like I'd told the funniest joke he'd heard. "You're from the city, aren't you, hon? I find myself real curious on how you managed to find your way out here."

He didn't give me a chance to answer before throwing up his hands in surrender and backing toward his car. "Tell Grady it was sure nice meeting one of his lady friends."

I didn't move from my spot until he was behind the wheel of his car and heading toward the county road I'd driven in on.

Once alone, I shifted my gaze to the metal building my brother had disappeared into. The garage stood back far enough from the house that I wasn't willing to walk to it dressed as I was, so I climbed back in my car and drove the short distance.

Never having visited a garage before, I was a little fuzzy on drawing attention to my arrival. The large bay doors were open, but I didn't see a smaller entrance that might lead to an office. Slamming the door to my car certainly hadn't made my brother magically appear, so I was at a bit of a loss.

Wandering closer to the wide opening, I tried a tentative "Hello?" but the inquiry died to a whisper before it was fully voiced. There was a rhythmic banging coming from the depths of the building, giving me a general direction to walk.

Curiosity, as much as the banging, pulled me deeper into the shop. Two car lifts were across from each other and there were several red metal cabinets scattered about the space. The interior walls were lined with shelves, and they were filled with mysterious gadgets. It was overwhelming and nothing like what I'd pictured.

A part of me was willing to admit to having been guilty of underestimating the sophistication of his mechanical skills. My city-bred snobbery had imagined something more in line with Goober's Garage from Mayberry. Thank you, Sawyer, for having put that image in my mind.

Even as foreign as this was to me, I could appreciate that beyond the smells of oily motor parts, and the overwhelmingly testosterone-juiced surroundings, there was order and cleanliness. Grady must be a neat freak like me. Something we certainly hadn't inherited from our momma. Wow, it would take some time to get used to it not being *my momma* but *ours*.

I came to a stop next to an old Ford pickup. The hood was up and one of those rolling cabinets filled with tools stood open next to it. I'd located the spot where the noise came from. Denim-covered legs sticking out from the undercarriage of the Ford helped locate the man. From the banging and cursing, it was easy to understand why my arrival hadn't been heard.

Pausing beside those legs, I ran a nervous hand down

the front and sides of my floral sheath dress, smoothing out any wrinkles the seatbelt might have left. I'd learned my lesson on wearing heels and had opted for a pair of Jimmy Choo flat sandals. Not exactly garage wear, but important people deserved the respect that came from putting effort into your appearance. They didn't come any more important to me than Grady.

Once every wrinkle had been twitched out of existence, I got down to the business of getting his attention. I didn't quite yell, "Excuse me," but it did come out louder than planned.

A violent jerk of his legs was followed by the sickening thud of flesh meeting metal. That was punctuated by "Gawd damn!"

Grady was now aware he had company.

I stumbled backward in surprise as his body shot out from under the truck. The speed with which he moved was explained by the board he was lying on. Wheels were attached to the bottom. Clever. His head had no sooner cleared the pickup than he jumped to his feet to advance toward me, an arm raised in the air clutching some sort of long metal tool.

"I told you I'd get to your fu—" Grady froze mid-step.

My gut reaction was to run. When I saw the trail of blood flowing from a cut high on his forehead, all thoughts of retreating fled. I rushed forward instead.

"Dear God, you're bleeding. You need to sit down." Reaching his side, I scooted under the arm he had raised in threat. Anchoring him to my side with an arm around his waist, I began shuffling us toward the open door of the truck he was working on.

"Kelli? What are you doing here?" He stared at me, then at his arm draped over my shoulder, as if wondering who it belonged to. Then he glanced at the tool he still gripped in his hand. His fingers went slack, and the piece of metal dropped with a clanging ring. What little color remained in his face drained to a sickly gray.

"Shit, Kelli! I could have seriously hurt you," he yelled, wincing in pain. Shouting at me had been a mistake.

"But you didn't. You're the one who got hurt. Please, Grady, let's find you somewhere to sit while I call for help." His feet had stopped moving while he yelled at me. I was desperate to get him seated, not caring if that meant laying him out on the floor.

"Whoa, nobody's calling nobody. Just let me rest against the side of the truck here for a minute. I'll be fine." Despite my protests, he refused to budge one step further, instead he eased back, letting the pickup take the brunt of his weight. Settled, he fished around in his back pocket and pulled out a red rag, none too clean, but he used it to wipe the blood running down his forehead and across the bridge of his nose. Once the mopping up was completed, he pressed that nasty rag against the cut to prevent any further leaks. I couldn't help but grimace thinking about all the germs pressed against his wound.

"What are you doing out here? You promised to stay away." His anger was still there but uttered at a volume less likely to add to the throbbing in his head.

"No, I didn't. I promised to not tell anyone about us. Two completely different things." I received a squinty glare from Grady. "I'm driving you back to the house. You can yell at me after that cut is cleaned properly."

"If this is what it's like having a little sister nosing around, you might as well shoot me now." I was sure he meant for his grumbling to be discouraging. Too bad. To hear him refer to me as his sister did nothing but make me smile inside.

CHAPTER TWENTY-THREE

Kelli

"HOLD STILL. I'm about finished here." I leaned over Grady where he sat on the rim of the bathtub.

I'd expected him to put up a fight when I insisted on cleaning and disinfecting his wound. But he'd been quiet as he led me to the bathroom and handed me a washcloth, alcohol, and first-aid kit.

The aspirin I'd fished out of his medicine cabinet had also gone down without a complaint. He wouldn't admit it, but I suspected he had a raging headache and wasn't in any shape to argue.

"That shit stings." Those were the first words out of his mouth since I'd refused to let him slap a Band-Aid on his head and call it quits. The gash that ran into the hairline above his left eye was accompanied by a goose egg so impressive that it made me nauseous just to look at it. The cut could have used a couple of stitches, but Grady wouldn't even discuss me taking him to the emergency room.

"It's all those germs screaming in their death throes making it sting." I dabbed at the cut one last time with the alcohol-soaked gauze before tossing it and applying the butterfly bandages. Finding out he had a well-supplied first-aid kit had been a relief, and no doubt a necessity for a man who worked in a garage.

"Screaming germs, huh?" Grady chuckled under his breath.

"That filthy rag you used to mop up the blood was covered in them." I stood back to inspect my handiwork. It would have to do.

"Aww, man, your dress."

"What's wrong with my dress?" I checked to see why he sounded upset.

"It's got blood all over it." Grady seemed more upset about the blood on my dress than he'd been about the knock on his head. I glanced at my very favorite, very expensive Dolce & Gabbana and sighed inwardly. It was ruined.

"What, this old thing?" I shrugged. The next lie rolled off my tongue as easy as the first: "No big deal. I don't even like it."

"Guess we both look like something from a crime scene on *CSI*." Grady pulled his t-shirt away from his body and surveyed the liberal splashes of blood dotting it.

"Grady?"

"Hmmm?" He didn't look up.

"Why'd you come out from under that pickup ready to attack? Are you in some kind of trouble?" The question had been burning my mouth.

"You surprised me. That's all." He wouldn't meet my eyes as he pushed to his feet. He braced a hand against the wall, collecting himself. "You can't go home looking like you just slaughtered a pig. I've got a tee and some old sweatpants that'll work until you make it back to your place."

Blocking his exit was easy in the small bathroom. "You didn't answer me. Do you have a reason to be afraid? Has someone threatened to hurt you? Is that why you were ready to smash me in the head with that tool?"

"Where'd you come up with a crazy idea like that? I'm not scared of anybody." He met my eyes with a cold look, body stiff.

Uh-oh. I'd wounded his pride. Terrible way to get answers from a man. And really...did I honestly expect him to confide in me? He just found out who I was. As hard as it was to pull back, I hoped the effort would pay off in the long run. "Okay. Can I take you up on that offer of clean clothes? While I change, you should pop an ice pack on that knot."

His whole body visibly relaxed when I dropped the issue. He might as well not get too comfy thinking I would always drop my questions, though. Only reason I was willing to let it go right now was because of the damage to his head.

"Yeah, sure. Hang on a sec." Moving with care, he started towards me. I let him pass and stepped into the hall to watch him as he slid a hand along the wall all the way to his room. I suspected he needed the help to maintain balance. Once through the door, he closed it behind him, shutting me out. That made me nervous. He wasn't steady and there was a very real possibility he had a concussion. He needed someone to keep an eye on him and make sure he was okay. That he would let that someone be me was doubtful, but that wouldn't stop me from trying.

He was gone so long that I began to worry he might

have passed out. I'd made up my mind to go check on him when the door opened. A clean shirt had replaced the blood-covered one he'd had on. He moved with the careful steps of someone expecting his head to fall off his shoulders, the promised change of clothes clutched in his left hand.

"You can put these on in Dad's room." He held the tee and sweats out to me and motioned to the closed door across from him.

"Thanks." Worry over Grady took second place to curiosity the moment I stepped into Emmett's room.

It was stupid, but I took a deep breath, hoping a trace of Emmett's smell would still linger. And strangely enough, I would have sworn there was the faintest hint of tobacco in the air. It was a bit fanciful to connect the smell to some ghostly dad hanging around a bedroom that used to be his. Like he would pop in to check out a long-lost daughter while enjoying a smoke. Common sense said the lingering scent came from years of cigarettes having been lit in that room. Being logical didn't stop a shiver from crawling up my spine.

To combat my crazy imagination, I gave the room a more realistic scrutiny. The walls were painted a bright white, the same as every other room in the house I'd seen. Even the curtains that framed the only window in the room were white. I crossed to the window and was able to see the garage in the distance. Turning back to survey the interior didn't take long. There wasn't much in the space besides a queen-size bed, oak-framed and covered with a bright quilt. The quilt was the only bit of color in the room. The matching oak nightstand was on the left, making me think that was the side of the bed he probably slept on. At the foot, snugged up against the opposing wall, was a dresser made of the same wood as the rest of the furniture. Above the dresser, a mirror was attached to the wall. Everything very generic, practical, and sterile.

There were no mementos scattered around the room. No tiny bits of foolishness that everyone collected during their life and put in their private space to remind them of days past. I tossed the change of clothes on the bed, then turned a small circle in search of anything that might have been personal. The door to the closet was closed. I stared at it. The temptation to take a peek was crazy strong. It was a physical pain to shift my attention to the rest of the room.

On top of the dresser a plastic comb lay beside a milk-white bottle sporting the red outline of a yacht in full sail. Old Spice. I moved to the dresser and picked up the men's cologne. Pulling the gray stopper, I took a cautious sniff. The heady scent of spices with a woodsy background tickled my nose and triggered a warm glow in the center of my chest. It felt like a memory. Swallowing a lump in my throat, I replaced the stopper and turned away.

Nothing good would come from snooping further. It was an invasion of privacy. Yes, the man had been my father, but he was a stranger to me. It felt like cheating to learn who he might have been by pawing through his belongings. If Grady decided to include me in his life, I wanted him to be the one to share stories with me about our dad.

I quickly stripped out of my dress and pulled on the faded tee and sweats. A couple rolls to the pant legs shortened them enough that I wouldn't fall over them, and a knot tied in the hem of the tee was the best I could do. I gathered my ruined dress off the floor, ready to join Grady.

When I pulled the door open, my brother was leaning against the wall across from me. As I stepped into the hall, he raised his bowed head enough to peer at me with wary eyes. He searched my face as if looking for the answer to a question. He spoke so low that I had to strain to hear. "That didn't take long. Figured you'd be in there for a while."

I was puzzled. Just how long did he think it took to switch clothes? Then it struck me what he'd been searching my face for. "I didn't do any snooping. Well, not much. I smelled his cologne. It was nice."

Grady shrugged. "That's all he ever wore. He always smelled like Old Spice, peppermint, and cigarettes. The mints were to hide smoker's breath and the cigarettes are what killed him."

"I didn't know. Lonnie only said he'd passed. I'm sorry for your loss." I ached for Grady and was angry for the years I'd been denied the chance to have a dad.

"You could have looked at his stuff if you wanted to. No big deal. It's all boxed up in the closet." His offhand manner didn't fool me. Whatever was in the closet was a big deal. That he offered to share it with me an even bigger deal.

"I hope someday you'll go through it with me." I held my breath, waiting to be rejected.

Grady nodded, slowly straightened from the wall then headed for the front room. I fell into step beside him, relieved he seemed willing to explore forming a connection with me.

My eyes stayed glued on Grady as we exited the hall into the living room. His pace was steadier, and he didn't appear to be confused, but his gaze stayed on his feet. The harsh lines around his mouth and deep creases across his forehead were signs of a monster headache. The sooner he sat down and got an ice pack on that epic knot, the better we'd both feel.

Trying to lighten the mood, I teased, "You really made a

mess of my dress. Next time, I'll be sure and bring a change of clothes when I visit."

"What the hell happened to you?"

We both froze in place. Standing in the middle of Grady's living room was a thunderous Sawyer.

CHAPTER TWENTY-FOUR

Sawyer

I'D FINALLY RECEIVED the call from Grady I'd been expecting. From the tension in his voice, the dumbass was ready to ask for help. Driving down his lane, I had plans to keep the talk short because of a beautiful blonde who was hopefully waiting for me back at the lake cottage. There was just one problem with my plan; Kelli's SUV was parked in front of Grady's house.

I pulled my truck beside her car and sat there studying the house. What the hell? There was no reason for Kelli to be here. Was it because I'd been straight with her about how things would be between us? You'd think a woman would appreciate not being lied to. I hadn't made a lot of promises, but I had said she'd be the only woman while we were together. I was remembering she hadn't done the same. The thought of Grady tangled up with her in the house had acid burning a hole in my stomach.

No damn way. I hadn't imagined her heat last night. There had to be something else going on.

I'd been suspicious of a woman like her showing up at Skeeter's. When she asked for a job, I'd wondered if she was there to get something on me or one of the other men who hung out there. Was Grady her target all along? It didn't fit. Nothing about her said she was anything other than what she appeared. A debutante out of her element, a mystery, but not a threat. Could I have fucked up? Had she used her job at Skeeter's as a way to get close to Grady?

Friday night had been the first time he'd met Kelli. I'd swear to it. But thinking back, I wasn't so damn sure she hadn't known who he was. I remembered the way she kept staring at him, and she'd made it a point to get his full name. Her tricks to pry people's names loose had amused me. When she'd used those tricks on Grady, I hadn't thought it was so damn funny. Her interest in him had brought out a possessive side. I didn't do possessive when it came to women. Not until her.

I had ignored the mystery surrounding Kelli Radcliff. I'd wanted in her bed bad enough that I didn't care why she'd shown up in my bar. Cocky enough to believe I could manage her. Time to figure out who the hell she was. It was also time to find out what kind of shit Grady had gotten himself mixed up in. Damn big coincidence her showing up a few days before Grady suddenly decided he was ready to ask for help. Anger and suspicion rode me hard.

I climbed out of the truck and crossed to the porch before stalling out at the front door. In all the years I'd been dropping by Grady's, I'd never knocked and waited to be invited in. The truth ripped through my guts. I didn't want to walk in and find Kelli had played me for a fool. She had me acting like a pimply-faced teen getting his first sniff of pussy. That shit was over. She was about to find out why I'd asked if she was afraid of me last night.

After walking through the door, I wanted to slam it hard enough to bust the frame, but closed it softly to prove I was in control. An empty living room wasn't what I'd wanted to find. Voices could be heard approaching from the hallway that led to the bedrooms. Fuck that. I started toward the voices at the same time Grady and Kelli appeared in the opening, looking cozy as hell.

"You really made a mess of my dress. Next time I'll be sure and bring a change of clothes when I visit." Kelli's words and light laugher cut deep. The sight of her in Grady's sweats and a tee set off the redneck crazy in me. I'd never hit a woman, but Grady was a grown man, nothing was going to stop me from beating the shit out of him if it came down to it.

My fingers were already curled in readiness when I got a good look at the face I was about to plant a fist in the middle of. What the hell? Looked like someone had gotten to Grady first.

"What the hell happened to you?" My question had them jerking to a halt, looking guilty as hell. My eyes darted back and forth between Grady and Kelli, waiting for someone to explain what was going on.

* * *

KELLI

I FROZE when I heard Sawyer's voice. There was no reason for me to feel guilty at being found alone in Grady's house. He didn't feel the necessity to tell me where he went or who he was with. When he left my bed at four in the morning, I trusted it was business and not another woman. His business was his and mine was mine. Same went for our friends. Two nights in his arms did not mean I was committed to him. Commitment wasn't even on the table for us because, according to Sawyer, I was just a curiosity that needed to be worked out of his system.

"Dammit, Sawyer. Scare the life out of a body, why don't you?" Grady glared at his friend before continuing to make his way to one of the two leather recliners centered in front of a massive TV mounted on the wall. He dropped onto the seat with a sigh, laid his head back, and closed his eyes. His show of weakness—especially in front of Sawyer —reinforced my determination to stay and watch over him.

"I asked what the hell happened to you." Sawyer didn't sound like he was in a mood to be reasonable. It didn't take a genius to figure out that finding me here at Grady's had him thinking the worst. If he wanted to know what happened to Grady, then Grady could tell him. If he didn't trust me, he had no reason to believe anything I said.

"I'm heading to the kitchen to put together an ice pack. I'll leave you to explain what happened," I told my brother, doing my best to ignore Sawyer—something I'd had a hard time doing from the first day I'd met him. I had the perfect excuse to escape and was taking it.

Goosebumps skittered across the back of my neck, a sixth sense letting me know someone was tracking my movements. Before I was out of the room, I heard Grady answer Sawyer: "A dumbass move on my part. I hit my head while working under Char's old pickup. Kelli had dropped by the garage and was there when it happened. She wanted to help out, so she patched me up."

After turning the corner into the kitchen, I paused, wondering if my brother would explain who I was.

"Looks like she's the one got helped out of her clothes while playing doctor."

Sawyer's words hurt. Did he honestly believe I'd let him in my bed, then move to another man's the next day?

"Since you don't have any idea what's going on here, you need to shut the hell up. Kelli ain't like the women you're used to hanging with."

Not waiting to hear more, I continued to the kitchen. Grady hadn't admitted I was his sister, but hearing him defend me was a salve to the cut Sawyer had just opened in my heart.

I started the search for plastic bags in the upper cabinets, but finding something to put ice in was proving to be a challenge. I'd just opened another door when a hand reached past my head and slammed it shut. There was no need to turn around to see who'd joined me. Sawyer's presence had an effect on me that was uniquely his own. He pressed his body along the length of my back as he reached to open a door adjacent to the cabinet I'd been searching.

You'd have thought the world tilted on its axis and I was in danger of falling off from the way my fingers gripped the counter's edge. Despite his anger, my nearness was affecting him just as much as his was me. After last night, I knew exactly what was behind the zipper of his jeans. And it was definitely growing hard as Sawyer pushed his hips into my butt.

"You grabbing that or not?"

Shock held me in place. Then outrage had me twisting and elbowing to gain distance before placing hands on hips to sputter, "What is the matter with you?"

"That's what you're looking for, ain't it? Or were you wanting something else?" His voice was cold. He jerked his chin up toward the open cabinet.

Confused, I looked to where he'd motioned. There sat a

box of Ziploc bags. Mortified, I decided the best way to handle it was feigned ignorance and frigid politeness. "Thank you."

I stood there, not willing to trap myself between him and the counter again. Sawyer made no move to give space or pull the box down for me. We were at an impasse. Sawyer broke the stalemate first.

"If you are looking for something else, you're not gonna find it with Grady." There was fire in his eyes. "This shit about not screwing someone else while we're together goes both ways. Should I have paid more attention when you didn't swear off other men last night?"

"You don't have a clue what's going on here. Grady's right; I'm not like your usual women. I don't have to climb into the bed of every man I talk to." My tone was hateful and bitchy. Didn't he realize he was a powerful drug that only took one hit to become addicted to?

"You got the clueless part right. Stay away from him. I'm not about to let some walking wet dream screw with his head. Either one. You need someone to screw around with, it's gonna be me. Any way you want to play it, sweetheart. I marked you last night. I don't know what the fuck you're doing here alone with him, but this shit won't happen again."

"You're disgusting." How many times did he have to prove he didn't know me before I got the message?

"Yeah? Then you better like the shit out of disgusting, because Grady's off-limits."

"Back the hell off, Sawyer. Kelli's my sister." Grady's flat warning had Sawyer pivoting quicker than I would have thought possible.

Hard to say who was more surprised to hear Grady challenge Sawyer. Fear for Grady had me rushing past Sawyer's tense figure to stand beside my brother. I had a feeling that not many men confronted Sawyer and walked away from it.

Sawyer didn't give his thoughts away by as much as a twitch of a muscle.

"How long have you known?" Sawyer's question to Grady lacked the intensity of his earlier warnings that I should stay away from him.

"She told me Saturday night. I asked her to not tell anyone else until I had a few things worked out. When I called you to come out, I didn't know she'd be here." Grady lost his defensive stance. He deflated into more of a defeated slump as he answered Sawyer's question, and I didn't think it had anything to do with his injury.

Sawyer narrowed his eyes as if running something through his head. "Is that why you called me? To tell me about your sister?"

CHAPTER TWENTY-FIVE

Kelli

GRADY TURNED to meet my stare. The determination in his eyes made me think whatever he was about to say, I didn't want to hear it.

"Kelli, I need to talk to Sawyer, so you're gonna have to leave. Give me your number. I'll call you later. I'd already told you there were things to work out. Until I do, you're still gonna have to keep quiet about being my sister."

He got a hard look on his face and said, "It'd be for the best if you left town and went back home to your mom. Things settle here, I'll get a hold of you and we'll have that talk about Dad."

It was kind of sweet, the way he thought I would walk away. Too bad—for him—that wasn't happening. "If you're planning on discussing me with *him*," I rolled my eyes in Sawyer's direction, "then I'm not going anywhere."

Sawyer didn't say a word. He simply took a step back, leaned against the counter, and crossed his arms.

"What I've got to say to him is private. It doesn't concern you." Grady started to drag a hand through his hair, remembered at the last second that wasn't a great idea, and let his hand drop.

"In that case, I'll sit on the front porch until you're through with your *man* talk. I'm not leaving. You won't go to the emergency room," I shrugged, "then you're stuck with me for as long as it takes to make sure you don't go passing out."

Grady's stare went past me and straight to Sawyer for backup.

"She's your sister. You were the one telling me how fuckin' delicate she is and to back off." It was good to see Sawyer had found his sense of humor.

I wouldn't be laughing with him. Just because he was all happy now that he knew Grady was my brother, didn't mean I'd miraculously forgotten he believed I would crawl from his bed straight into another man's.

"Dammit, this is serious." Grady gritted his teeth. He was growing paler, a sheen of sweat glistening on his brow.

"If it's that damn serious, you should've come to me months ago when you first got your balls in a vise." Sawyer pushed away from the counter, his good mood showing cracks and anger leaked out every one of them.

"That's enough." I'd had it with idiot men. Turning to my brother, I told him, "You need to sit down if you won't lie down." Switching back to Sawyer, I said, "And you need to come back later when he's feeling better."

"She's right," Grady said. "I need to sit before I fall on my ass, but what I have to tell can't wait. If the men I've gotten mixed up with find out I've got a sister, she's as good as dead." Grady headed back into the living room. That left Sawyer staring at me with questions I had no answers for.

Sawyer went charging after my brother. "What the hell are you talking about?" He almost ran into Grady's back when my brother stopped abruptly.

Grady spun and gave me with a wild-eyed look. "Did you see anyone on your way to the garage?"

I was still trying to wrap my head around him saying I was a dead woman. "What?"

Sawyer spun on me too. A grim mask settled over his features. This was the dangerous man I'd heard everyone whispering about at Skeeter's. I'd gotten a good look at *this* Sawyer when he'd come to my defense against Mason. It emphasized how different he was around me that I'd forgotten how deadly his reputation was.

The silence had stretched too long for him. "Kelli, answer Grady."

He'd called me Kelli. Yep, this was serious. "Yes, I talked to the customer you were arguing with when I first got here."

If possible, my brother grew paler, visibly shaken. "How the hell did that happen? I didn't see you when Andrew and I were at the garage."

"Andrew?" Sawyer narrowed his eyes at Grady. "Get your butt in a chair. I need information, and I need it now. You pass out on me, I'll kick your ass until you wake up." He grabbed my brother by the arm and hustled him onto a chair.

"Sawyer, be careful—"

He barked over his shoulder at me, "Not one word. Get him some water."

Spinning around, I ran back into the kitchen, grabbed the Ziploc bags from the shelf, and filled one with ice. A dishtowel wrapped around it and I had an ice pack. After filling a glass with water, I rushed back to the living room. My brother was seated and Sawyer paced in front of his chair. At my entrance, he stopped and watched as I passed the water and ice bag to Grady. He pointed at the other chair next to Grady. It wasn't worth arguing, so I sat.

He stabbed a finger at me. "Now explain how you ended up talking to Andrew."

Again. Not worth arguing. "I'd stopped at the house looking for Grady and was on the porch when I saw him and another man come out of the garage arguing. When the customer was leaving, he either saw my car or me, and he stopped. He started asking me questions like was I lost, or a friend of Grady's. I denied being a friend and said I was here to have my car worked on. I could tell he didn't believe me."

I glanced over at Grady, not sure what I expected to see, but he wasn't liking my story, not one bit. Sawyer had stopped pacing. The intensity of his gaze sent a shiver down my spine.

"That's it? Did he leave after you told him you were a customer?" The total lack of emotion in Sawyer's voice was frightening on a whole new level.

"No. He asked my name, and I refused to give it to him. He then offered to go back to the garage with me, and that's when I told him he was scaring me. Said I would call 911 if he didn't leave."

Sawyer interrupted. "Did he touch you?"

I shook my head, and Grady let out a breath as if he'd been afraid of my answer. Sawyer nodded, encouraging me to continue.

"He laughed. Called me a city girl. Just before he left, he said, 'Tell Grady it was sure nice meeting one of his lady friends.' Those were his exact words. I remember because the way he said it sounded more like a threat than a social nicety."

Grady frowned at me. "You've got to leave. Now,

tonight. I don't want to hear any shit about you staying. I'm serious."

Before I could agree or refuse, Sawyer spoke up. "She's not going anywhere until I get the whole story and figure out the best way to protect her. That means you're up, and don't leave out one fucking detail."

"Dammit, she's my sister, and *I* say she needs to get away from here." Grady's eyes met Sawyer's, glare for glare.

"She's my woman, my responsibility. You have a problem with that, too damn bad. You were too proud to ask for help when your dad died, and your damn pride has put her in danger. From now on, I make the decisions on how to keep her safe." Sawyer leveled his gaze on me, daring me to contradict him. I actually got as far as opening my mouth, but the ice that came into his expression had me closing it without saying a word.

It was all good and well to roar *I am woman. I belong to no man.* It was different when one special man claimed you and the right to protect you. Reject his claim, reject his protection, and you risked losing the man. I was mad at him, not stupid. And the mad was disappearing, real fast.

My brother sighed, sounding so defeated I was sick for him. "This all started about eight months ago. It'd seemed like easy money when Andrew showed up offering a couple extra thousand for a rush job on one of my traps."

"What's a trap?" I asked. Any trap worth thousands of dollars wasn't used to catch any kind of mouse I'd ever seen.

Grady glanced at Sawyer as if asking for help, then went ahead and answered my question. "I make hidden compartments in trucks, cars, trailers; you name it, I can put one in. They're worth a lot of money because it takes special electronics to make them work. Not everybody knows the electronic systems as well as I do, and they're not exactly legal." He was quick to add, "They're not exactly illegal, either. As long as their use conforms to the law."

He left a lot out of his explanation, but I could make some guesses on who would want these hidden compartments installed in their cars. None of them legal. He watched me, waiting for me to turn on him and denounce him for being a scumbag. Sawyer watched me silently too.

I took a deep breath and said, "Okay, I'll add that to my list of things to not ask questions about."

Both men stared at me, clearly wondering *What the hell is she talking about?*

"Zane and I have an agreement of sorts," I explained. "She tells me about things I shouldn't ask questions about, and I add them to a Don't Ask, Don't Talk to Stranger About It list. Yours is short compared to Sawyer's." I slid a glance Sawyer's way.

Sawyer just grunted, but Grady went to run a hand through his hair again, and this time the ice pack reminded him it wasn't a good idea. "I'm afraid my list is about to get a hell of a lot longer."

"It doesn't matter. Whatever goes on the list won't affect my feelings for you."

He nodded in agreement, but I didn't think he believed me. "Getting back to the traps: Andrew said if I put his Denali in front of legit repairs and custom jobs already scheduled, he'd pay me extra. I needed the money. Dad's hospital and doctor bills were more than I could cover each month. Business had slowed after Dad got sick, and I was spending more time at the hospital than working. It was still slow even after I went back to working full time. I figured one job for Andrew would give me a little breathing room. I did the job and everything was okay for a couple of weeks. Business picked up, and with the extra from the Webber job, I was feeling better about not losing everything." He met Sawyer's gaze. "I know you were sending a lot of those jobs my way."

Sawyer shrugged as if it was no big deal. The man really didn't want anyone to know he had a good heart. At least where his friends were concerned.

"Anyway, a few weeks later, Andrew showed up again, only this time he had a couple big bastards with him. Figured they were from out of town, 'cause I'd never seen them before. They had come wheeling in with another vehicle they wanted customized, an older one-ton Chevy. It was one of the trucks Webber uses as a car hauler."

Seeing my puzzled look, he stopped his story to explain, "Andrew Webber's old man owns the Ford and Chevy/GMC dealerships in Copper Ridge. They're just two in his lineup of car lots. He has them scattered from Little Rock to St. Louis and plenty of small towns between. Andrew manages the ones here."

"Is Andrew Webber any relation to Mason Webber?" I remembered Mason being insulted I hadn't been impressed when he'd given me his name. He'd also threatened to kill Sawyer that night.

"Yeah, him and Andrew are brothers. Both worthless pieces of shit," Sawyer gave his opinion of the brothers in a flat voice.

Awareness flared in his eyes. He asked Grady, "Was Mason at Skeeter's to meet up with you last Friday night? He got anything to do with what's going on between you and Andrew?"

"Hell no!" Grady said. "I don't know why he was there that night. If he's in on this shit, I don't know anything about it. They bring me the trucks; I put in the traps. That's it."

"We'll figure out what he knows." Sawyer sounded grim.

I didn't want to know how Sawyer planned on finding out what Mason knew.

Grady slowly nodded, then continued. "They showed up with one of Webber's trucks and wanted more traps installed. But I was busy and told Andrew he'd have to wait. I still needed the money, though, so I didn't turn the job down, just said it'd be slower. That's when he told me life was about to change for me. Said I was working for Tommy Jefferson now—"

"Fucking hell." The curse exploded from Sawyer's lips. It was the way he'd said the words that let me know whoever this Jefferson person was, he was bad news.

Grady went on as if he hadn't been cut off, "—and when Jefferson had a job for me, I dropped everything else and did his job. Said he'd be sending a lot of work my way for the next few months 'cause they were partners now and would be using the Webber company trucks to carry Jefferson's product. That meant a lot of trucks would need to be customized."

Grabbing the back of his neck, he squeezed his eyes shut. When he opened them, he looked ashamed. "I told Andrew I didn't want any part of Tommy Jefferson, and next thing I know, one of those big bastards has me pinned against the wall of my garage, choking the shit out of me. Last thing I remember is Andrew yelling at him to let me down. I woke up kissing the concrete floor. The minute I'm awake, Andrew's in my face giving me a list of the number of traps he wants put in the truck.

"When I could stand, I made a move on the sum'bitch that throttled me and the other bastard stuck a gun in the middle of my forehead—"

My gasp stopped Grady in the middle of his story.

He didn't offer me any reassurances. I guessed he didn't have any to give. "Andrew told me once I got used to the way things would be from now on, I'd see this was a good thing. I'd make plenty of money, and after I finished custom-fitting all of the company trucks, I could forget this had ever happened. Business would go back to normal and I'd only have to do a job for Jefferson once in a while. Told me to be smart, keep my mouth shut, and we'd all live to get rich. Said if I didn't, Jefferson wouldn't just be *my* worst nightmare if I crossed him. Claimed he'd inflict a horror story on anyone I cared about and have a damn good time doing it."

Grady met Sawyer's stare straight on. "When Andrew walked away, that asshole was scared shitless of his own partner. How the hell do I ask you for help when it pits you against Tommy Jefferson? If it wasn't for Kelli, I wouldn't be getting you involved now."

When Grady finished, the silence was deafening. Guilt ate at me as I thought about all Grady had gone through alone. Being there for Emmett in his final days and then being buried under a mountain of medical bills. It didn't matter I hadn't known about any of this. I'd always carry the bitter memory of what my mother's deceit had put him through.

"You see why she has to leave?" Grady said. "Now he's seen her, Andrew won't stop digging until he figures out who she is. She called it the other night. Plenty of people around here remember Denise running off with her when she was a baby. Once he figures out she's my sister, he'll run to Jefferson and I'll never get away from him. If she leaves, they won't have anything to hold over me." Grady sounded exhausted and looked worse. "I'm sorry, Kelli."

"She's not going anywhere." Sawyer's words had the ring of finality.

CHAPTER TWENTY-SIX

Sawyer

"ARE YOU CRAZY? Of course she has to leave." Grady tried to stand, but Kelli grabbed his arm to keep him seated.

"Grady, I'm not going anywhere as long as you're in trouble. I trust Sawyer and if he says I need to stay, I'm staying." She ran a soothing hand up and down his arm.

Hearing her say she trusted me eased something inside. She trusted me, even though I'd stormed through the door ready to believe the worst. She radiated anger, and yet she trusted me. I'd screwed up.

"If you go back to Little Rock, nobody will know where you are," Grady argued. "Your family's rich. Tell them enough to make them understand your life is in danger. They'll be able to keep you safe. While you're gone, we'll work on the problem from here."

"She goes running back to Mom, she'll just draw Jefferson's men after her. Then it's not just her in danger. Mom's ass is on the line." I understood him wanting to get Kelli out of here, but it wouldn't work. It'd spread the reach of the problem.

"Grady, you're my family," Kelli said. "Momma is the only one I have in Little Rock, and we're not exactly talking right now. As for the Radcliffs," she scrunched her nose in distaste, "if any of them find out there's a way to eliminate the two of us? They'd wrap us up, put a big bow on top, and hand us over to Jefferson as a gift."

"What the hell are we supposed to do? Just sit on our asses and hope it all goes away?" Grady slung the ice pack across the room in frustration. Kelli flinched when it slammed into the side of the wood stove. Nobody bothered to go pick it up.

"You're gonna go about business as usual, and I'm moving Kelli to my place until I can fix this." A foreign stab of emotion tightened my chest when she claimed Grady and her mom as her only family. I might not be family, but she was mine to protect.

"Wait! What? No, no, no, no." Kelli was furiously shaking her head. "We just started..." She shot a red-faced peek at Grady, then whispered to me, "You know."

Her brother sat right next to her. Did she really think he couldn't hear her or figure out what we'd "just started" doing?

In a normal tone, she continued, "Why can't I move in with my brother if I need to stay with someone?"

Grady jumped in, "Because what he says makes sense. We're the only ones who know I'm your brother. Wait. You said Lonnie knows. Right?" Grady raised an eyebrow in question.

"And Zane. She knows." Kelli gave him a tiny smile.

Grady shut his eyes and his lips stretched until they were two thin lines. "Anyone else you've shared this with?"

She kept her lips clamped and shook her head. I noticed

she didn't get as mouthy with Grady as she did me. That made me want to smile. She really wasn't afraid of me.

"The point I'm trying to make is you can't move in with me 'cause we don't want any *more* people knowing you're my sister." Grady opened his eyes in time to catch her head shake. "If you're worried I'll figure out what you and Sawyer just started doing? You can stop worrying. The cat was pretty much out of the bag when I heard the two of you arguing in the kitchen. The safest place you can be right now is with Sawyer."

Before she could come up with another excuse, I gave her the most important reason: "Nobody is stupid enough to take something of mine. And they sure as hell aren't stupid enough to come on my property to take my woman." Wade had been right yesterday when he'd said I was the meanest bastard around. Jefferson would be as aware of my reputation as I was of his. Sometimes that was all the checks and balances necessary to keep a war from breaking out.

My eyes met Grady's. "Andrew can't find out you've told me any of this. If you're supposed to be working on something for Jefferson right now, do it. Keep him and Andrew happy."

He looked grim, but nodded his agreement.

"I'm taking Kelli to the Dog House tonight. There's always a crowd there on Tuesdays. The quicker word gets around she's with me, the quicker she'll be safe. Showing her off in front of that bunch of damn grannies is the fastest way to spread gossip." For the first time in my life, I wanted everyone know a woman was mine. Getting word to Webber that she was off-limits was only part of it.

"Fine. Moving in with a nasty person to keep other nasty people away makes sense," she gave in.

"You fuckin' like me nasty." Having her agree to move

in took the sourness out of my mood. Watching her turn pink made me want to remind her how much she liked it when we got nasty together.

"Damn, Sawyer! Can you not talk like that to my sister in front of me?" Grady looked like he was in real pain.

Kelli's squinty stare said I was going to pay. She jumped up ready to do battle. "I'll move in, but Grady can't be left alone tonight. He probably has a concussion, and someone needs to stay with him. That someone is going to be me." Her smug smile said *so there*.

"Dammit, Kelli," Grady said. "If you're trying to prove sisters are a pain in the ass, you're doing a great job. You've been trying to get me to lie down ever since this knot showed up. You leave, that's where I'm headed. To lie the hell down. And I don't want you creeping around, staring at me while I sleep." Grady pushed out of his chair and glared down at her. No way was he letting her get height advantage over him. I would've done the same.

We didn't have time for this shit. "Princess, we're leaving now. The only choice you have is if you walk out the door, or I carry you out. You have ten seconds to decide."

"This is a mistake." She curled her hands into fists and glared at me.

"You've got five seconds left."

She did that flounce thing and turned to her brother. "Promise me you'll call if you start feeling worse?"

"I promise. Now go. You've worn my ass out." He gave her a weary smile.

"Okay, in that case—" She shrieked when I spun her around, bent down, put a shoulder to her stomach, and stood back up. She would learn that when I said something, I meant it. When she tried to move, I slapped her ass, and that brought out another shriek. "Are you crazy? I was coming!"

I was so damn tempted to tell her she would be later. But after slapping her ass and carrying her out on my shoulder, she probably wouldn't find it funny.

"I told you ten seconds. That's what the hell I meant. You want a chance to clean up before we go to the Dog House, you'll stop wiggling. Unless you want me to slap your ass again." I didn't even try to hide the grin when she went limp as a wet dishrag. Only her hands were clenched in a death grip on the waistband of my jeans.

I turned to Grady. "I'm gonna bring Vernon in on this. He'll be at the poker house. Call you tomorrow and let you know what we come up with. I'll send one of the boys to get her car later, to take back to my place."

A muffled voice sounded about halfway down my back. "Are you going to let him do this to me?"

Grady sighed. "Kelli, I know Sawyer would never hurt you physically. If I didn't believe that, concussion or not, he would not be walking out my door with you. I'm thinking you must like him a lot to have let him in your bed. You told me you trust him. Now you need to show it."

I didn't move, waiting to see if she would say anything else.

She said in the same small, muffled voice, "Goodnight, Grady."

* * *

KELLI

SAWYER CARRIED me to his truck then managed to open the door and dump me on the seat. Okay, he didn't exactly dump me. He was careful as he transferred me from his shoulder to his truck. No bumps on my head or anywhere else as he got me inside. The only thing stinging was my bum and my pride.

My hair was a tangled mess as I pushed it off my face with both hands. Masculine fingers joined mine in combing through the snarls. I let my hands drop and watched his face through my lashes as he continued to tame the strands.

He had a beautifully harsh face. The heat from his body blocked the cool autumn air from sneaking into the cab. When satisfied with my smoothed hair, he pulled the seat-belt across my body, leaned in, and clicked it home. He didn't straighten, staying curved over my body. My eyes were captured by the darkness in his as he brushed the back of a finger from my temple to my chin. Tipping my chin, he placed a soft kiss on my lips.

As he backed away, the chill of the night took over, and a shiver having nothing to do with the cold crawled down my spine. The door closed with a quiet snick and darkness filled the space.

I didn't know what to do with his tenderness.

A moment later, he was seated beside me and the rumble of the engine covered the silence. "It won't take long for the heater to kick in."

The timbre of his voice washed over me. The anger and the hurt were hard to hang on to.

He didn't trust me. *You were in another man's home and wearing his clothes.*

He spanked me. *He wants to protect you.*

He was domineering. *You knew what he was when you welcomed him to your bed.*

He was vulgar and embarrassed me in front of my brother. *He's a wolf and plays rough.*

"Are you going to give me the silent treatment again?"

"No. I'm sitting here arguing with myself."

"Who's winning?"

"I believe you are."

"I like to win." There was laughter in his voice.

Sighing, I shifted in my seat to see him better. The dim light from the instrument panel accentuated the angles in his cheekbones, the straight line of his nose, and the perfection of his lips.

"I'm sorry for not telling you that Grady's my brother." There, I was first to give in and admit I'd been wrong about how I'd handled the situation. "In my defense, He asked me to— Scratch that. He *told* me not to tell anyone."

"I'm not anyone. I'm the man who makes you scream orders at me to do *nasty* things to your body." His lips lifted in a smirk. "And when we get to the Dog House, we're going to share some *nasty* kisses. If we get caught, all the better. It'll keep all the other *nasty* men away from my woman."

Please let him be teasing about that part of tonight's program. Well, not the kisses. The getting caught part of the kissing. "You finished with all the *nasty* references?"

"Princess, I'm just getting started."

CHAPTER TWENTY-SEVEN

Kelli

CARS FILLED the front yard of the house. There were so many that they spilled over onto the adjoining lawn. Someone had very tolerant neighbors. When Zane and Sawyer had called this place the Dog House, I hadn't expected it to be a house. But there it was, a sprawling ranch-style home surrounded by a sea of cars. There were so many that the only space left to park was close to the road. I exited the truck and Sawyer wrapped an arm around my waist, pulling me against his side.

I was grateful for the warmer clothes. Nights were getting chillier the deeper into fall we got. Jeans and boots were becoming something of a uniform for me. Stopping to change clothes almost derailed Sawyer's plans for the night. He'd refused to wait in the living room. Said he'd spent all day wondering what kind of *nasty* panties and bra were hiding under my clothes. Yes, he was still using *nasty* every chance he got. The pink satin corset and matching thong led to kisses, and that lead to groping. It was a miracle we made it here at all.

Nerves had me hanging on to Sawyer tighter than necessary as we went through the door. The exterior gave every appearance of being someone's home; inside, it was all business. I hadn't known what to expect, but it hadn't been a real house turned into a poker den. The place was packed. It was strange seeing the professional gaming tables scattered around what should have been a family home.

We stopped in the entrance and he took his time scanning the interior. I wondered if he surveyed every building he stepped in before committing to joining the crowd. Tonight, his routine had the added advantage of giving everyone in the open living/dining/kitchen area a good look at us. And were they ever looking.

Not one to waste the moment, he leaned over and whispered in my ear, "Ready for your first night in the Dog House?" The nip on my earlobe was unexpected and sharp, startling a tiny squeal out of me. If anyone missed our arrival, they certainly noticed us now.

"Get a room."

The derisive snort and familiar voice had me searching the room for Zane. I finally spotted her at a long oval table placed in front of a heavily curtained window. Her comment had broken the spell, and everyone went back to their gambling.

She had both men and women crowding her table, but there were a couple of empty seats available. I went to untangle myself from Sawyer, intending to claim one. He pinched my waist, his way of saying no. But he did start moving in her direction.

We skirted other poker tables that flanked the sides of the room. A few people tossed greetings at us; he did his chin tip at a couple and ignored the rest. He was in full asshole mode. What amazed me was everyone seemed okay with it.

Once we reached her table, Sawyer sat, pulling me down to settle on his lap. Zane cocked her head and studied us. I braced for whatever was about to come out of her mouth. She earned my everlasting gratitude when she kept those thoughts to herself.

After dealing the cards she'd been shuffling since I'd spotted her, she informed the players, "Last hand before the break."

She thumbed up to a small flat screen mounted high on the wall. A countdown ticked off on the screen. Checking around the room, I spotted two more mounted on the other walls. All easily seen from anywhere in the room.

The only thing I knew about the game being played was the name, Texas hold 'em. Bradley had loved to attend the charity poker nights at the Country Club of Little Rock. It was the only game played on those nights, and drew huge crowds. Apparently, it drew crowds wherever it was played.

Hesitant to talk to Zane while she worked, I stretched to whisper in Sawyer's ear, "How do you get away with this? Gambling is illegal and this place is next to a state highway. You're not exactly hidden."

Cheek to cheek made it easy for him to answer as quietly. "There's no money on the table. All these people are simply here playing a fun game using chips. It's in a private home and the sheriff never misses the cash games on Sunday nights. He owes me too much money to shut any of my houses down. Put that on your list."

"Guys. Would you mind? Not everyone is as lucky here tonight."

I twisted to find the speaker and ended up facing Evan's

belt buckle. I tilted my head and got a wink from him. Sawyer stood, landing me on my feet.

"Losers usually *leave* when they run out of chips," Zane grumbled.

I turned to Sawyer to see if he knew what she was talking about. He was eyeballing Evan, and he wasn't smiling.

"Lightning, splash the pot one more damn time and you'll forfeit your entry and you're heading home," There was no playing around in Zane's voice. "You know damn well that every time you toss your chips in the middle of the pot we have to delay the game while the pot's counted."

A bearded man I took to be Lightning jumped to his feet and almost fell across the table. The alcohol fumes rolling off the man drifted to where we were standing. Face red enough to catch his beard on fire, he argued, "Fuck that, little girl. You and what damn army is kicking me out?"

Sawyer nudged me behind him and smoothly stepped forward. The movement snagged everyone's attention, dragging it away from the two facing off over the table. Like the night Mason attacked me at Skeeter's, people began making space. They abandoned their chairs and backed away from Lightning. He might as well have had a spotlight on him as he stood alone.

"She doesn't need an army. She's got me." Evan moved passed Sawyer to challenge Lightning.

Zane's chair fell over as she charged to her feet. "I don't need an army and I don't need you to fight my battles. He has a problem with me. I'll meet his pasty-white ass outside and kick it up and down the road for him."

"Fucking hell." A muscle twitched in Sawyer's jaw as he moved to stand beside Evan.

Sawyer stepping forward caught Lightning's attention.

He weaved as he tried to get his eyes to focus. The minute he realized exactly who was watching his tantrum, his face went noticeably gray.

"Stop the clock." Sawyer's face lost all expression and his voice went flat. Whoever was running the clock heard him, and every TV froze.

Footsteps could be heard pounding in our direction from deeper in the house. A lean man loped into the living room, joining Evan and Sawyer. He was average height, but he looked short beside the other two men. "What the hell is going on?"

"Vernon, Lightning's leaving," Sawyer said. "Clear his chips and turn his entry fee over to Zane. Anything he's already put in the pot stays. Have a couple of the men dump his drunk ass in the storeroom until he's sober enough to drive home."

Vernon looked over the spectators then called out, "Joe, Tillis. Get his keys and haul him to the back."

Two men came forward out of the crowd. One grabbed Lightning's arm and the other followed behind.

"Show's over. Clock starts in thirty seconds. Five minutes till break." As soon as Vernon made the announcement, people started talking again, but no one lingered.

Vernon blew out a breath. "Damn it. Lightning's been warned more than once about getting drunk and pulling dirty moves. It's not Zane's fault it got out of hand. He saw a woman and figured he could bulldoze right over her."

Sawyer told him, "Decide what you want to do with the asshole and I'll back you. When I turned this place over to you to run, that's what the hell I meant."

I noticed Zane bending to right her chair, and darted around the table. "Are you okay?"

"I'm fine. Made an extra fifty-five bucks thanks to

Lightning being his usual asshole self." The hard edge to her eyes said she wasn't fine.

I knew Zane well enough to know it wasn't some drunk spewing bullshit, either. That would roll off her back without another thought. No, something else was definitely going on with her tonight.

"Hey, we'll get a chance to talk during break. Okay? I gotta get back to work." She flashed me a tight-lipped smile.

Nodding in agreement, I slowly walked back to Sawyer. Not wanting to interrupt the three men, I stopped a few steps behind them. The man had some kind of radar when it came to me. The moment I stopped, he swung around and started in my direction. He grabbed my hand and turned me toward the kitchen. Talking over his shoulder, he told the other two, "Let's move this to the kitchen."

He didn't wait for them to follow.

"I need to work out some things with Vernon." Sawyer stopped us by a granite counter. If it weren't for the industrial-sized refrigerator and the coolers lined against the wall, this could've been a kitchen found in any home. "You gonna be okay on your own for a few?"

"Sure. Zane and I'll keep each other company." I'd love to be in on the conversation between him and Vernon. But I doubted he could be talked into letting me be there. Just as well—something was going on with Zane, and I'd agreed to spend the break with her.

Vernon joined us and gave me a smile that had a lot of *who the hell are you?* in it. Knowing Sawyer would never make introductions, I smiled back and did the work for him. "Hi. I heard Sawyer call you Vernon. I'm Kelli."

Sawyer didn't give us time for any more pleasantries. He leaned against the counter, pulled me in front of him, and wrapped me up in both of his arms. It was a temptation to relax against him. It would be so easy to let his shoulder be a pillow for my head. But there were too many people interested in watching us. He hadn't been kidding about showing people I belonged to him.

"Soon as Zane's free to keep Kelli company, you and I need to have a talk," Sawyer told Vernon. He absently ran his hands over my arms where they crossed on my stomach. For a guy who'd never had a girlfriend before, he sure knew the moves.

"Halftime is starting now. I'll go help color up her table." As Vernon headed back to Zane, everyone started pushing away from their tables. A few wandered into the kitchen. A woman had moved to stand in front of the coolers and was taking money for beer, pop, and water as people started gathering in front of her.

The ones who'd stayed with their chips carefully watched those chips being switched out for different-colored ones. Only after they'd counted the new chips did they make their way to the kitchen.

While we waited for Zane, I noticed a man who looked familiar coming from one of the back rooms. Then it struck me where I'd seen him. He'd been with Sawyer last Friday night. He noticed us about the same time I did him. He paused for a minute, as if not sure he wanted to join us, then started walking our way.

"Hey, Sawyer. Surprised to see you here." His smile was cautious.

"Wade." Sawyer didn't sound overly happy to see him, but then, he never sounded thrilled to see anyone.

"Eh, can I talk to you a minute outside?" Wade glanced at me, then added, "Alone."

Pretty easy to tell he wanted to straighten something out with Sawyer. Zane was heading in our direction, and I squeezed Sawyer's arms where they rested at my waist.

"Zane and I are going to do some catching up. I'll see you when you get back."

He pushed us both off the counter and set me free. Almost. He snagged my elbow before I walked away. "If I'm not back by the time break is over, wait for me at her table." He waited for me to nod before brushing a kiss across my lips and walking away with Wade. He kept surprising me with these tiny shows of affection.

"Let's go this way." Zane reached me and kept walking. I checked to see what had happened to Evan.

He was still by the gaming tables, but not alone. A group of women had him surrounded and he was laughing at something one of them said. They were working to capture his interest, and he didn't seem to mind the effort they were putting in. Despite what Zane said about being over him, seeing him flirt with other women hurt her.

I turned and followed Zane through a door at the end of the kitchen. It opened to a laundry room equipped with a washer and dryer. The only items out of place were a couple of lawn chairs crowded together at one end. Zane claimed one and motioned for me to take the other. She dragged a small cooler out from under hers and drew out a couple of pops. After handing one to me, she popped the tab on another and took a long drink. "I was ready for something cold." She reached back into the cooler and brought out a pint jar filled with a clear liquor. "This is going to make it even better."

She carefully added it to the remaining soda in the can. When finished, she offered the jar to me. I shook my head. She shrugged, upended the can, and took an even longer draw.

When she came up for air, she heaved a sigh. "I needed that about two hours ago."

"What's up?" I was willing to bet Evan was what had Zane sucking her high-octane pop like it was water.

"Evan's been acting weird as hell ever since the bonfire." Zane brushed a curl off her face with the back of her hand.

"Weird how?" This being only the second time I'd seen him, I had nothing to gauge his weirdness against.

"He's hanging around." She bugged her eyes at me like that was supposed to mean something.

"Yes, well, he is here playing poker." I was lost.

"You don't understand. He's hung around my table ever since he lost all his chips. He didn't even make it to half-time, but he's still here." She sounded bewildered. "Nobody hangs around if they run out of chips."

"Maybe he's just being friendly." Or maybe after Zane flashed her breasts at the bonfire and told him kids didn't have boobs like hers he was hoping for another peek. That incident seemed to be one of those blank spots from that night for her. I didn't have the heart to tell her about it.

Her brows scrunched in confusion. "He isn't trying to talk to me any more than he ever did. He just watches me. Most of the time with a frown on his face. Like I said, weird."

"Could be he's realized you've grown up and is inter-ested in finding out who a grownup Zane is." I didn't know whether to be happy or sad for her. I was still afraid he had the potential to do serious damage to her heart, nice guy or not.

"He can get uninterested. I've decided we won't work." She finished off her can of mixed something or other. An impressively loud burp followed. "Tell me what the hell is going on with you and Sawyer. Talk about weird. He has never, n-e-e-ver hung on a woman before. Usually they're the ones doing all the hanging. What's up with that?"

Zane wasn't fooling me. She'd closed the discussion on Evan using my situation with Sawyer as a diversion. Too bad for both of us, on our way over here Sawyer had more or less—okay, it was a lot more than it was less—ordered me to not tell Zane anything about the whole Grady/Jefferson problem. He didn't want her getting involved. She would jump in with both feet if she thought she could help. To keep her safe, I had agreed. We'd come up with a story that was the truth, just not the whole truth.

"Yesterday, after you left, he said he wanted me to be his girlfriend." My excited giggle fell flat.

"He said that? He came out and said, 'I want you to be my girlfriend'?" Zane had a doubtful look on her face.

"Not those exact words."

"What were his exact words?" She reached over, took my hand, and patted it. She thought I was delusional.

"That he wouldn't be with other women while we were together and I couldn't be with other men." I took a breath and added, "I'm moving in with him. Tonight."

Her expression went blank. Totally. Blank. Was she waiting for me to yell "psych"? The silence was starting to get awkward. Finally, she blinked. "You're not shittin' me, are you?"

When I shook my head, she grabbed my hands. Her squeal sounded a lot more genuine than my giggle had.

"Holy hell, I'm so happy for you. I knew that when he finally fell for a woman it'd be hard, fast, and deep."

Her description sounded a whole lot like mine and Sawyer's last session in the bedroom. The thought had heat crawling up my neck into my cheeks.

"Eewww! You were thinking about screwing him when I said that, weren't you?" She scrunched up her nose in disgust.

I cleared my throat, neither confirming nor denying.

"Anyway, I suppose he's just letting people know we're together."

"You mean he's warning off other men." She nodded, satisfied she'd figured out what tonight's display was about. "Does he know Grady's your brother?" Her face went serious.

"I told him today. We're a couple now. It was the right thing to do." Lordy, I sounded prissy. Lying to Zane was as hard as I'd thought it'd be.

A knock on the door interrupted any further questions she had for me. A man I didn't know stuck his head in. "Halftime's over, Zane. We're waiting on you."

She narrowed her eyes at me. "This isn't over. You're not telling me something."

I trailed after Zane, feeling miserable. She was going to be furious when she found out the parts of the story I hadn't shared with her. Especially when a part of that story was being played out here, right under her nose.

CHAPTER TWENTY-EIGHT

Kelli

"How can you already have everything set up?" I rested my chin on my hands as I lay on top of Sawyer and stared into his face. Being on top was fast becoming an addiction. And not just for sex.

We were in his living room stretched out on his ratty floral couch. It wasn't dirty or anything; it just should've been replaced a decade ago. Pretty much everything in his house was in the same condition. Clean but worn. It wasn't hard to figure out material things didn't mean a lot to him. He put on a show for nobody—so different from the people I'd grown up with, and one of the things I loved about him.

Thinking about loving him didn't freak me out like it probably should have. No big epiphany had slapped me in the forehead, saying, *This is the moment you fell in love*. I'd been in his house all of three days, and when I'd awoken this morning, I just knew. His big body wrapped around me was where I wanted to be for the rest of my life. He'd made me no promises of forever, and I knew if he ever said we were finished, I'd be ruined. But I wouldn't miss one moment with him, not even to save me from pain should I lose him.

"When you're in certain lines of business, you get your ass in gear when there's a threat. Jefferson wants this meeting as badly as we do." He was twisting and untwisting a strand of my hair around one of his large fingers.

The man loved to touch me. When we'd gone to the Dog House, I'd thought all the touchy-feely was his way of showing everyone I was his. But nothing had changed since that night. If we were in the same room, he liked me close and he liked to touch me. He might play with my hair or run a hand along my spine—there was always a connection.

"Did you make a threat?" My little bubble of content-ment popped. I pushed against his chest with my forearms to lever myself higher. My voice came out all screechy. "Don't tell me you threatened a fucking drug lord!"

Our change in position was so fast that it made me dizzy. I was pressed into the saggy cushions while he glared down at me. "Watch your fucking mouth. You talk dirty when we're not screwing, and I'll wash your mouth out with fucking soap."

Double standard much? I was wise enough not to say that out loud. He wasn't kidding. He had this crazy idea that being around him was going to reduce me to a white-trash ho. Zane's colorful description. He needn't have worried. I'd learned my lessons too well growing up in the Radcliff household. Only moments of extreme stress, or passion, would make me utter such vulgarities. Momma's disdainful description.

"Please, tell me you didn't threaten Jefferson." I searched his face for an answer.

"Shhh, princess. I'm an asshole, not stupid." He braced one arm as he brushed away the hair his wild flip had flopped in my face. He traced one of his rough fingers back and forth across my brow, smoothing the worry lines. "We're meeting to talk. That's it. He no more wants a war than I do. It draws too much attention from the wrong government agencies."

"What do you mean wrong agencies?" The dark world of illegal business was a mystery to me. Sawyer wanted to keep it that way. Zane told me he'd been pulling away from that way of life more and more in the last few years. I'd never change the man he was. But I couldn't help feeling relieved there was less chance of him going to prison. I was pretty sure they didn't allow daily conjugal visits.

"I mean the ones that you can't buy off. Not without spending more damn money than it's worth. Jefferson has more to worry about in that area than me, and from a hell of a lot more agencies."

He leaned forward and kissed my frown lines. More kisses were feathered down the bridge of my nose. I tipped my chin back to make my lips easier to reach. He moved in, and I could feel the heat before he touched me. His lips were a whisper away when he shifted his aim to the side, landing them on the corner of my mouth, nipping instead of kissing. He was a tease. Whether it was kissing or in the middle of the most intimate act, he would do something to drive me crazier.

I slapped a hand to the middle of his chest and pushed. I might as well have been trying to move a mountain. "If you're not going to kiss me proper, back off and tell me about these plans. Details. I want all the details."

"I plan on starting with your mouth and working my

way down your hot body to suck on these sweet titties of yours." He pinched a nipple in case there was any doubt which breast he was talking about. "Then the plan is to shoulder between your thighs and work on making you scream my name three times before I nail your ass to this couch."

Man, I wanted to hear more about this plan, but worry had me twisting my face away when he lowered to claim my lips. My other hand joined the first one planted on his chest. "No. You're trying to distract me. I want to know what you and my brother are going to do when you meet with Jefferson."

He ignored my attempt to stop him. My puny efforts at holding him back were pathetic. With my face turned, he placed lazy kisses from my temple to my ear. My body was demanding I give in. My mind screamed at me to find out what was going to happen.

"Please. Don't." My whispered plea hung in the air. He froze then eased away. I turned back to meet his questioning eyes. After searching my face, he rose to sit on the couch and pulled me to straddle his lap. His hands splayed across the tops of my thighs, anchoring me in place. Physically, there was no way I could've stopped him. But he would never use his strength to force me into something I truly didn't want.

"Hell, princess. I leave in a few hours. Sure you'd rather talk about this shit than get a good fucking in before I go?" He squeezed my thighs in encouragement.

"It's hard to resist such a romantic offer, but yes, I need to know what's going to happen at that meeting." Dark strands of hair covered parts of his face. I finger-combed it back, loving the silky feel across my skin. All of his flips and flops, ups and downs had his hair looking like a wild man. It suited him. I dropped my arms to rest on his shoulders when I was finished, fingers weaved together at the back of his neck.

"Fuck romantic. It's the results that count." He tapped his forehead against mine.

I couldn't agree more. Especially when the results were so spectacular. He didn't need to know that, though. He was already overly proud of his bedroom performance.

"Are you and Grady going to be safe tonight?" I hid my fear. It was important he realized I was strong enough to handle whatever he told me. Worry was acceptable. Fear wasn't.

He cradled my face between his hands, capturing my gaze. I expected to see tenderness, but what I saw was raw determination and power. He wasn't showing me weakness.

"Kelli, I'll never lie to you. If you ever ask me a question, you better be sure you want the truth, because that's all you'll ever get from me."

I understood what he wasn't saying. If I didn't *ask*, he wasn't volunteering information. There were things he didn't want me to know. Things *I* didn't want to know. This was a perfect example of being careful what you asked for.

"Are you and Grady going to be safe tonight?" I repeated.

"I'll have backup with me. We'll have guns. They'll have guns. Nobody's going to want to use their guns. I'm meeting Jefferson to talk, not place a bullet in his head. He's meeting me for the same reason. If things go the way we want, this will be the end of it. If not, it won't." He met my eyes with a watchful stare.

My guy wasn't the sugarcoating kind. His world was a rough one, and if I wanted him, I accepted it. I didn't flinch when he mentioned guns, and my voice stayed level when

I said, "You said *you* have backup. What about my brother?"

Sawyer's gaze lightened. "Grady is staying here with you. He put up a fight to be there, so I used you as an excuse to keep him from going. Told him you needed protection and my best men would be with me. He wasn't happy, but he agreed."

"Why don't you want him there? This is about him, after all." I frowned.

"I don't want him anywhere near Jefferson. We're not giving that bastard a chance to pull a damn Solomon deal. He's the kind of asshole who'd think it was funnier than shit to split him down the middle." His steady gaze told me his grim words weren't an exaggeration.

Okay, I might have flinched at that.

"You'll have to watch each other's backs. Men I can trust for the serious stuff are spread thin right now; most of them will be with me. There'll be one with Grady when he shows up later. Name's Clay. He doesn't talk much, but he knows his way around a gun. You'll be safe with him and Grady here." He lowered his hands back to my legs. This time he slid them underneath and pulled me closer.

"Well, looky here, we're all through talking with plenty of time to calm my nerves before the boys show up and I have to leave." He winked.

"You're nervous?" I raised an eyebrow in disbelief. I wasn't ready to drop our talk about the meeting, and he wanted to play.

"I'm about to face a *fucking drug lord*. Of course I'm nervous." His slanted smile gave him a wicked look. The tightening of his hands was the only warning as he shot to his feet. I tightened my arms around his neck and my ankles automatically locked in the small of his back. His strength would never stop amazing me.

"Very funny. Now put me down. I'm serious. What do you mean 'the serious stuff'? There has to be more to the meeting. How are you going to convince him to leave Grady alone?" The more he ignored my questions, the more heated I was getting. And not in the way he wanted.

"Now you're hurting my feelings. I need comfort and you think I'm funny." He jerked his hands out from under my legs. The sudden loss of support had me squealing and wrapping around his body even tighter. He grabbed hold again, only this time he filled his hands with my butt cheeks.

When I was sure I wasn't going to fall, I peeked through my lashes at his face. "You're an asshole."

"Oh, princess. You're going to be paying for that one." He took off running for his bedroom, making sure the trip was extra rough so I clung tighter and couldn't hold the laughter in.

A playful Sawyer was a rare creature, and irresistible beyond the limits of what the law should allow.

CHAPTER TWENTY-NINE

Sawyer

I STOOD at the edge of the abandoned campgrounds and looked out over the lake. This close to the head, it was more river than a wide expanse of water. There were still a few hours of light left, but the sun was low enough in the sky to start throwing color on the scattered clouds. Purple bled into pink before turning into a blazing orange at the horizon. Kelli would love the shit out of this show. I wasn't immune to the spectacle, but it wasn't the kind of shit I usually wasted time on. The woman was turning me into a pussy.

I'd picked this spot for two reasons: isolation and famil- iarity. If things went wrong, it was always good to have home-court advantage. I'd been suspicious as hell when Jefferson let me have it.

Arriving early with several of my men gave us time to search the area for any surprises he might have planned. Just because his home base was in St. Louis didn't mean he lacked contacts that could set up a *screw you* welcome. I hadn't really expected to find anything, but being a distrustful bastard made me cautious by nature.

The muted roar of more than one powerful engine pulled my attention back to business. Turning away from the water, I watched the opening in the woods where the vehicles would enter. I didn't bother checking to make sure my guys were out of sight. This wasn't the first meet-and-greet for any of them. They knew their jobs and were good at them.

Two black Suburbans with blacked-out windows crawled out of the woods and came to a stop thirty feet back from where I stood. There was no movement for a good five minutes before four men exited the rear SUV. Each was armed with what appeared to be M16s. They fanned out around the front car, scanning the area. Only when they were in place did the man I'd come to see emerged.

Jefferson wasn't anything I would've expected. The thirty-something had a crazy Hawaiian shirt on over board shorts, his feet covered by some big-ass gold tennis shoes. He would have been at home on a beach with his tanned skin and the Corona he carried in one hand. He even had a messy man bun to complete the picture of an uncomplicated dude chilling his way through life. In this setting, he just looked like a moron. If the image he projected was to get me to relax my guard he'd wasted his time. Morons didn't run a drug business with the reach and power behind it this one had.

The boss man started strolling my way, keeping to the center of his bodyguards. When he was about ten feet away, he threw his arms out in greeting. "Hell of a place! Just look at that fuckin' sunset." He winked at me. "You're rockin' it on our first date, bro."

I didn't bother returning the goofy smile plastered across Jefferson's face. "You normally bring chaperons with you on dates, Jefferson?"

"What, these guys? They're just window dressing. Hell, I figure you've probably got at least two more than what I brought, and they've all got their guns sighted on me and my friends. Right? Am I right?"

"Everybody keeps their hands to themselves and you leave here still breathing." I saw no reason to lie to Jefferson. We'd both shown up expecting the other to have backup. I was willing to bet Jefferson had more than a driver waiting in the lead Suburban.

"That's cool, that's cool. I feel ya, bro." Jefferson took a long pull at his beer then tossed the empty off to the left and slightly behind me. "Shit, man. Sorry, sorry. I come to your party and I start trashing your pad. Jerry, don't be a pig. Run over there and grab that bottle."

As one of the gun-toting chaperons went to move forward, I slid a hand around to the middle of my back. I grasped the handle of the Glock 19 tucked into the waistband of my jeans but didn't remove it.

"That's close enough." The hard edge in my command had Jerry coming to a halt after only two steps. I didn't take my hand off the pistol's grip as I said, "Don't worry about the mess. It's going to be a hell of a lot easier for the cleanup crew to pick up that bottle after you leave than what's left of Jerry if he takes one more step."

Jefferson started laughing as if I'd said some funny shit. He motioned for Jerry to return to his previous spot. "Get back over here, you knucklehead." Jerry didn't say anything, just backed up the same two steps he'd moved forward.

Jefferson's laughter died, but he was still grinning at me

when he shrugged. "Hey, can't blame a dude for checking boundary lines. Right? Am I right?"

Easing my hand away from the gun, I slid it into my back pocket, keeping the Glock within easy reach. "Boundaries are exactly why we're here, Jefferson. One of your people took a fuckin' running jump across the line into the middle of my business."

He slapped his hands together. "Look, call me Tommy. All my friends call me Tommy. I really want us to be friends because we've got a situation we need to straighten out." He gave a solemn nod.

No doubt his laid-back dude act had served him well in the past. The *hey, bro, let's be buddies* wasn't working for me, though. I'd done my homework on this motherfucker, and he was one ruthless piece of shit.

"Only situation we have here, *Tommy*, was carried out by one of yours, Andrew Webber. He poached one of my guys and put him to work for you. In the interest of staying out of each other's business, I'm willing to give you a chance to straighten this out before I handle it my way."

"Now, see? Right there is why I think we're going to be tight. You're willing to be reasonable. I've heard about you, you know?" Jefferson made a really good show of being impressed.

"You don't take shit off nobody. They move in on your business interest...BAM! You clean that shit up. But you're smart about it. Now, you claim one of my guys screwed up." Jefferson shook his head, frowning deeply to show his disappointment. Then, just as quickly, he beamed a toothy grin. "But like I said, you're smart. You contact me. That gives us a chance to work together to figure this out.

"This is how I see it. You and I, we both have employees. Pains in the ass. Right? Am I right?" Jefferson paused as he looked at the men surrounding him. "Course, I don't mean you guys, 'cause you're the best. Dudes, you're awesome!" He did a fist pump, turned back to me, and mouthed *not that one* while tipping his chin in Jerry's direction. He drew tiny circles in the air close to his temple with his index finger.

I didn't crack a smile. Jefferson's antics and all the joking around in the world weren't going to change the fact I didn't like the man. When we'd set up this face-to-face, I'd hoped we'd come to an understanding that would avoid a lot of people getting killed. I was never a big talker, always more a believer in actions speaking louder than words. It usually worked to my advantage to let others run off at the lips. Right now, though, I would gladly blow this fucker's head off if it would shut him up.

"Okay, back to the ones that are pains in the ass." Jefferson heaved an exaggerated sigh. "Andy boy has become a big ol' boil on my left ass cheek." He slapped himself on the ass. The man was big on giving visuals.

"Thing is, I didn't realize how big a pus-head he'd become until you contacted me. Made me do some checking into the only part of my operation that had the potential to bump up against yours. It's embarrassing as hell to admit, bro, but I've relied on my reputation to keep people in line. After all, that's why we build one. To let people know what to expect if they step out of line. Easier on everyone. Being comfortable and all, I've been letting things slip that wouldn't have gotten by me a few years ago. Turns out I've got to do some house cleaning. Thing is, *friend*... so do you. As a show of good faith, and in the hopes of establishing a possible working relationship, I've brought you a gift."

What the hell was Jefferson playing at? I watched as he raised one of his arms in the air and flapped a lazy hand in a beckoning motion. It must have been the signal the men in the first Suburban had been waiting for. Both back doors opened and two more gunmen emerged. After one of them exited the SUV, he reached back inside and pulled a man out who had a hood over his head and his arms tied behind his back.

I moved my hand from my pocket and tightened on the handle of the pistol once more. I didn't want to pull it unless absolutely necessary. Drawing the gun would signal my men that things had gone to shit and to start shooting.

"Who the hell is that?" I kept my voice level.

Whoever was behind the mask froze at hearing my words then struggled against the hand clamped to his upper arm. Frantic, unintelligible sounds erupted from deep within the cloth sack. A gun barrel pressed against his head put a stop to both the struggles and the noise. The prisoner was jerked to a stop next to Jefferson, and a swift kick to the back of his knees had him dropping to the ground.

"This is just a little something from me to show I'm willing to believe that you're not a part of what's happening within your organization." Jefferson wagged a finger in my direction. "Bro, you're going to be as embarrassed as me when I tell you what two of our more stupid employees have been getting up to.

"Now, stupid in an employee isn't always a bad thing." He did a little nod in Jerry's direction, then winked. "But stupid and ambitious is just annoying enough to be dangerous. Right? Am I right?"

I ignored the man on his knees and kept my eyes trained on Jefferson. For all I knew, the bound man could simply be a distraction to get me to drop my guard. If that was one of my men, tied and hooded, Jefferson better have a damn good reason for doing so. "Are you claiming one of my men has been dealing meth on the side? If that's what's going on here why are you bringing him back to me? I've heard about you, too. Not your style to leave anyone alive when they screw with you."

Jefferson spread his hands and shrugged his shoulders. "Let's be honest with each other. This part of the state is pretty as hell, but I'm not going to make money selling product here. Any dude with access to YouTube and an empty Gatorade bottle is shakin' and bakin' that shit at home.

"All those regulations on allergy pills has pretty much shut down the mom-and-pop operators who used to cook the good stuff. It's getting hard as hell to get their hands on the right ingredients, and that right there is killing off an entire cottage industry." He was back to shaking his head as if saddened at the thought of all those good ol' mom-and-pop crystal cookers being run out of business.

"The smart money is in transporting and selling ephedrine and pseudoephedrine to major players. Only place you're going to get those kinds of customers are in the larger cities. That's where Andy comes in. Because of his daddy's car dealerships, he has access to an established and secure network to move items from Little Rock to St. Louis. Use a few of my customized trucks as transporters to move vehicles from lot to lot, and there you have it. A company that's been in business for years moving product, and other things"—he winked at me like we were fucking buddies sharing secrets—"safely in this little section of my operation."

"Mind getting to the part where any of this shit matters to me?" I said. "Your Andy still hijacked one of my men to work for you." Nothing he said came as news to me. Grady had told me much the same story. The only thing I cared about was finding a way to get Grady out of the drug business and keep Kelli safe.

"To get to the part where this shit matters to you brings us back to our pain-in-the-ass employees." The grin Jefferson flashed was filled with anticipation. The idiot looked like he actually thought I was going to get a kick out of what he was about to revel.

"While I don't want to dis on Grady's trap-building skills, I don't need him. I have my own guys to do all my custom work. But I'll tell you who does need him." Jefferson whipped the hood off the man kneeling beside him with all the flash of a magician unveiling a fantastical trick. "This asshole right here."

I'd been prepared to see one of my men under that hood. I didn't betray by so much as a flicker of an eyelid my surprise at seeing Andrew Webber. I said nothing as I took in the beaten and swollen face of the man in front of me. Looked like Jefferson had asked his partner a few questions. Andrew blinked the one eye that wasn't swollen shut, adjusting to suddenly regaining his sight. When Andrew's panicked gaze landed on me, I was surprised to see hope lighting his busted-up face. Why the fucker would be glad to see me was a mystery. We both knew he was a dead man.

"That's it? You're just going to have a staring contest with him?" Jefferson was clearly disappointed in my reaction, or lack of one.

"I'm still waiting for the part where any of this shit matters to me." My voice came out as cold as the ice taking over my stomach.

Jefferson looked a little more satisfied after he heard the unmistakable threat of *someone's about to die* in my voice. Why he was confident that *someone* wasn't going to be him probably had to do with his hints that one of my men was screwing me over.

"Hang with me here a little longer, bro." Jefferson

patted the air in front of him with both hands. He used one of those placating hands to reach over and deliver a slap to the back of Andrew's head.

"Took some persuading to get answers out of my boy Andy. Then again, not as much as others I've had *talks* with in the past." Jefferson's mouth twisted into an ugly sneer. His eyes narrowed in malicious glee. I was finally seeing the Jefferson I'd expected to meet.

"You're not going to fucking believe what he told me. It's like a damn soap opera." Jefferson was back to laughing, but there was a vicious edge to it now.

CHAPTER THIRTY

Kelli

THE MAN PLAYED DIRTY. I had to admit that he made dirty feel really good, though. I'd been angry at him for not discussing the meeting in more detail. By the time he'd finished smothering my flames with his blanket of passion, the only thing I fought was sleep. That had been a losing battle. He'd more than made good on the only plans he'd been willing to talk about. Those he'd followed to the letter once he got me to the bedroom.

Waking to an empty bed cured the sappy, lovesick smile I'd gone to sleep with. I dragged one of the twisted sheets off the bed, wrapped it around my body toga style, and went in search of Sawyer. My mood went further south after my search turned up nothing but an empty house. Surprise! He'd left without leaving a note. We seriously needed to work on his communication skills. I grabbed my phone to call his cell, but it went unanswered. As did the text I sent.

I broke a personal best getting dressed. Not bothering to hunt for clean clothes, I pulled on the ones he'd peeled off me hours earlier. In the bathroom, I made do with a smear of lip gloss, finger-combing my hair before pulling it into a high ponytail. My, how I'd changed since moving here.

I wondered where my brother was. If he wasn't here, did that mean he'd gone to the meeting after all? See? This was why we should have discussed the plans more. We could have made a Plan B if something happened and Plan A had to be scrapped. As I marched out of the house, I began to punch in Grady's number. If he didn't answer, I'd head over to Skeeter's. I'd rather be working than sitting around the house worrying.

My Plan B was squashed after jogging down the steps and seeing the trucks parked on either side of my car. Grady and Wade sat inside my brother's truck, staring at me. I had a feeling they'd been there for a while. Grady pulled out his phone as I watched, checked the screen, and rejected the call. Sawyer got bonus points for having them watch over me from outside the house. The embarrassment could have been worse. My brother could have been inside when I'd traipsed out of the bedroom wrapped in a sheet.

Both men climbed out of the truck and strolled over to where I'd come to a halt. Great, I wasn't the only one feeling weird. Grady's eyes skittered around the empty yard, searching for anything to fasten on besides me.

Wade didn't have any problems letting his eyes do some roving over my figure. I didn't like the smile that slowly spread across his face. He winked as he asked, "Nice nap?"

"Shut the hell up." Grady curled his hands into fists. If he'd seen how the man had checked me out, those fists would already be flying.

"Whoa... hold up there. Just having a little fun. I didn't mean nothing by it." Wade held up a hand and took a step back from Grady. He looked over at me and said, "I'm real sorry if I made you feel uncomfortable, miss."

I was willing to believe he meant what he said. He was used to a different type of female sharing a bed with Sawyer. No doubt Marilee would've giggled and invited him in to take another *nap*. Grady waited to see if I was satisfied with Wade's words or if he needed to beat some respect into the other man. I didn't want him starting a fight on account of me. But having him act all big brotherly was still new enough to give me warm fuzzies.

"It's already forgotten," I dismissed the incident, more interested in why he was here. "What's going on, Wade? Sawyer told me to expect a man named Clay. Did something happen?"

"You'd have to ask your boyfriend. I do what I'm told and keep my mouth shut." He shrugged, but an emotion crossed his face that made me wonder if his talk with Sawyer last Tuesday hadn't worked out the way he'd hoped.

"Where you headed in such a hurry?" Grady's question dragged my attention back to him.

"To Skeeter's. I didn't want to stay here alone. Work will make the time pass faster." I gave him a smile. "We could all go there to wait."

"Give it up. Wade said Sawyer wanted you here, and I agree with him." Grady headed for the house, not giving me a chance to plead my case.

I followed in his wake at a slower pace, and Wade trailed behind me. Sawyer was slick. He knew the one person I wouldn't fight was my brother.

* * *

KELLI

IN THE LAST hour I must've checked my watch a dozen times, but that didn't stop me from checking it again. The meeting should be starting about now, *if* everyone had shown. Not knowing what was going on had to be killing my brother. After all, it was his life being decided while he was here keeping me safe.

Wade didn't seem too concerned about anyone being in danger. He'd been flicking through the channels on the TV while Grady kept watch out one of the windows. I stood at the other. The only sign he was restless was the way he kept checking his watch. Talk had been mostly nonexistent. The only sound in the room came from the TV.

Staring out the window, I admired the colors painting the sky. The spectacular sunset made me wondered if Sawyer ever took the time to notice such things. There was so much about him I didn't know. When I'd first seen this place, I couldn't picture him living here. I'd only been here a few days, but I still had a hard time understanding why he would choose this house. He didn't seem to have any emotional attachment to it. When I asked, he'd muttered something about it being an investment.

I loved it. It was so different from the magazine-perfect mansion I'd grown up in. It could be homey if Sawyer ever took the time to add the touches needed. Maybe he'd let me change a few things to make it more welcoming. It was a house that deserved a family with lots of kids to play in its big yard.

I studied the wide porch that begged for huge pots of flowers to add life to the broad expanse of bare space. Growing up, I'd never hung out with the gardeners hired by Jackson to keep his lawns immaculate. How to grow anything was a complete mystery to me. That didn't stop me from picturing beds filled with blooms decorating the yard. Thinking of flowers reminded me of the two tiny pots of mums on Zane's small deck. Bet she'd know what kind of flowers we could plant. If she ever talked to me again.

I hadn't seen her since Tuesday night because Sawyer wouldn't let me go back to work after moving in with him. He'd said until the Jefferson and Andrew situation was handled, he wasn't taking any chances. Zane and I had talked on the phone a few times, but it'd been awkward. She knew I was hiding something and she was starting to get mad. More than mad—she'd sounded hurt the last time we'd spoken.

"Hey, Kelli? Sawyer got anything to drink around here 'sides water?" Wade shifted his gaze from the TV to me.

"Yes, there's sweet tea, some beer, and a few different kinds of pop." I'd already mentioned all of this earlier. We might be in a stressful situation, but Southern Hospitality demanded refreshments be offered. Both men had declined at the time.

"I'll take a beer." He went back to flipping channels. I narrowed my eyes. Hospitality was one thing, but being treated as if I was his waitress was something else.

Grady turned from the window and caught my glare. It was the first time he'd smiled all night. "I could use a beer myself. I'll go get them."

"Oh, no. I wouldn't think of it. Let me see if I can find a tray in the kitchen to carry them out on." I straightened from the wall.

Grady barked out a laugh, but the sarcasm went over Wade's head. "Nope, bet I manage just fine without a tray."

He took off for the back of the house where the kitchen was located. Open floor plans were all the rage, but I loved the intimacy that came with smaller rooms. I went back to staring out the window. Footsteps coming my way had me turning around to find a gun aimed at the middle of my stomach. For a first reaction, mine was pretty lame.

"Wade, if you're going to play with your gun, take it outside." My voice was sharp.

"Well, darlin', that's the dumbest thing to ever come out of someone's mouth when they had a gun pointed at them." His grin confused me. Was he playing around? If he was, I didn't like the game.

"Are you crazy? This is how people get shot." Grady would be in the room soon, and he would go ballistic if he walked in on this.

"It sure as hell is. So don't move and nobody gets shot." The grin dropped, and hate filled his eyes.

Not moving wasn't a problem. If he'd *asked* me to move, *that* would have been a problem. My body had turned to stone.

"You're not so high class now, are you, bitch?" He moved close enough that his sour breath slapped me in the face. "If you don't do what I say, I'll kill you and then Grady."

Grady. I had to warn him. My eyes or my face gave me away. Wade saw my intent. He shoved the barrel of his gun against my mouth before I could open it to scream. The skin on my lips split and the pain of the metal grinding them against my teeth turned my knees to liquid. Before they buckled, he had a vicious grip on my upper arm and had transferred the barrel to my temple.

"Damn, where's all that smart I keep hearing you have? Do as you're told and you both come out of this alive. Understand?" He wiggled the gun to highlight his point.

Before I could reply, Grady strolled into the room.

"Took forever to find a bottle ope— What the fuck are you doing?"

Bottles hit the hardwood, beer gurgling as they emptied. Fear sank razor teeth into my heart and shook its head viciously. I'd just found my brother; I couldn't lose him now.

"You want your sister to live, you'll sit down and keep your mouth shut," Wade threatened. The metal pressed to my temple ground in harder. I controlled the grimace but there was nothing I could do about the blood trailing from my lips.

"Hurt her one more time and you're sure as hell gonna have to kill me." Grady's rage was barely contained. His body vibrated with tension.

"Please, Grady. It's worse than it looks. Just do what he says." I was terrified Wade would attack Grady at the first opportunity.

"I said sit down and shut the hell up." Wade's grip on my arm couldn't hide the tremors in his fingers. Grady wasn't the only one vibrating with tension.

He moved to the couch, his eyes hooded and locked on Wade. "What now?" His voice was so rough and gravelly it sounded as if it hurt to talk.

"Now we wait." The gun barrel didn't ease one bit.

* * *

KELLI

TIME PASSED SLOWLY when you had a gun pressed to your head. It didn't help not knowing what we were waiting for. Grady sat hunched forward on the edge of the couch, his left leg bouncing and his fists clenching and relaxing on top of his thighs. His heated gaze never left Wade. He'd given up trying to talk to him a long time ago.

Wade had moved us to the wall across from Grady. He leaned against it and I was caught in his arms, the barrel of the gun now digging into my side, our stance a cruel parody of the way Sawyer had held me at the Dog House.

Blood oozed from my lips and dripped off my jaw. The gun had caught me on the right side of my mouth and not dead center. My teeth ached but I still had them. Small things. Zane had said that to me once. When I'd asked what she meant, she'd said, "Be grateful for the small things".

The sound of a car pulling up had Wade straightening from the wall and looking out the window. Whatever he saw made the taut cords in his arms relax.

"About damn time." He moved us to the center of the room to wait for whoever had arrived.

When the door opened and Mason Webber walked through, I wasn't entirely surprised. I cut my eyes to my brother; the look on his face said he certainly hadn't been.

Mason zeroed in on me. He tapped the gun he held against his forehead in salute. "Hello, bitch."

Wade didn't give him a chance to exchange any more pleasantries. "What the hell, man? I expected you an hour ago."

"I don't jump when you say frog. You say Andrew's missing, you think Jefferson has him and I'm supposed to take your word? I had to do some checking." Mason lost his sneer for a second. "We both know my brother's a dead man. Nothing I can do about it but save my own ass."

"We need to get out of here and finish this. We're in Sawyer's damn house. We do not want to be here when he gets back." For the first time, Wade sounded worried.

"You think I'm scared of that bastard? Fuck him. We've got plenty of time. Jefferson loves the sound of his own voice. He'll keep dickhead locked down for hours with his dumbass chatter. I intend to get a piece of this bitch before we leave." Mason stuck his tongue out at me and gave it a lewd wiggle.

Grady exploded off the couch, fist drawn back. Mason fired into the floor at Grady's feet, freezing him in place. "Next one goes in you." Then he smirked at me. "Or maybe her. You I need. She's disposable."

"Touch her, and like I told Wade, you'll have to kill me. I'll do whatever you want as long as you leave her out of it." Fury painted Grady's face red. His chest heaved with the intensity of his hate.

"You'll do whatever I want anyway because you want to keep her alive. In the end, I don't think it's going to matter what condition she's in as long as she's alive." Mason taunted Grady by grabbing one of my breasts and giving it a vicious twist. I refused to scream but couldn't control the whimper.

"What the hell, Kelli? You don't have time for me, but you can throw a damn party—"

Zane marched through the door furious and ready to give me a piece of her mind. She faltered to a stop. We'd frozen at her appearance. The bizarre scene in front of her took half a beat to process. When what she was seeing sank in, she summed it up nicely: "Fucking. Hell."

Mason swung his gun on Zane. I believed he had every intention of shooting her, but Wade pushed both of us in front of the gun. Since he held me in front of him, he probably figured he'd live if Mason pulled the trigger.

Grady unfroze the quickest, lunging at Mason. Mason twisted before he could get to him, and the gun ended up centered in the middle of his chest. Zane was still where she'd come to a halt. I wanted to scream at her to run but knew she'd never leave us.

"Would everyone just take a breath for one damn minute?" Wade sounded at the end of his rope. "Grady, are you trying to get Kelli killed? Because I'm not moving this gun. I will kill her. I'm kinda out of options here, and if anyone is gonna die, she's first on the list.

"And you." Wade glared at Mason. "You arrogant moron. You're not killing Zanie Mae. She's has nothing to do with any of this. We stick her in the cellar where she's not a problem. Sawyer is going to know who did this and he is going to be after our asses. Jefferson has your brother, and that bastard is spilling his guts, so Jefferson is going to be after our asses, too.

"I let your brother fill my head with bullshit and now I'm trying to get out alive. You are not going to fuck this up for me. We leave now, or I end it right here. I kill her"— Wade wiggled the gun in my side—"and Grady dies trying to kill both of us. You can't use him if he's dead. So make up your mind."

Wade would kill me, I had no doubt, but he was protecting Zane. Small things.

"I won't forget this, asshole." Mason's mouth stretched in a hideous smile. "Where's the cellar? I'll dump your girlfriend's ass and we can get out of here."

"No way. We're all going." Wade narrowed his eyes at Mason. Then he turned to Zane and softened his voice. "Honey, I'm sorry you got tangled up in this. Nothing for it now—you've got to do what I tell you. Things have gone too far, I can't never come back from them. I *will* kill your friend if you don't listen to me."

Zane studied my bloody mouth and the way Wade's fingers were bone white from gripping my arm. When her glare got to the gun pushed into my side, she bit her lip and nodded.

"You know where it's at, honey. Head on outside." Wade pushed me toward Zane and the front door. I was the means to control everyone, and my stomach rolled with sickness and regret.

"You heard him. Move it." Mason waved his gun at Grady.

We trooped through the dark, guided by the light escaping through the windows. The cellar was located under one of those windows. I wanted to grab Zane and not let go. Not for me, for her.

"Open 'er up." Mason used the gun pointed at Grady and flicked it toward the double doors angled between the house and the ground.

Grady hesitated, his body stiff when he finally reached down to lift first one side and then the other. The opening revealed steps leading to the underground vault. The darkness was terrifying.

"Damn it, Wade, you can't make her go down there alone," Grady said. "Send Kelli with her. I'll do whatever you want. It doesn't matter what it is, I'll do it. Just let Kelli stay with her."

"Wade don't have a say in this, asshole. I'm giving him Zane. Kelli goes with us." Mason wanted us to know he was the one in charge.

Zane's teeth were chattering as she said, "He's gonna kill you, Wade. You and Mason. Let us go and I'll talk to Sawyer for you."

"Either get her ass down those steps or she's dead. I'm through wasting time on this sobby shit." Mason turned his gun on Zane again.

Zane stiffened her back. "Fuck you, Mason." She turned to Wade. "You too, asshole."

I held my breath as Wade squeezed my arm until I thought the bone was going to snap. "Please, Wade, don't send her down there." He didn't so much as blink as I begged.

As she went to walk past Grady, he snapped, "Wait." He reached to grab the back of his shirt, jerked it over his head, and held it out to her. "Put this on. It's not much, but it should help a little bit."

"No way." Mason went to snag the shirt from Grady's hands, but Wade growled at him, "Let her have the damn shirt and let's get out of here."

The last I saw of Zane was her clutching the shirt to her chest as the doors closed her into the darkness.

CHAPTER THIRTY-ONE

Sawyer

MY PATIENCE WAS THREAD-THIN. Jefferson was enjoying the moment and not in a hurry to bring it to an end. An urgency had taken hold. It told me shit was happening right the hell now and I needed to be there.

"This piss-ant has been going around telling my suppliers, and select customers, he was my partner," Jefferson said. "Not one of those customers or suppliers thought to come to me and question anything said in my name."

Jefferson got a thoughtful look on his face. "Huh. If I think about it that way, my reputation worked too well. Those dudes were afraid not to follow Andrew's instructions because they thought they'd offend me."

I didn't have time for this shit. Jefferson could go brag to Jerry about his greatness. He paid the guy to listen to him. All the money in the world couldn't get me to hang here one more minute than necessary. My guts were screaming that I had to move. "Give me the damn name. That's all I care about. You say Grady is in the clear. Great. Andrew is your embarrassment and I don't give a shit how you handle it. Give me a name and I'll handle my embarrassment."

I knew the name but needed it confirmed. It'd been staring me in the face for months. I'd been arrogant enough to believe one of my own wouldn't betray me. Not someone I'd known all my life. It was Wade. He hadn't shown with the rest of my men this afternoon. By the time I'd gotten here, it'd been too late to track him down. But I knew.

"I'm getting to the fucking good parts." Jefferson's laid-back demeanor slipped. He didn't like having someone call him on his bullshit. His guards caught the shift in mood. Shoulders got straighter, feet shuffled to a wider stance, and hands tightened on their rifles. "I brought you a fucking gift. Yeah, it's your party, but I'm not leaving until I get a fucking party favor."

"I'll give you a fucking party favor," I said. "The name you're hanging on to is Wade Hobson. And you're not here to bring me a damn present. You're here to add me to your list of piss-ants. You put on this big show of how you're my bro and I'm supposed to suck your dick for coming to my rescue." I placed my hand back on the handle of my Glock. This party had a really good chance of ending in fireworks. "Well, keep your pants zipped."

"Your party favor sucks. When do you get to the part where any of this shit matters to me?" Jefferson sounded like a kid pouting.

"Who the hell knows how long it would've taken you to figure out what was going on with Webber if it wasn't for me?" I said. "But after checking into what he was up to, you got to thinking he was onto something. You got to thinking adding my contacts would be productive. What none of you numb-nuts considered is my delivery routes are worthless to you, to them, to anyone who is trying to push anything but booze. Any motherfucker willing to move crystal is already doing it. It's like you said. They're shakin' and bakin' the shit out of it and they ain't interested in your high-grade crap." I needed out of here and I needed out of here fast.

"Sonofabitch, see? I knew I was going to fucking like you." The stupid asshole was grinning at me again. His damn mood changed faster than a woman PMSing. "So, you ain't gonna suck my dick, huh?" Jefferson looked over at Jerry. "Guess you're not getting a night off after all."

If any of his guards thought he was funny, they didn't laugh.

"Yeah, we're fucking BFFs. You need to get the hell out of here. Party's over." I braced to see if he was going to do another one-eighty and order his men to kill me.

"You heard him, boys. Load up the piss-ant. And put him in the other car. That dude stinks. I need a beer. Jerry, you knucklehead, did you forget to bring the beer?" And, that quickly, it was over. Two of his guards watched me while Jefferson and the other two headed back to the lead Suburban.

Jefferson was standing on the running board when he shouted over to me, "Hey, dude. You see Andrew after tonight? Don't ghost his ass. I still need his routes and I think he's learned his lesson." He gave me a wink. "You see his brother Mason, though? Kill him, would ya? I've always hated the arrogant little shit."

The door closed and the same two who'd hauled Andrew out jerked him up and dragged him to the rear

SUV. The two remaining men turned and headed for the trucks. When they were even with the one Jefferson was in, the door popped open and he stuck his head back out. "Hey, I forgot. Don't bother looking for those two dudes who were helping Andy haul trucks out to Grady's garage. Jerry made sure they're enjoying a permanent vacation in hell." When he ducked back inside, his laughter could be heard through the closed door.

By the time the engines roared to life, I had my phone in my hand. There was a text and a missed call from Kelli. They did nothing to lessen the darkness threatening to swallow me whole. The text said, *Where are you?* She hadn't left a voice message. My call to her phone went unanswered. Clay was next on my call list. I ran for the truck as his phone kept ringing.

Vernon and Willis reached the truck the same time I did. "Tell the guys to split up. Two go to Clay's place and two to Wade's."

While they loped off to hand out instructions, I called the one man I would always be able to trust to hold the light for me. I wasn't a man for prayer, but I breathed a thank you when he picked up.

"Hey, Sawyer," Jase answered. "Where the hell you at? Evan talked me into coming out to Skeeter's and your ass isn't here." The background noise feeding through the phone confirmed his whereabouts.

"Calling in a favor, Rydan. I'm about ninety minutes out. Need you to get to my house and check on Kelli and Grady. If you don't have any guns on you, tell Charlie to give you my special reserve. He'll know what you're talking about." I didn't have time to go into details, and Jase didn't need them.

"We can be there in fifteen. I'll call soon as we know anything." The line went dead.

* * *

KELLI

THE DRIVE TO THE CHEVY/GMC dealership was uneventful. If you didn't count the gun sticking in my side as I drove Wade's truck. We'd split up at the house and Grady had driven Mason's Denali. The dealership was on the outskirts of town. Not isolated, but certainly not in the middle of the action. Once here, we'd driven around back to a fenced lot and straight through its open gates. There were several trucks with Webber logos on them, and we'd parked at the end of the row.

I stood in front of Wade, his gun pressed to the middle of my back. He'd been careful to keep me between him and Mason ever since he'd challenged him over Zane. The thought of her left underground in the cold and dark made me want to throw up. Silently repeating, *She's safe,* over and over didn't lessen the pain of leaving her there.

Mason and Grady had been arguing for the last five minutes over how to get in a truck. Well, Mason was arguing. Grady had been stoic ever since Wade and I had joined them beside the hauler.

"Unless you have the keys, the only way to get to the electronics is to get inside the truck. To do that, without the keys, you have to break a window," Grady explained slowly to Mason as if he were a five-year-old.

"Break the damn window, then." Mason wasn't as quiet as you'd think someone breaking into trucks would be. It didn't matter if they belonged to his dad. What was hidden in them should have elicited some caution. I didn't really care how loud he got. Maybe someone would hear us back here and come to investigate. Not sure who, since the lot backed up to an open pasture dotted with trees.

"I can't break a truck window with my bare hands." Again, the talking-to-a-child tone from Grady.

"Damn it, we can't hang around all night," Wade yelled at Mason. "You screwed around so long getting to Sawyer's, we're running out of time here, asshole."

"Shut up. Everyone, shut the hell up." Mason slammed the back of the heavy-duty flashlight he held into the driver's-side window. It sounded like a grenade going off. He reached inside and flipped the locks. "You're in the truck. Now open the traps."

"I'll need something sharp to cut and strip the wires." Grady stood with a hand out.

It was as if a light came on in my brain. My brother was stalling. Ever since we'd gotten here, he'd done whatever it took to waste time. Time for Sawyer to make it back to the house. Time for Zane to tell him who we were with.

"You think I'm stupid or something? I'm not giving you a knife," Mason sneered.

Grady shrugged. "You got the 'or something' right, but I still can't do it without a knife. Wade has a gun on my sister. I'm not going to do anything to get her killed. It's simple, if you think about it. I'm not getting into a gunfight with a pocket knife."

Wade's arm swung beside me and a small knife landed on the ground at Grady's feet. "Let him have the damn knife. He's not going to get his sister killed."

"I'm damn tired of you trying to run the show tonight." Mason might not like it, but he didn't say anything when Grady picked up the knife.

Knife in hand, Grady crouched in front of the driver's seat. He glanced up at Mason. "You're gonna have to shine the light under here."

Mason didn't argue for once, and held the light for my brother as he worked. In no time the truck was running, and he crawled back out. He stood beside the open door and stared at Mason.

"What the hell are you waiting for? Run the damn sequence." Mason ordered.

CHAPTER THIRTY-TWO

Sawyer

I'D CUT twenty minutes off the ninety-minute drive getting back to town. Jase had called to let me know they'd found Zane locked in the cellar. It was Zane who pointed us in the direction we needed to head next. I pulled into the back parking lot of the First Baptist and stopped beside Evan's white Silverado. The truck was empty, but I'd expected it to be. Jase was at the dealership already and Evan was back at my place with Zane. Vernon and Willis joined me at the front of my pickup.

"Remember, Jase is on the lot somewhere," I said. "Make sure you know who you're shooting before you pull the damn trigger. We're cutting in behind the building to the fenced lot. Once we're in, shouldn't be too hard to find them. If you can get to Wade or Mason without shooting, do it. Gunshots are going to be noticed this close to town."

Vernon and Willis nodded. I headed for the highway

and we jogged across. There was no way to hide our approach—if they were there in the back, it wouldn't matter. I didn't stop moving until we hit the corner of the building closest to the fenced area.

Jase leaned against the block wall, hidden in the building's shadow. The security light's glow didn't reach around the corner to where he stood. His whisper carried through the shadows, "I haven't gone any closer. Didn't need to. They're making enough noise I could keep track of them from here."

I held my hand up and we all went still. Loud arguing and the sound of busting glass came from deeper in the lot. It gave us a direction to move in. "Vernon, you and Willis fan out on the left," I pointed in the direction I wanted them to head. "Jase and I are taking the right. We ain't got time for fancy shit. We're going through the gate. There's only two of them and they're all going to be together. Make it fast—get out of the light and behind some cover. Once we get there, be ready for anything."

Vernon and Willis took off in a silent run. The light exposed them for less than a minute as they slipped through the gate. They disappeared into the rows of vehicles. I strained to hear any sounds they might make that would give away their approach. All I could hear was the racket coming from Wade's group. He better hope Kelli didn't have a mark on her when I got her back.

"You ready for this?" I glanced over at Jase.

"I didn't expect to be doing this kind of shit with you again." Jase's faint laugh was grim.

"You and me both."

We took off running at the same time.

* * *

KELLI

"I TOLD you I didn't put the traps in this one. I don't know what electrical sequence was installed." Grady stood by the open door of another truck. This one had a flatbed in place of the normal pickup bed found on the rest of the trucks in the lot.

"Then figure it out," Mason yelled at him.

The longer we'd been here, the more agitated Wade had become. "We've got enough shit from Andrew's trucks," he kicked one of the three duffels at our feet. "We need to get our asses out of here. How the hell do you even know this is one of Jefferson's transporters?"

"Because, asshole, my brother's flatbed car haulers are white, Jefferson uses black. This look white to you?" Mason sneered as he jerked a thumb over his shoulder at the black cab of the truck. "We're not leaving until I find out what that bastard hid in this one."

He dropped the light he'd been using to bust windows and moved to where Wade and I stood. He jerked me away from Wade, my back hitting his chest. He slipped an arm around my waist and stuck the gun under my chin.

Wade didn't fight to keep me, and panic flared. It was funny how you could get used to the same person holding a gun on you. You didn't really relax, but you started believing they might not kill you after all if they hadn't done it by now. Let a new person take control and the original terror returned.

Grady went stiff. He realized the level of threat had escalated.

Mason rested his chin on my shoulder. "Figure out the damn sequence or you can watch me put bullets in this

bitch. There are lots of places I can shoot and not kill her."
He pulled up one of my arms and waved it at my brother.
"How about I start with her hand?"

"You're going to fucking die." Grady turned back to the
truck and reached inside. The hood made a popping
sound. He stomped to the light on the ground and snagged
it before jogging to the front of the truck, where he
finished raising the hood.

He used the front bumper as a step to give him the
height needed to lean over the side of the engine compartment then yelled, "Wade, get over here. You're gonna have
to hold the light while I trace the wires in the electrical
harness."

Wade had backed away from the three of us. I expected
him to cut his losses and make a run for it. The intent was
there in his body language. We all held our breaths as he
made up his mind. But greed won out and he moved to
Grady's side.

Minutes ticked by. Grady muttered and barked at Wade
to shift the light to different spots as he worked.

"What the hell is taking so long?" Mason edged us
closer to get a look.

"I'm trying to figure out how many jumpers this guy
used, and which electrical components were added in the
fuse panel. He'd didn't leave a damn instruction manual for
me to follow, asshole." Grady glared over his shoulder at
Mason.

A few more minutes passed and the silent engine
rumbled awake. Grady hopped off the wheel, loped back to
the cab, and slid inside. Mason pushed me forward, but he
stopped when we could see what Grady was doing.

Grady mashed the brake, then reached for the seat
controls. The seat rose, lowered, and then moved back as

far as it could go. Last thing he did was turn the defroster on, and we all heard the faint click that said the circuit had been completed. I watched for some type of hydraulic to kick in and reveal the opening to the trap hidden in the cab. Nothing happened.

Mason wasn't happy. "Where the hell's the trap?"

Grady jumped out of the cab and moved to the back of the flatbed. A center row of lights was popped out of their normal frame. Behind them was a recessed box with a lever. Grady pulled the lever and the entire top of the flatbed began to rise. "There's your damn trap."

We all stared at the huge compartment that was revealed. What was inside had Mason dropping his hand from my waist. Even the hand holding the gun under my chin dropped to my side.

"Holy motherfucking shit," Mason said in awe.

Money. Stacks and stacks of money, all shrink-wrapped, filled the entire length of the compartment. There had to be hundreds of thousands of dollars.

"Oh, hell no. That shit belongs to Jefferson. There won't be a place on this planet you can hide if you touch one dollar of it." Wade backed away from the flatbed, shaking his head.

"You're not fucking walking away from this. With this much money, we can disappear to the point we were never born." Mason slung a hand in the money's direction. He no longer had that arm wrapped around me, but the gun stayed near my side.

I watched my brother as the two argued. Something had changed. His head was up, his muscles bunched, ready to attack.

"I'm through." Wade swung around to leave.

Mason pulled the gun from my side and aimed at Wade.

Grady made a leap for him, knocking me to the side. The explosion of a gun firing made me stumble back farther.

* * *

Sawyer

How the hell had Jase handled it when Char had been held at gunpoint? I was about to lose my fucking mind. We were two trucks away from the drama being played out at the flatbed. Jase had moved one truck over on my right side. I didn't know where Vernon and Willis were, only that they'd be close.

When it looked like Wade was going to make a run, I thought we'd caught a break. But he'd stayed. I wasn't about to go in guns blazing as long as Mason had the barrel of one stuck under Kelli's chin. Now Wade was getting ready to rabbit again and I took the chance to move closer. Mason was going to have his hands full controlling Kelli and Grady on his own. He'd need to figure out a way to do that and unload whatever the flatbed held. My best guess was that he'd kill them, which meant we were running out of time.

Grady's eyes locked on me. My movement had caught his attention. His whole body went on alert. I hoped to hell he didn't try something stupid. But if he was going to try anything, now would be the time to do it. Mason was arguing with Wade and his attention was split.

Suddenly Wade about-faced to take off. Mason jerked his gun up and pointed it at his back. It was the moment Grady needed. He charged Mason and pushed Kelli out of the way. I was already running to join the fight when Mason's gun went off. I watched as the bullet connected with Grady, punching him back, causing his head to connect with edge of the flatbed frame. Kelli's screams pierced the night as she crawled across the ground to get to him.

I slid to a stop, lifting the gun, and squeezing the trigger. The 9mm round entered the back of Mason's head and mushroomed out the front. He dropped where he stood. I twisted to get Wade in my sights, but the bastard had dropped his gun and stood with both hands in the air. Not wasting any more time, I broke into a run to get to my woman. I trusted Jase and the other guys to have my back.

"Grady. Oh God, Grady." She had him cradled in her arms, sobs racked her body. I knelt beside her and tried to pull Grady from her. She wasn't letting go.

"Princess, I need to see where he's hit. Let me help him." She nodded and loosened her hold, giving me a chance to tug him out of her grasp.

It wasn't hard to locate the wound. He didn't have a shirt, and the entry point streamed blood. I shifted him and the saw the exit hole, a through-and-through. One less worry. If he had to get shot, it wasn't a bad location. Mason had hit the fleshy part of Grady's shoulder. Seeing no air bubbles in the flow of blood had me hoping the bullet missed the lungs. The blow to the side of his head had me worried the longer he stayed unconscious. I started tugging on my shirt, but Kelli already had hers off and passed it to me to press against the torn flesh.

"Is he going to live?" Her tear drenched eyes searched my face.

"He's too stubborn to die." My assurance had her nodding in agreement, but the way she chewed her lower lip said she wasn't sure whether to believe me or not.

Jase squatted beside me. "Here, give this to her." He passed me his jacket and eased Grady out of my hold.

Pulling her up as I stood, I helped her slip on Jase's coat. Once she was buttoned up, I pulled back to examine her. Needed to make sure she was truly all right, and that's when I got an eyeful of her swollen and busted lips. The rage that had been banked came roaring back. I searched the area until Wade landed in my sights. Vernon and Willis had their guns on him. I gently eased Kelli behind me as I addressed Wade, "You're a fucking dead man."

Wade had been staring at the ground. At my words, he raised his head and the bastard smiled at me. It was a tired-to-the-soul kind of smile. "See. Now this Sawyer I know. He's been missing for so damn long, I thought he was gone forever."

"Lucky you. He showed up in time to bury your ass."

Kelli laid a hand on the arm holding the gun. "Sawyer. Please, not like this. Not when he's standing there without a gun." Her voice was still hitching from her tears. She moved until she stood in my peripheral. "He saved Zane, you know."

No, I hadn't known. I'd yet to get her part of the story.

"Mason was going to kill her and Wade stepped in front of his gun," she murmured as if trying to soothe me. She rubbed my arm. "I don't think he would have really hurt me."

"Damn it, Sawyer. Look at her. That lip of hers? I did it. Me." Wade pounded a fist on his chest. "And when I stepped in front of Mason's gun? Shit, man, I was using your fucking princess for a shield. And Clay, shit, I busted his head and left him in his house so I could take his place. Don't let her turn you into a pussy. We both know I'm dead, whether it's you or Jefferson who does it."

I swung around and searched her face. Her eyes pleaded with me to let Wade live. A tipped a chin was the best I could do to let her know I heard her. Pulling her into my side, I kissed her temple. The one with the big damn bruise on it.

"Wait here." I set her away and moved to where Wade slouched. When I got there, I leaned in and whispered, "You want to die so damn bad? Let me see your face anywhere in the state after tonight and it will happen. She wants you alive for some crazy reason, and I'm giving it to her, tonight. Disappear and stay gone."

I backed away from him. He met my stare for half a beat then turned to walk away. I watched him until he was out of sight. Looking over at Vernon, I said, "Follow his ass."

I returned to Kelli, and she tried to smile, but those lips reminded her it wasn't happening. Regret hammered for letting Wade walk away.

A groan from the ground had us both turning to look at her brother. She dropped beside him and I squatted next to her. If he was coming to, we needed to get our asses out of here. Two shots had been fired, someone was bound to have heard. This one was an easy cleanup. The scene spoke for itself. The bags left behind by Wade painted the picture of a drug deal gone wrong with Mason caught in the middle of it. We'd close the flatbed and let Jefferson worry about getting his property back from whoever ended up with it. End of story.

"Grady, are you awake?" Kelli smoothed a hand over his forehead. The one that now sported two serious bumps.

"Shit. What happened?" His gravelly voice sounded weak.

"You got shot." I answered before Kelli could. "If we can get you up, we gotta get out of here." I didn't like his color, but he'd live.

"Kelli?" Grady's eyes shot open.

"I'm here. You saved me. You all did." Her soft voice had a tremble in it.

His eyes closed for a beat then opened and met hers. "This being a big brother is turning out to be harder than I remembered. Not sure I'm gonna survive you, sis."

She let the undamaged side of her mouth lift. "If I can survive Sawyer, you'll be able to manage me."

EPILOGUE

Six weeks later

KELLI

"MOMMA? WHAT ARE YOU DOING HERE?" I should have known something earth-shattering was about to happen. Nobody ever knocked on my brother's front door. When I pulled it open, it took me a minute to recognize my momma. It wasn't that she looked any different. There wasn't a hair out of place and her makeup was flawless. She didn't look old enough to have a son in his thirties. A good plastic surgeon was an older woman's best friend. She was wearing the camelhair Burberry coat. The one that said, *I'm meeting someone important.* The one meant to impress. No, she didn't look different—she was just out of place. If she had belonged here at one time, she no longer did.

"Well, are you going to just stand there? I raised you

better than to leave your momma standing in the cold. Close your mouth. You look like a fish gasping for air." Her tart words left no doubt that this was my momma.

Instead of inviting her in, I stepped outside and closed the door behind me. "I don't think this is a good idea."

"Obviously, I'm the kind of woman who doesn't care what her children think, or I wouldn't have run off with one and abandoned the other one." She picked at something only she could see on the sleeve of her coat, she wouldn't meet my eyes. I had my second shock. Momma was scared.

"How did you find your way out here?" Her Beamer was parked a good distance from Sawyer's truck and Zane's Buick. It was as if she'd purposely distanced her car in case she wasn't welcome. And that was exactly what I was doing. Not making her welcome. Thanksgiving Day, she had no other family, and I was going to turn her away from Grady's door.

"Don't be silly. The trailer Emmett and I lived in sat right over there." She fluttered her hand in the direction where her Beamer sat. Maybe I'd been wrong about why she'd parked away from everyone else. Had some long-dead habit caused her to park in the same spot she'd used when she had lived here in the past?

"Momma, I love you, but you need to leave..." My words trailed off as the door opened behind me. Momma's eyes traveled past me and widened. Afraid it was Grady behind me, I froze, but when an arm slid around my waist and tugged on me, I relaxed back onto a hard chest. The door snicked shut behind him.

"Who's your friend?" Sawyer's gravelly voice would never stop raising goosebumps. The way he slipped his other arm around my waist, cocooned me in his warmth, made me suspect he had a good idea who she was.

"Yes, Kelli. Who's your friend?" Momma arched a brow.

"Momma, this is Sawyer Garrison. I love him." Nerves had me blurting out the last part. I knew what she saw when she looked at Sawyer. A dangerous man who was incredibly handsome but not even close to the class of people she considered acceptable. I braced, ready to defend my man against her catty remarks. Not that he needed to be defended. He was equipped to handle anything she dished out. But I suspected he would show her respect for my sake. Whether she extended him the same courtesy was the doubtful.

He removed his right arm from around me, leaving the other firmly in place. He offered his hand and politely said, "Pleased to meet you, Mrs. Radcliff."

I suppressed a smile when he leaned over to whisper in my ear, "I know how to fucking act when meeting a parent."

She narrowed her eyes as she studied him and the way he wound around me. What she didn't do was make a move to take his hand.

"Should I spit in it and rub it on my pants?" he whispered in my ear. Despite the seriousness of her showing up, he was making it hard for me not to laugh. In length of time, it hadn't been that long since we'd first met, but in terms of emotions, it felt like years.

"Are you related to Jesse Garrison?"

"He's my dad." Sawyer straightened from leaning over me. "You knew him?"

"Of him." Momma appeared thoughtful. "He was a sexy devil and a dangerous man to cross. He knew how to make money. Most of it illegally. Small-town criminal."

"There was nothing small about him, ma'am." Sawyer managed to be polite while he smirked at her.

"Does he treat you well?" she asked me as if Sawyer

hadn't said anything.

"I would never hurt her. And I'll make damn sure no one else does." He answered for me and this time he wasn't smirking.

"I suppose if he's what you want." She shrugged. "And coming from the Garrison family, at least he has money."

"Momma!" I was mortified.

"Oh, hush." She waved my protest off. "He's not a hypocrite who can't appreciate plain speaking. He's not going to run when the road gets bumpy the way your ex-fiancé did." After she, unknowingly, dropped that bomb, she took his hand and gave it the shake he'd been waiting for.

"Ex-fiancé? What the hell, princess?" He didn't bother to whisper this time.

Before I could offer the same explanation I'd given Zane, the front door jerked open again.

"Holy hell, Sawyer. Can't you keep your hands off my little sister longer than five minutes?" Grady was laughing as he stood in the doorway. He couldn't see Momma yet because Sawyer's broad back blocked his view. "Who was knocking on the door?"

Panic flashed in Momma's eyes, she was about to meet the son she'd abandoned so many years ago. She didn't let it linger. She threw her shoulders back as if preparing to face a firing squad. She very well might have been.

Sawyer pulled me to the side, making it possible for Grady to see past him. I was still wrapped in his arms, but I could now see both Grady and Momma.

"Hello, Grady." Momma made no move toward him.

The laughter died on Grady's lips. He turned into a pillar of stone.

Momma continued as if Grady wasn't staring at her with a blank expression. "Kelli looks like Emmett, only she has my eyes. But you... you are your father's mirror image."

"Come on, Kelli. Let's leave them alone." Sawyer started moving me toward the door.

"No. I want to stay. I have a right to stay." I planted my feet.

"Kelli, go back inside. Mrs. Radcliff and I need to talk." Grady's voice was firm but emotionless as he moved out of the door and farther out on the porch.

"Kelli, go inside. Your brother and I have things to discuss." Momma shooed me away.

Sawyer again started moving me toward the door, and this time I didn't resist as he pushed me back inside the house.

"About time you decided to get back in here," Zane said. "This meal ain't gonna cook itself. Just because I'm the only one that can boil water without burning it doesn't mean you get out of all the work." Zane stopped her complaining when she saw me pacing back and forth across the living room. "What's going on? Where's Grady?"

"Momma showed up. Grady wanted to have a talk with her, in private." The strain in my voice was evident. Sawyer snagged me on one of my passes and held me captive in his arms.

"What the hell?" Zane headed for the door. She had her mad face on.

"Stop right there," Sawyer barked. "Grady's a big boy. He doesn't need an audience for this. If he sends her on her way, then that's that. If she comes through the door, it will be because he wants her to stay." He gave Zane a warning glance. "And you're going to keep your mouth shut if their mom stays. Understood?"

She wasn't happy about it, but gave a grudging agreement. She spun on her heel to walk back toward the kitchen, firing off orders as she went. "Everything's about ready, so his *talk* better not last long. Kelli, check on the rolls. If they're brown, pull 'em out and butter the tops. I've gotta get these potatoes mashed."

The sound of the door opening had Zane turning around, and I twisted in Sawyer's arms to see how many people came through.

Momma walked through first. Sawyer dropped his arms from around me and moved toward her. He reached her in two strides and helped her shrug out of her coat.

Grady followed slowly. He looked from Momma to me. "Mrs. Radcliff is going to stay for supper." He crossed to Sawyer and took Momma's fashion statement out of his hands. He headed down the hallway to deposit it on Dad's bed with the rest of our coats.

Zane broke the silence that gripped us. "Well, somebody's gonna have to set another place at the table, and those rolls are gonna burn if you don't get to them, Kelli." Zane stomped into the kitchen, not waiting to be introduced. "The potatoes ain't gonna mash themselves," she called back over her shoulder.

I ignored Zane and rushed after Grady. Sawyer called, but Momma shushed him.

The door was shut on Emmett's room when I got there. I opened it cautiously. Grady was sitting on the bed. "Are you okay?"

"Come in and shut the door." He scooted over to make room for me.

I sat down beside him, not sure what to say.

Grady ran a hand through his hair and stared into the corner of the room. "I've been mad at her so long I don't know any other way to feel about her. And now here she is, just showin' up at my door like she's got the right."

"Why are you letting her stay?"

He met my eyes and shrugged. "She's not my momma, but she's still yours. I didn't want to do that to you. You know, kickin' her out on Thanksgiving. You're my sister, my family, you don't do that shit to family."

"I wouldn't have—"

He put a hand over mine. "You're mad at her now, but you'll get over it. She's alone and she was there for you growing up. It's different." He turned his face away, but not before I saw the sadness. "When I was a kid, I hated her for leaving me and taking you away. As I grew up, I hated her for the way she hurt our dad. He never got over her, but he still managed to be a great dad."

"Did she apologize?"

"No." He turned back to me and smiled. "Told me she was a selfish bitch. Said the only good thing she'd ever done was leave me with Emmett." He shook his head. "Personally, I think it's a bunch of bull. The shit she pulled finally caught up with her and she's scrambling to not lose you. She wrote me off a long time ago, but it doesn't matter. I'm not letting her stay for me."

"What now?" I honestly didn't know where we went from here.

"Now we're gonna go back in there. Sawyer is going to hover over you all evening, Zane is going to pick at your mom, and we're going to have an awkward Thanksgiving meal. Just like everyone else in the country who is lucky enough to have family to spend it with."

When we returned to the rest of the family, I was in for another shock. Momma had a stick of butter in her hand and was smearing it on the last of the perfectly browned rolls.

"Don't go crazy with the butter," Zane grouched at her while she mashed the potatoes. She kept shooting the evil eye over at Momma.

"If you don't like the way I'm doing it, you should have done it yourself. I could have mashed the potatoes." Momma appeared to be having fun quarreling with the diminutive ball of fire.

"I thought you couldn't mess up the butter. Don't make me rethink it and kick your ass out of the kitchen."

Sawyer took my hand and headed for the door. Zane caught us slipping out. "I swear to hell, if you ain't in the house by the time food's on the table, I ain't waiting." I heard Momma admonishing Zane for cursing as Sawyer pulled me through the door. Zane was going to eat her alive.

The minute we were outside, he pulled me to his chest. I draped my arms over his shoulders and tangled my fingers in his hair at the nape of his neck. He gave me a deep kiss. One of those *nasty* ones I loved so much. When we came up for air, he asked, "You okay?"

"I don't know about anyone else, but I am." I was cautious with my answer.

"Good. Now you want to tell me about this fucking fiancé?" His tone said he wasn't playing around.

"Ex. My ex-fiancé. He was out of the picture long before I met you." I gave his hair a gentle tug.

"Kelli, I'm the only one in the fucking picture from now on. I lied when I said I wouldn't come after you if you ever got tired of roughing it. I would hunt you down, drag your ass back, and tie you to our bed. You're mine, I'm not giving you a choice from this point on."

In all the weeks we'd been together, he'd not once said he loved me. He'd shown me in a hundred different ways, but had never given me the words. Not going to lie, it had bothered me. But he had just said *I love you* in his way, and it was beautiful.

ABOUT THE AUTHOR

New Book Release Email List

Thank you for reading Crystal Moon! Hope it was as much fun for you to read, as it was for me to write. If you loved Zanie Mae then you're about to be very happy! Next up in the Copper Ridge series will be Zane and Evan. So excited to get started on their story! If you would like to be notified when future books are released, please click the link above to sign up for my mailing list. Pinky swear not to load your inbox with emails, nor will I share your email address with anyone else. I'm also including my webpage and my Facebook page if you'd like to stalk me. HAPPY READING!

www.donnatayloreauthor.com

Facebook

Twitter

ALSO BY DONNA TAYLOR

Copper Moon

www.ingramcontent.com/pod-product-compliance
Lightning Source LLC
Chambersburg PA
CBHW020725210626
46807CB00016B/28